The Long Way Home

NEW YORK TIMES BESTSELLING AUTHOR

HARPER SLOAN

Cover Design & Interior Formatting by Devin McCain, Studio 5 Twenty-Five Designs
Editing by Jenny Sims with Editing4Indies

To Andrew:

I'M NOT SURE THIS BOOK WOULD BE HERE WITHOUT
YOUR ENCOURAGEMENT AND LOVE.
YOU HELP MAKE ME A BETTER PERSON DAILY.
I AM OH SO LUCKY TO BE YOURS.

TO CONTACT HARPER:

Email: Authorharpersloan@gmail.com
Website: www.authorharpersloan.com
Facebook: www.facebook.com/harpersloanbooks

OTHER BOOKS BY HARPER SLOAN:

Corps Security Series:

Axel

Cage

Beck

Uncaged

Cooper

Locke

Hope Town Series:

Unexpected Fate

Bleeding Love

When I'm with You

Drunk on You

Loaded Replay Series:

Jaded Hearts

Standalone Novel:

Perfectly Imperfect

Coming Home Series:

Lost Rider

Kiss My Boots

Cowboy Up

Hearts of Vegas Series:

Unconscious Hearts

Disclaimer:
This book is not suitable for younger readers due to strong language and adult situations.

Playlist

ONLY EVERYTHING BY QUINN LEWIS

HERE, RIGHT NOW BY JOSHUA RADIN

PLAY IT COOL BY MONSTA X FT. STEVE AOKI

MAKE YOU FEEL MY LOVE BY ADELE

YOU WERE MEANT FOR ME BY JEWEL

SHOW ME WHAT I'M LOOKING FOR BY CAROLINA LIAR

SIMPLE THINGS BY ALEXANDER CARDINALE FT. CHRISTINA PERRI

UNBELIEVABLE BY WHY DON'T WE

HURT BY JOHNNY CASH

SAVE ME BY BTS

THE BONES BY MAREN MORRIS

IT'S YOU BY HENRY

BROKEN BY SEETHER AND AMY LEE

BAD INTENTIONS BY NIYKEE HEATON

MERCY BY SHAWN MENDES

HOLD BACK THE RIVER BY JAMES BAY

PLEASE NOTICE BY CHRISTIAN LEAVE

HOW TO BREATHE BY MATTHEW MAYFIELD

IN MY VEINS BY ANDREW BELLE FT ERIN MCCARLEY

DISAPPEAR BY ELI.

I.F.L.Y. BY

BAZZI

WITH ARMS WIDE OPEN BY CREED

FARAWAY TREE BY BOATKEEPER

CUZ I LOVE YOU BY LIZZO

NOBODY BY KEITH SWEAT FT. ATHENA CAGE

SHALLOW BY BRADLEY COOPER AND LADY GAGA

OCEAN BY LADY A

SOMEONE'S SOMEONE BY MONSTA X

DAYS LIKE THIS BY VAN MORRISON

SALT AND THE SEA BY THE LUMINEERS

ANYONE BY DEMI LOVATO

FEELS LIKE THIS BY MAISIE PETERS

I WAS MADE FOR LOVING YOU BY TORI KELLY AND ED SHEERAN

HOLD MY HAND BY LADY GAGA

YOU BY LOUYAH

WANDERING CHILD BY WILD RIVERS

BROKEN BY SEETHER

BE MY FOREVER BY CHRISTINA PERRI AND ED SHEERAN

STARTING OVER BY CHRIS STAPLETON

GOLDEN HOUR BY JVKE

RUN BY TAYLOR SWIFT FT. ED SHEERAN

STONE BY WHISKEY MYERS

FIND THE PLAYLIST

ON SPOTIFY:

CHAPTER 1

Olivia

"SAVE ME" BY BTS

"Livi." My beautiful niece's sing-song voice breaks through the silence in our condo, pulling my attention away from cleaning the kitchen island clutter and over to her inquisitive gaze. "You're going to be super-duper unhappy when you see what the sky looks like today." She cocks her head to the side in an overexaggerated jerk of the chin toward the full-length wall of windows showcasing our spacious balcony and the stunning city view beyond.

"That bad, hmm?" I question with a smile, loving that she still does this as a part of her routine in the mornings. Every morning since she could stand, she's pressed her adorable little chubby cheeked face against the glass to check the weather. She's so cute … even though the smudges on the glass she leaves behind will drive me insane, I can't imagine my morning not starting off with a Riley weather report.

To this day, it still shocks me that she is such an intuitive five-year-old. Much more so than my sister and I ever were at her age. If I didn't know better, I would say she could feel my moods almost as if they were her own. However, it wouldn't take an empathic soul to know *and* understand how much her aunt's moods are affected by weather like this. Thankfully, she doesn't understand just how much it impacts me or the actual cause. To her young and innocent eyes, it makes me all the more lovable.

"I'll have you know, little bean of mine, I have the best reason to be upset with my pal Mother Nature. Her rainy day messes up our plans."

Her little button nose turns up, and she purses her lips.

"Never fret, pet … I have a feeling that, together, we'll be able to find all sorts of fun adventures to go on. We may miss a day outside, but who wants to walk around with boots full of puddles and wrinkly toes? You don't like wrinkly toes, do you?" Her giggles bubble up her throat, and she covers her mouth.

I give her a wink and think back to my morning when I realized it would be a gloomy, depressing day. My energy always seems to wane on days like this, making it almost impossible to motivate myself. I heard the sounds of raindrops dancing across the glass windows well before I was even fully awake this morning. For a moment, I couldn't even force myself to open my eyes, let alone get out of bed. If it wasn't for Riley being in my life and the need to get her to school on time without getting yelled at again, I likely would have just accepted defeat and waved the white flag. Unfortunately, responsibility won out, so here we are.

It's been a slow-moving morning ever since. It will take some effort for this not to be a down in the grump's kind of day.

She laughs softly, my serious little Riley bean, and turns away from the window. Her eyes assess me the whole walk across the room, seemingly slicing right through me and seeing way too much. I've always thought she was an old soul, wise beyond her years, stuck inside her tiny little body.

I watch out of the corner of my eye with a smile tipping my lips as she huffs while climbing up on the stool at the island. She sits back with her arms crossed over her chest, watching me with an expression laced with pure exasperation.

Wearing a small smile, I move around the kitchen island toward the wall of cabinets next to the fridge and reach up to open the one where we store the bowls.

As much as I prefer her getting a warm and well-balanced meal to start the day, you can count on one thing with rainy days like this … we *always* have cereal for breakfast. However, the overthinker in me pauses before I can get my fingers on the bowl, realizing she doesn't hate rainy days like I do and might prefer a nice warm breakfast of her favorites instead: cheesy scrambled eggs and cinnamon sugar toast.

"What are you in the mood for this morning, bean? Cereal or would you prefer something warmer on this bleak morning to soothe that wee little wild dancing soul of yours?" I ask, turning my head slightly to look at her over my shoulder.

I almost lose control and laugh when she contemplates my question with a fever pitch of seriousness, forgetting her judging eyes moments before changing plans, and decisively nods to herself after making up her mind. I wait patiently for the little wise one to inform me of her vast knowledge of life, which I'm sure is coming.

"I would have picked cereal, but I suppose cheesy eggs might be nice this morning, Livi. You know, you shouldn't be thinking about cereal if you want to stay warm in the rain. Which is why eggs and toast should be our pick," she responds, her proper demeanor that of someone way older and more mature than the five-year-old little princess that she is. How she's able to channel so much sass and seriousness at the same time is beyond me. It does take a herculean effort to keep my smile to myself, though.

I didn't have a great childhood, so it's always been important that Riley's not be anything close to what her mom and I endured. When I was growing up, in my family, any kind of behavior that wasn't silent was frowned upon. From the moment my sister and I spoke our first word, we were in finishing school training with the strictest of teachers. Poise and perfection, that was the key. It was drilled into our heads that we must never be children, but mature always, even at Riley's age. Riley's childhood experience, compared to her mother and me, has been nothing even remotely close to resembling what we lived through.

Her mother, my late sister, and I weren't raised by loving parents who were present during our lives at all. We were raised by a continuously changing wave of staff and nannies—seven days a week and twenty-four hours a day. Our parents didn't want *their* prime years to be consumed by doing the actual parenting thing. Instead, they chose to travel the world. They had one thing they truly did care about—making

3

appearances at every high-society gala they could find and making sure that our family name and standing never dropped below the upper crust.

Riley, though, has never spent a day in her life outside of the care of her mother or me. That is, until this year. Now that she's in kindergarten for a handful of hours each weekday, she's getting another thing that was a big no-no for our family. An education outside of carefully chosen upper-class private schools with the best of the best tutoring us after each day.

The day that I opened my coffee shop—Olde Mug by Bean and Co.—I struggled for a bit getting my groove going. It's important to me, beyond all words, that Riley never experience the harsh upbringing her mother and I had to endure. Just like that day three years ago, when she came to live with me, she's been by my side every step of every day. Which is exactly why, when choosing the name of my shop, I made sure my sweet Riley girl had the biggest stamp smack dab on the heart and soul of the business. There will never be a day when she will ever have to doubt her importance over everything in my life. It doesn't hurt that she runs that place with an iron fist of the toughest dictators. My employees think it's the cutest thing in the world, which is good because otherwise, I would have to fire all of them. My little bean will always be my number one priority. It's Riley and me against the world.

I think about my sweet Riley as I place slices of sourdough bread into the toaster oven, smiling at the vision of her flitting through the shop with her raven hair in pigtails as she demands that things get done her way. I continue cooking breakfast, stirring the eggs. My Riley girl soothes the restless soul inside me that this weather always precipitates. The best medicine, that girl.

I jump, realizing that I must have been completely lost in thought, stuck in my own head and mentally zoned out, when I hear Riley shouting a demand to that know-it-all robot she said we just *must* have. I'm convinced that a little stalker gremlin lives inside the screen that I've come to disdain greatly at times. Who knew a machine that was only supposed to offer simple conveniences could also be used as an annoying torture device as well once a very bright little girl taught herself how to use technology to her advantage?

"Alexa, please play BTS!" she yells with a burst of joy only slightly higher than her normal pitch.

I turn my head in question, watching her bounce in her seat with excitement.

And of course, that little know-it-all machine responds immediately, and I'm convinced that brat Alexa directs her mocking tone at me when she does.

"Okay. Shuffling songs by BTS on Amazon Music."

And just as suddenly as my calm appeared, it vanishes as the stillness of my beautiful kitchen becomes riddled with music at an ungodly level. My little bean begins to sing along, complete with what sounds like perfectly spoken Korean lyrics. Riley doesn't even know Korean, so it's got me transfixed as she just keeps going and going.

"Save me! Save me!" Riley yells.

Yes, someone please save me.

"I need your love before I fall!" she continues. "Save me! Save me!"

The music picks up, and even in my shock, I have to admit they're good. She keeps dancing, clearly knowing a good dance break when she hears one.

"Beep, beep!" she yells, her smile getting bigger, and I feel one creeping up on my face, despite my complete confusion. "Save me! Save me!"

"Kim Namjoon! Kim Seokjin! Min Yoongi! Jung Hoseok! Park Jimin! Kim Taehyung! Jeon Jungkook! BTS! BTS!" She shocks the crap out of me with the weird chant at the top of her lungs, sounding completely possessed as her little eyes are closed tight, smile huge, face pointing at the ceiling. She repeats herself, pumping her little fist in the air when she yells, "BTS!"

What on earth is going on?

Of course, I know who BTS is. You'd have to be living under a rock not to have at least heard about the Korean pop megastars. They're her favorite group at the moment. It still gives me pause when she, having no prior connection to the Korean language or culture, can sing along to every word in every one of their songs she falls in love with. They don't have to be my favorite band for me to value the joy that their music brings to her, but maybe I can value them just as much for her with a touch lower volume. I smile, letting her have a little more time with the music playing way too loud. She doesn't pay me any mind while I keep cooking, completely lost in her BTS-loving world. I'll never admit it, but I enjoy them almost as much as she does. I've fallen down the rabbit hole of their fandom, complete with my own bias and wrecker. But it will forever remain my secret, and they'll never steal the top spot from my favorite band, Queen.

I watch her with a smile while plating her breakfast, tapping my foot to the beat. It takes me longer to cover her eggs with her favorite cheese and put the toast on her plate, too content to watch her close out her performance until the very last line of the song. I love watching this girl shine. As soon as the song finishes, I act quickly before the next song has a chance to queue up.

"Alexa, volume four," I order her nicely, pretty proud of myself for not outwardly showing how much I dislike that know-it-all bitch of a robot. I see Riley's lip twitch, and I wait for her to remind me to say please to Alexa. She skips it, though, scowling at the device that's no longer giving her a mini concert, making me contemplate electronic murder again.

Today, setting an example for the child that will undoubtedly repeat anything I say stops me. The possibility of that happening and showing the prim and proper teachers at St. John's Day School some of my gold-star parenting is the last thing I want to deal with. No doubt I would be called into the headmaster's office to be reprimanded … again. I thought my days of being on the naughty list in school were in my past, that is until Riley decided to yell "shit" when she broke her pencil one day. Now I'm right back on the very top, only on the parent list instead of the student one.

I'm pulled from my thoughts when I hear my phone's text notification sound, and I glance around the kitchen to see where I placed my phone. It could only be one person this early in the morning, and a burst of happiness hits me, despite the mood the weather has me in. Everyone else would wait until they know the other person is at least halfway through their morning routine and available. Okay, maybe that's a little dramatic for seven in the morning, but come on! Sleeping in is the best thing ever. There isn't a day that I wouldn't prefer to sleep until noon and then start my day.

Walking over, I pick up the phone from where I placed it well before the sun came up and glance at the screen, confirming the text is, in fact, from Ella.

Ella: Greetings, my bestest friend. All is well here. Sold out of the chocolate chunk muffins right away this morning, but we still have a lot of the other flavors. People keep asking for them, so I had to take the featured item off the wall menu. Wanted to let you know, I think it's rain and things are slower than normal. Don't rush in. No need to save us from any fires just yet. Go run some of your errands or something after you drop bean off at school.

Me: Another reason to hate rain—it's bad for business.

Ella: I wouldn't say it's bad for business, per se. The lull gives me time to catch up on the tasks we don't always have time for during big rushes. We're prepping, stocking, and cleaning when we aren't helping customers.

Ella: Do you have any idea how many slaughtered trees we had in this shop just from all the old newspapers left behind? I was momentarily overwhelmed with guilt watching one of the guys pile that stack in the recycling canister.

Me: I'm certain the recycling center is very happy that we have so many murdered trees. I don't think the old newspapers left behind are supposed to be the biggest impact on your morning and overwhelm you with guilt. Instead, my precious friend should count her lucky stars and relax while you can for once. Maybe ask one of the baristas to make you a super complicated drink to test their skills and keep them on their toes. Then relax with an old paper while you can and enjoy your beverage. ;) See you in about 30.

Ella: See! Another reason you're such a rock star. Now I need to think of a tricky order so I can try to throw them off. You know… For training purposes, not to be mean. I guess it's kind of mean, but justifiable since it's with good intentions to help them grow and learn and all. Right?!

7

Me: Insane. You. Are.

I toss my phone in my handbag and glance over my shoulder at Riley.

"Okay, little bean. Let's shake a tail feather, okay? It's a short day at school, so let's get going so I can get back to you. Maybe we can go see *Frozen 2* again and avoid the rain?"

Riley screams, shoving the last bite in, and just like that, my girl is ready to take on the day with a burst of energy I wish she would share.

Oh, to be young and blissful again.

CHAPTER 2

Olivia

"THE BONES" BY MAREN MORRIS

Olde Mug by Bean & Co. never fails to give me a massive rush of pride every time I'm walking up Newbury Street and see it in the distance. Each step brings me closer to the little dream I always imagined but never had the courage to break away from the family expectations to build.

Sadly, it took losing my sister for me to take that step. I needed a purpose other than the one drilled into us. The high-society bullshit was never my thing. I played the part and did what was expected of me, but when our parents died, it was just motions of what I had been conditioned to keep up with.

My life had no color.

I'll never forget the day I bought the building, which had once housed the Cole Haan store. It took an exorbitant amount of money to buy the building from the retail giant to build my coffee shop. The previous owners had been fighting the Historical Society for the changes they wanted to the outside, and it just was my lucky day that I gave them the out they had been looking for. They just moved their store farther down Newbury and knocked out three retail units to give them what they wanted in the end. What their new place isn't, though, is the gem of Olde Mug.

It took me longer to talk the sweet old man who owned the unit behind the space to let me buy that as well, giving me not just the shop but also the ability to renovate and add a kitchen and living quarters that took up the whole back end and top level of both.

Ella has been living above the shop for two years now as part of the perks of being manager and working such long hours. It also helps so that I can be with Riley.

I wait for a car to pass so I can cross the street, taking me one block closer to Olde Mug. I can see the dove-gray awnings over the outer windows from my vantage point, the glint of the sun shining off the glass intricately designed as a belt, so to speak, wrapping around the whole building between the levels. One more "belt" of copper and then more windows. It was the first thing that made me know it was where I needed Olde Mug—that natural light was a must. But it was the roof that made me crave. I would have paid millions more just to have this building. There's no other way to describe my pride and joy other than looking like a castle. Two high peaked Victorian-style turrets on either side of the roof, pieced together by some of the finest craftsmanship I've ever seen in a gable. Every time I see it, I feel transferred back to the little girl who grew up wishing her prince would steal her away from my life and into one of pure happiness. Which is exactly what I get every time I walk in the door.

Now nothing about my world is colorless.

Between the shop and Riley, the only thing that would make it better would be having my sister back. Unless you ask Ella, and then she'd tell you what I was missing was a man.

With a laugh, I wrap my hand around the iron pull on the door and step into heaven. The first thing that assaults me is the scent. Nothing on this earth is better than the smell of ground and roasted coffee beans. The sweet scent of different foods intermingling make it almost too euphoric.

I step around the eclectic mixture of couches and chairs I hunted down to fill the vast floor area, each carefully placed to break the room into different seating areas. A variety of tables are sprinkled between. A large area serves as a workspace for those who prefer to relax while working as well as ones that take up a decent chunk of the room on each side, just to the side of the front windows. My eyes flit up, and I smile at the three chandeliers above me. So classy, my coffee heaven castle.

"You're late!" someone bellows from farther back in the room, where the bar of coffee machines and food display counters are.

I shake my head and glance over at our large clock, complete with coffee mugs as number placeholders, and roll my eyes.

"I'm ten minutes early, just like I always am," I call back to Ella.

"Morning, Olivia. Lovely morning, isn't it?" someone says from my side.

When I see who spoke, I can't help the smile that grows.

"Well, good morning, Mr. W! It's a wet one, that's for sure. How are you feeling today? I missed you here last week, but I heard someone wasn't being a good boy about taking his medication."

My favorite customer just laughs, his weathered voice heavy with age and the pneumonia his caregiver, Grace, had told me he had last week.

"That nosy little girl doesn't know what she's talking about. You know she isn't even a doctor!"

I pat him on the shoulder. "She's qualified enough to know when you need your medication, you stubborn man."

"In my day, you just took a few shots of Jameson to get rid of a little cough."

"Well, in my day, you still do the same, only you make me hide it here so Grace doesn't know you're being a bad boy."

He grumbles under his breath, but smiles nonetheless.

"You doing okay? How about the wee one?"

"We're doing just fine. She's just as energetic and opinionated as ever. Reminds me of someone I know," I respond with a wink.

His grin gets mischievous, and he grumbles out a laugh, his face showing every one of his eighty-three years.

"She reminds me of my beautiful Rachel. So full of life, she was. That little girl is going to take the world by storm one day. Mark my words."

"I don't doubt that for one second. You'll let me know if you need anything, okay? No rowdy for you today, Mr. W."

He gives me another one of his famous winks and goes back to his morning paper. I don't miss the bottle of Jameson tucked at his hip, the one I keep behind the counter just for him. What can I say? I'm a sucker for his beautiful soul and stories of a life well lived. There isn't much I wouldn't keep hidden for him if it keeps him here for hours on end. And Grace, bless her heart, can use the break from her full-time charge.

"The rush came just as soon as I hung up with you." Ella sighs, leaning against the counter and tossing the towel over her shoulder that she had been using to wipe off the counter next to the vintage register.

"Was it bad?"

"No. Just a little more crazy than normal. It must have been a party night for every damn college kid around us. I'm convinced those Ivy League brats who come in here just to talk about which boy they're going to sleep with that night pay for their passing grades. No way they can be passing if they party as hard as they talk. One of them looked like she had been ridden by the entire MIT senior class, and if her words were true, she was damn well close to it."

"Someone's in a good mood," I respond, not even touching the rest. She isn't wrong for the most part. A few groups of girls are regulars after a long night of partying, and it drives me nuts when they loudly boast about their "conquests" when I have Riley here.

"I'm good. Just didn't sleep well last night."

"You want to talk about it?" I ask, focusing on my friend.

"Nothing to talk about, just the usual." She lifts off the counter and straightens her back. "Anyway, look alive. Incoming."

I don't even need to look toward the windows to know what she's talking about. My body acts instinctively, too. My back straightens, I brush my hands down the front of my camel-colored blouse and slip off the cardigan I pulled on to keep the chill away on my walk to work. Ella laughs under her breath but takes it from me.

I grab a white apron from the hook, drop it over my head, and move to the coffee machine, the large monstrosity that looks like a work of art. Even as I hear the door chime, my movements don't stall as I continue the task I set myself to complete. My heart picks up with each heavy-booted step. Even through the low hum of people enjoying their time around the room, I can hear them.

I feel his energy the moment he's near. It hits me like a battering ram. If he's ever felt it, he's never let on. If he ever noticed my reaction, he's never let on to that either, though.

Today, it feels different.

I peek out of the corner of my eye, using the veiled curtain of my hair, and see he isn't alone. The order may change occasionally, but it isn't uncommon for him to have someone else with him. Three men seem to cycle out periodically, but today, it's Evan. Well, damn. Ella must not have seen him at first. Ella has affectionately nicknamed him the Latin lover. My never-shy friend, she can't hold her tongue around him either. It helps calm my nerves to watch her around him and to keep from focusing so much on the giant at his side, that's for sure.

I finish the coffee, putting the lid in place, and turn to the counter where they're both standing side by side with Ella. My eyes connect to his dark-green orbs instantly. I'm used to his silence, and I stopped expecting anything, but today, it looks like a storm brews behind them. My hand shakes as I hold out his drink, the one he hasn't had to order in over six months. There's another reason I'm never late, and it has everything to do with the blond Viking in front of me.

He gives his usual nod but doesn't speak. More normal behavior, but still those eyes rage their silent storm. His fingertips brush mine, and I feel a zap of electricity snake down my spine.

"You want anything, hunk?" Ella asks Evan.

"Don't I always, princesa."

"You want anything other than a drink and a muffin?" She leans over the counter, and I feel my lip twitch.

"Ella," I warn.

"What?" she responds firmly but still playful.

"What did I tell you about offering yourself as part of the menu?" I question, moving my gaze to Evan as he has his own issues holding back his laughter.

"That it's illegal if I accept money for sexual services."

"Or that maybe it isn't appropriate?"

"Oh, yes. That one." I look at her, knowing what's coming because it's the same every time—almost daily. "I quit." She smiles, and her eyes are back on Evan. "Wanna go upstairs, hunk?"

His wide, toothy smile comes out, and bright white teeth bite into his thick bottom lip. I hear Ella make a sound and I elbow her before she can continue.

"Would you like anything, Evan?" I ask.

"Just a black coffee, darlin', and one of those blueberry muffins."

"You got it." I look at Ella. "You wouldn't quit because you love me too much. Now, go get Evan's order ready."

"Anything else for you guys?"

"We're good. Do you mind if we use one of the rooms today?"

It takes me a second to realize he means one of the two private rooms we have here. Well, private isn't the best term since the double doors and much of the room's wall—carved perfectly into the brick surrounding the room –are made of glass. You can see in to the main floor, but they're perfect for larger groups that need a quiet space for conversation. They're typically booked during the day by study groups, but luckily for them, they're both empty today.

"Of course. I'll fill up a carafe for you. Anything else?"

"The other guys will be here soon. They'll let you know. Thank you, darlin'."

"No problem, Evan."

I look back up at the silent Viking—Drew—I've heard him called. His hair is up today, which is shocking since I'm so used to seeing his shoulder-length dark-blond hair and not the shaved parts on each side of his scalp. You would never know he had such beautiful straw-colored hair if he didn't keep the top long. His normal wardrobe of all black is in place, his thick muscles carved under his skin making him look not just giant but carved from stone as well. The intricate black tattoos decorate every bit of skin that isn't covered from the neck down.

My eyes land on his full pink lips between the blond beard and mustache hairs, willing him to speak. When he doesn't, I look over at Evan.

"Let us know if you need anything. With the iPad next to the door, you can send us a text with anything you want to order. We'll bring it in, or you can have someone come out to get it. Just make sure to settle your bill before you leave. You can pay for these drinks later if you have friends coming. That way, they can just add theirs to the room. Easy as pie."

"Thank you, darlin'. We'll do that if we need anything. Send the boys in when they come?"

"Just the two of them, or is anyone else joining you?"

"Just Hunt and Saint."

"Sounds good. I'll send them in. Don't forget the button next to the painting, center wall, if you want the shades to go down on the windows."

"No offense, but they're kind of pointless with the glass door, darlin'." His eyes dance, and I have to admit, I get Ella's obsession with him.

"I'll find a suitable solution to install just for you guys next time," I sarcastically drawl.

With a deep grunted laugh, he turns and walks to the left of the room, where our two private rooms are tucked next to the bathroom space. I look back over at Drew, who is still looking at me with his silent storm.

"You need anything else?" I ask, proud of myself for sounding calmer than he makes me feel.

He's silent, as usual, and I'm about to turn and clean up the machines before I'm stopped dead in my tracks.

"Soon."

That's it.

Just one word.

The first he's ever spoken to me in the three years he's come in here. His voice sounds like he never uses it at all.

Rusty, deep, and full of masculine seduction.

I'm so stunned, I didn't even realize he had left until I feel Ella's fingertip at my chin, closing my gaping mouth.

"What was that?" she exclaims on a shocked whisper.

"I have no idea."

What was that, indeed?

CHAPTER 3

Olivia

"PLEASE NOTICE" BY CHRISTIAN LEAVE

"What do you think they're talking about in there?" Ella asks.

I stop restocking the clean mugs and look toward the room for the hundredth time since the other two men arrived.

"I don't know. Sports, maybe?"

"Have you ever seen men need to go into a private room to talk about sports?"

"Have you ever understood why men do a lot of the things that men do?"

"Fair played, my friend. Fair played."

"Why don't you go top off Mr. W? He should be leaving soon, and you know he doesn't like Grace to know he's been sipping Jameson all day. Don't forget to get the bottle so he doesn't try to take it home again."

Ella laughs and walks toward Mr. W. His face lights up the second she sidles up and places her butt on the arm of his chair, rubbing her hand over his bald head.

I look down at the mugs, each one unique and funky, and feel another rush of pride for Olde Mug. Even all these years later, I still feel like it was the first week I opened the doors, and I pray that feeling never leaves.

I've always had an affliction for beautiful old mugs. The older and unique, the better. It started from my grandmother, who had an extensive collection, but she never minded that I wanted to play with her expensive mugs like they were nothing but a cheap doll. She was, without a doubt, the kindest adult that I ever had in my life growing up. I knew when I opened Olde Mug that I wanted that part of her—and the happiness those memories gives me—into this place. The rest of the hippie meets Victorian era design was all me and Riley. Of course, she was too young at two to really understand what she was doing, but I purchased any couch or chair she gravitated to during our estate sale hunting. It didn't take long for the place to come together, and the result is nothing short of flawless—the perfect mix of old historical Boston, a reformed socialite, and a sassy little girl.

Bean & Co.

Riley and me.

Forever.

"Hey."

I snap my head up from the mug I had been holding in my hand, contemplating while my mind wandered. I adjust my eyes when I realize it's one of Drew's friends. Hunt, I believe. A quick glance at the room shows that all three remaining men are still heavy in conversation. I turn my attention back to the man before me, standing straight and keeping my voice calm. They all make me nervous, but more because they're huge, and larger men have always given me a little pause. For good reason, too.

"Hello, again. I'm sorry, but I've forgotten your name. It's Hunt, right?"

"Hunting, but my first name is Ben."

"Oh. I'm sorry. I wasn't aware," I start, confused. "Which would you prefer to be addressed by?"

"Doesn't matter," he responds, seemingly annoyed in tone even though his body language is completely relaxed and calm.

"Of course it does. It's your name, isn't it? Surely, you know which you prefer to be called. I have three first names as my full name, so I'm very used to the confusion of people not knowing how to address me."

"It's something," he mutters under his breath. "Call me Ben."

"That wasn't that hard, right?" I give him a smile, and his lips twitch. "Well, what can I do for you, Ben?"

He grunts out a laugh. "You always been this scripted?"

My back jerks straight. "Excuse me?"

He holds his hands up. "I didn't mean to offend you, just trying to figure out if you're like this with all your customers or if I just got the special treatment today?"

"I'm polite."

"You are. You're also someone who I would say would be more prone to the galas and fundraising luncheons, but here you are, rocking a kick-ass coffee shop."

"For your information, I could do both." I cross my arms over my chest, trying to relax the whole high-society aura he can clearly see.

"You could, but you don't."

"How do you know that I don't? For all you know, I might have a function tonight."

Oddly, his questioning and mockery of my upbringing doesn't bother me. I don't really have many friends, so this kind of teasing banter is a welcome change to the chatter of Ella and a five-year-old.

"Isn't much I don't know, Olivia Elizabeth Kelley."

"That isn't exactly master detective work, Ben. My name's listed on things all over the shop," I joke.

He just cocks a brow.

"For your information, I haven't been part of the galas and luncheon world of Boston for years. It's a product of my upbringing, I'm afraid. Ingrained in a way that you're just stuck with polite conversation," I continue, not annoyed anymore.

"You ever rude?"

"Not if I can help it."

"Well, this will be fun," he adds, not making any sense.

"Okay … well, Ben, is there something I can do for you?"

His large shoulders move as he laughs silently. "Just wanted to see if you had the room clear for a few more hours. Things aren't progressing as quickly as we thought they would. We can get out of here if you need us to, just figured I would ask since all our shit is spread out already."

I glance back at the room, seeing that papers are, in fact, strewn everywhere, and computers are open in front of each man.

"You're free to use the room for as long as you'd like. I only had the one booked, so it will be empty anyway. There's no sense in packing up and moving if you're in the middle of your work."

"Thanks, Olivia."

"No problem, Ben."

He walks away but turns around when the door bursts open, and I hear my name yelled.

"Livi! Liviiii! Oh, my Liv!"

Riley rushes into the room, stopping to toss her light-pink backpack on to the closest piece of furniture she can find. I look up to see Grace walk in behind her and smile. I love Grace. She's Mr. W's full-time caregiver, but when he's here all day long anyway, she is the one person I know I can trust when there's a conflict with Riley and work. Luckily, she's also a good friend, so she loves her Riley time, and it's not just a favor.

When the little tornado is done taking off her backpack, jacket, *and* shiny black shoes, she moves around the room greeting a few of the regulars like the world-class charmer that she is. She saves her favorite for last, climbing into Mr. W's lap and resting her elbows on his shoulders. She presses her nose to his and looks him wide-eyed into the face. I wait, knowing she'll be giving me my favorite sound, and I'm not disappointed when exactly ten seconds later, she giggles and backs away slightly. Her hands come up and frame his weathered face, still laughing.

"How come you always win?!" she exclaims on a giggle.

"Because in my day, if you moved, the big bad guys would find you."

"Were they monsters?"

"They were like monsters to a lot of people."

"That's not good. Monsters are bad. Did you put them in time-out?" she asks, completely oblivious with her childhood innocence.

Mr. Westchester, the gentlest man I've ever met, is a hero. He's spent a lot of time talking to me about his service in the Army, so I know the monsters he's referring to are from his time enlisted. He's opened up to me a lot over the years, and I always soak in his military stories. He always gets a twinkle in his eye when he tells me how he lied about his age so he could enlist and get to Korea. His first taste of war was in Panmunjom back in 1953. As he says it, he was a young man full of piss and vinegar ready to take on the world and make a difference. He doesn't talk much about his time in Vietnam, but I do know he was in Ia Drang in the mid-sixties. He didn't retire from the Army until he had given over thirty years of service, retiring as a Master Sergeant. He made me stop thanking him for his service after six months, but I still silently do it. Heroes like him make it so I can rest easy at night. There will never be a day that I'm not thankful for the sacrifices he's made for our country. I tell him often that he's lived so many lifetimes in his eighty-three years, and he just smiles and tells me another story.

"I put them in time-out forever," he whispers with the tone of the rascal I'm sure he's always been.

"Forever?" Riley gasps.

"Forever!" he booms, laughing so hard that Riley joins the instant his belly starts shaking, and just like that, they've moved on to something else. I leave them to it, knowing she's in good hands while Grace moves in close.

"Hey, you." She wears a smile, her blond curls dancing around her face.

"Hey," I greet, walking around the counter to hug her. "Thank you for picking her up for me."

"It's no problem. I knew Bobby wouldn't be leaving anytime soon, so it isn't like I have anything to do until it's time to get his Jameson-drinking cranky bones home."

I laugh softly, squeezing her shoulders affectionately.

"He thinks you don't know about his secret stash," I whisper.

"He thinks a lot of crazy things, but I still love the old menace."

"Let me go tell Riley that it'll be a later night than she thought, then let's have a cup of coffee so you can fill me in on that hot date you had Saturday night."

She rolls her eyes. "Bobby tell you about that?"

"You darn tootin' little girl! You think it's safe to be walking around town in those toothpick shoes? Just waiting for a young hoodlum to get the wrong idea, I tell you!" Mr. W bellows from his seat, Riley thinking he is the funniest man on earth with tears rolling down her face from her laughter.

"They were very subtle heels, Bobby." She sighs.

"In my day—"

"In your day, women couldn't even show their cleavage. We get it, you cranky old man. Finish your drink and your time with Riley, or you don't get to play poker while we watch *Jeopardy* tonight, mister."

He mumbles under his breath, Riley kicking up her laughter even harder. I look up and around the room, seeing that most of the customers are just watching the madness with smiles. Anyone who spends any time here knows about Riley and Mr. W. Before my eyes can get back to Grace, I glance toward the room that houses the four giant men. All four of their eyes are on us. The mix of amusement and … worry, a confusing hue of emotions on their faces. Surely, they aren't worried that she will bother them. Riley may be young, but she knows better than to go near those rooms.

The thought is immediately gone when my gaze clashes with the one who has always drawn me in. It's the heat in those stormy eyes that gives me pause. It feels like I've been physically burned.

What on earth is going on today?

CHAPTER 4

Olivia

"DAYS LIKE THIS" BY VAN MORRISON

"She's out cold, Ms. Kelley."

I look up from my computer screen, pushing the glasses that I wear to block out the blue lights to rest on the top of my head. Lewis, the sweet seventeen-year-old we hired last year, stands in my doorway. His glasses held to his face with an eyeglass chain pulled tight behind his neck. His pimple-covered cheeks blush profusely.

"When are you ever going to call me Olivia, Lew," I joke, standing and walking around the desk after I shut off my computer, thankful it was a slow night so Riley could play while I took care of payroll. Not that it would have mattered. Everyone who comes here loves her.

"My mom always said that I should address my elders with their proper title until I'm of age to be speaking to them as a peer."

"You're just the sweetest thing, Lewis," I gush, tapping his nose with my finger as I walk by.

"Thank you, ma'am," he says, his eyes looking away in embarrassment.

I giggle softly. "So polite. You're going to make someone very happy one day, you know."

His cheeks get even redder as I walk away from him and into the main room. I almost choke on my tongue when I see Riley. She looks like a starfish, clinging to one of the larger couches in the middle of the room, taking up every inch possible with her tiny body. One of her arms and one leg hangs off the side, dangling above the floor. The other leg lays straight down the couch body, and the other arm above her head. Her hair, tangled all around her head, covers her face completely. My Lord, she's perfection. And just like her mom. Right up until we lost her, Emma would sleep hard and just as messy.

Moving over to the register, I rest my hip against the wood on the other side of Ella and watch as she finishes changing out the receipt tape. She looks up and arches a brow but continues her task.

"When did the giants leave?" I ask.

"About a half hour after you went into the office. They were here one moment, gone the next. For men that big, they shouldn't be able to move without a single person even noticing."

I open my mouth to respond when I feel a tug on my cardigan. I look down to find a sleepy, wild-haired Riley.

"Livi, do you think we can get the white pasta from that place with the crispy bread?" she asks softly with a slight whine in her tone. She's more tired today than usual, which I pray doesn't mean she's getting sick. She takes naps often after school, but she only gets like this when she's not feeling well.

"Aren't you in luck, my sleepy bean. You must be a mind reader because I just had the thought that tonight felt like a great night for GrubHub delivery and a movie on the couch." I look down just in time to see her eyes light up a little more, some tiredness leaving her features. Bending down, I wrap my arms around her small body to give her a hug and kiss. She smiles back, and I happily note the exhaustion on her face hasn't returned.

Even though she tried her hardest, the weather zapped the energy right out of her. Since we weren't able to have a picnic and feed the ducks in the park, I hope this dinner will do the trick of easing the disappointment of missing our outing. It's one of our favorite afternoon activities when Olde Mug has bread leftover that couldn't be donated to the local soup kitchen, but the rain ruined that plan today. It may have stopped, but there is no way the ground isn't holding enough water to keep it soggy for the next couple of days. Which I hate because not only do we lose out on our time together in the park, but the bread will have to be tossed now. I almost told her we could go tomorrow regardless, but then I checked the weather forecast, and sure enough, the cold weather I've felt moving in will be here in two days. I used to love when Boston turned cold, but that isn't the case these days. The winter weather and chilling temperatures will make walking to Riley's school and then to Olde Mug more challenging.

"Let me go grab my bag, bean. Keep Ella company, okay? You know she likes to put the paper in wrong," I tell her with a wink.

I grab my purse off the hook behind the door and drape the strap over my head and across my body. Turning around, I lock the door to the office at the same time as I see Riley run over to where she dropped all her stuff earlier. She slides her backpack over her shoulders and then wobbles herself into her shoes. She's beyond ready to go home. She never complains when we need to stay a little later than normal, but you can see it in her movements at go time that she was silently wishing we were elsewhere. I ended up staying a little longer than even I had planned, but payroll needed to get done tomorrow, and I would rather have a little extra time in the morning with Riley than sitting here on my computer poring over numbers.

At times, Riley would have been in my office with me the whole time. She has her own little setup in the corner of what she calls "our" office. Having an office doesn't impress her as much as working the room, though. My girl prefers to be people pleasing, bopping around the shop while chatting with the regulars and meeting new customers. I guess you could say she's our little mascot.

She smiles up at me when I hold out my hand for her, taking it immediately. I feel so much pride for this kid every time her eyes meet mine. I give her hand a gentle squeeze, our secret code to get going, and we start walking toward the front door. I stop before pushing our way out to call over my shoulder and let Ella know we're leaving.

"So long, coffee gods!" Riley sings, letting go of my hand so she can start dancing around the room.

Ella's smile grows even bigger as she beams at Riley from across the floor. "I bid you farewell, Coffee Princess. Will you be coming to grace us simple folk with your beauty again tomorrow?"

"Silly El. Where else would I be? I work here, remember? My name is on the signs and alllllll the other stuff, you know," Riley tells her, annoyed at the slightest possibility she'd have somewhere else to be.

"Oh my goodness, how could I ever forget? I guess you do kind of run this place more than your silly auntie. What would we do without a boss like you, Princess Riley?" Ella snickers, giving Riley a curtsey that makes her mouth open to release a huge belly laugh.

I laugh along with them, knowing how much effort I put into this business, especially with all the behind-the-scenes stuff I do at night after Riley goes to sleep.

Ella's hours are a close second to mine. She cares about this business as if it were her own, which it might as well be since she bought shares in it two years ago. She's more than just reliable. She manages the staff and scheduling like a pro and puts in more hours than I'd ask of anyone purely out of choice. I consider myself lucky to have found her, which is why I pay her so well. It doesn't hurt that she actually does live here.

"Give me a call or text if you need anything later. I'm sure I'll be up late tonight. I need to do some ordering for next week, and I keep forgetting the list at home," I tell Ella as Riley skips back to me, taking my hand and pulling me toward the door.

"You got it, chickadee."

Both Riley and I wear smiles when we push through the front door into the slightly chilled air, the sun heating our faces despite the temperature. I pull the door closed and step onto the sidewalk, happy to see—and feel—the sun rays beaming through the clouds and the rain long gone.

I only get two feet away from the door when my back tingles with pinpricks of awareness.

I know what this is.

Or, I should say, who it is.

I can feel him.

I've always felt him.

Even though I sensed him, it still shocked me when he was just there, almost out of thin air.

My step falters for a moment, Riley jerking my arm when I don't continue walking with her peppy steps. I feel her turn to look at me, but

I don't look away from the man with his back pressed against the corner of the building. One leg kicked up against the wall, shoulders against the brick, both tattooed arms pushing his hands into the pockets of his jeans. He looks relaxed, but also … not.

As soon as his eyes lock with mine, I feel a shift in the air.

Even from the distance, however slight, I can tell a silent storm brews in those fierce dark-green eyes. It feels as if my heart will pound right out from behind my ribs, picking up speed every second he continues to hold my gaze. Other than his expressive eyes, eyes that I'm sure he has no idea give away so much, he shows zero outward sign that he is even as mildly affected by me as I am of him. It's always like this. I would love to have just a small view inside his mind. Maybe then I would understand what goes on behind the silence.

Something tells me this man has tons of shadows floating within his depths. I feel it right down to the center of me.

Curiosity most certainly will kill the cat, but I can't help but wonder what makes this silent giant tick.

Not that I have the guts to do anything about my curiosities.

Taking a deep breath, I try my best at a normal smile. No doubt my smile, however, is completely awkward and slightly off-kilter, making me look more possessed than polite.

"Hey. I know you, giant." Riley snickers, covering her mouth with her tiny hand and smiling through her fingers up at him.

He breaks our eye contact and looks down—way down—at Riley.

"Is the weather up there different, mister?"

He shakes his head but doesn't speak. I've never seen someone resist little bean.

"Do you hurt the trolls?"

He cocks his head but still no words come from his mouth.

"Do you know the trolls?" Riley continues as if his silence means something to her.

His blond hair, down now, moves as he shakes his head.

"Well, that's good. Trolls are nice. They sing pretty songs too." She looks back at me and smiles her beautiful smile. "Let's go, Livi. I'm ready now."

She's ready now? God, this child. My heart swells every time she opens her little mouth.

"Oh," I start, clearing the hoarseness out of my voice. "You are now, are you?"

"Yup," she responds, popping the p.

"Well"—I look up at Drew—"if you'll excuse us."

I start to walk around him, but he reaches out and grabs my bicep with the most gentle of touches. I look down at his hand, up to his beautiful eyes, then back at the hand on my arm again. Repeating the motion twice more before finally settling on his eyes. I hear Riley giggle, but all my focus is on him.

"I'll walk you."

Wow.

Again, that rusty baritone voice sends a jolt through me like my whole body has been hooked up to the entire electrical grid of Back Bay.

"Uh, that's very nice of you, but we'll be okay. We do this every day."

His eyes get hard, narrowing slightly, but otherwise, he doesn't move. Then, after a beat, he tips his head in the direction that we walk and raises one dark-blond brow—the one with the scar dissecting it.

"We don't need an escort."

He doesn't say a word, per the norm.

"Really," I continue.

"I'll see you home," he says, leaving no room for argument.

"Livi! Yay!" she exclaims. Riley rips her hand from mine, and she leaps at Drew. He's a little delayed but doesn't miss a beat in dropping my arm and grabbing her under her armpits before she just bounces right off him. "I'm going to climb a giant! Look at me, I'm like Jack, but I get to climb the giant and not the beanstalk. HEY! Beans. Like me, Auntie!"

The whole time she's jabbering, my jaw drops farther and farther as she continues to do exactly as she says, climbing the muscular giant like it's a completely normal thing for her—with his help, of course—which is even more confusing to me. I can tell the exact moment something changes for him. The storm settles a bit behind those eyes, the waters not churning uncontrollably but just calm and peaceful. He moves quickly, his arms dashing out as Riley's legs lose their purchase, and she's squealing in laughter as he tosses her up in the air in a spin, catching her so she's facing the street and not his body. Then, in a move that I will never forget until the day I die, he settles her little body on his shoulders and hooks her ankles with his big paws, securing her on her new perch.

"Livi, look! I'm a giant now, too!" Riley yells as if I can't hear her clear as day.

I clear my throat, blink a few times, and look from Drew's very calm eyes up to her wildly excited ones. "I see that, my precious bean."

"Let's go, giant!" she exclaims, pointing her hand toward the direction of our condo.

"Let's go, squirt," Drew rumbles down to me.

"Excuse me?" I gasp, so confused at this turn of events that my brain just can't move quickly.

Again, he tips his head and goes back to silence.

"This is the strangest day ever," I mutter under my breath, but do I do anything to detach my niece from him?

No.

Like the basket case I feel I am at this moment, I do the only thing that makes sense.

I start walking home.

CHAPTER 5

Drew

"HURT" BY JOHNNY CASH

A man experiences many things in life that scar him to the point that he'll never be the same again.

Some good.

So good that you let those moments fill the space inside you the best they can—pushing the bad out.

Some bad.

Some, for a few, are only everything that nightmares are made of.

Those moments will hit you out of the blue and knock you flat on your ass. You could be in the middle of something mundane and routine, and the next thing you know, you're struggling to breathe. Or, in my case, struck with so much desperate grief that you feel like you really are dead.

It's been a battle for me mentally the past few days. Ever since I started walking Olivia and Riley home. Things I had long since stopped thinking about and dreaming of stayed in the forefront of my mind, not locked away where they belonged. I haven't so much as explained myself to her, just made sure I was there every time she made that walk between her home and the coffee shop. It's insane. I know this. Yet do I stop? No … I let the monsters in the dark start whispering louder in my head and keep showing up.

I place one hand on the railing of my balcony and look down at the water of Boston Harbor. The other absentmindedly reaches for my shirt while the past enters my thoughts against my attempts to keep it away. I lift the cotton from my flesh, tucking my hand underneath. I don't stop until my fingertip hits the puckered scar directly between my abs. With my finger touching that old wound, I think about those nightmare flashes of pain that had just hit me and reach for the bottle of Bulleit with my free hand, consuming half the bottle with one gulp. I'll need it. When these days come, I always fucking need it.

I don't remember much from that first day. I know after I was patched up and my handler came in to explain what he needed from me, I demanded they take me to where I could see my family. Where I could watch them find out I was … dead.

My brother was the hardest. Though, I knew he would be. You don't have a bond like we had and not realize the news of my "death" would break him completely. Somehow, I managed to stay put as the doctor walked out. I had been ordered not to move, not unless I wanted to really die because I was foolish enough to be on my feet after having surgery to repair the bullet that tore through my gut. But when I watched him process what the doctor said, I had to be held back. I remember Clark, my point of contact, holding his hand over my mouth to keep me quiet while two of his men held my body back as gently as possible. It didn't matter, I still tore open what was just repaired the second my brother made a sound that came from his very soul being ripped from his body and fell to his knees.

There is no way to describe the pure heartache that comes from someone who has lost someone they love, but to have him experience that while I was watching from the shadows … there's no way to make anyone understand that. Everything inside me demanded I rush in and tell him it wasn't real, but I knew better. I knew the costs. And I would do it all over again and spend the past two-plus decades living the life of a ghost.

It wasn't just my brother.

When I saw the rest of my family, my five brothers who life had given me through our time in the Marines—their wives and girlfriends—it killed whatever was actually left inside me.

At least, that's what I thought before I had to watch my own funeral from the black windows of the SUV waiting to take me away from the life I had loved. The life I would never return to, not if I cared about what happened to the people I "died" to protect.

It wasn't seeing the men who had become my brothers not moving, staring at the casket they thought held me that killed the biggest part left of me. I knew they would hold themselves tight like that, but I didn't expect them to work so hard to keep their shit together. Not even the rifles going off got a single blink from them. I knew what type of effort they were putting into their grief. It hurt knowing they were in pain I essentially caused but knew was unavoidable.

It wasn't seeing the girls crying for me that did it either, though it made me want to rush out of the car and be the man they knew me to be. The one that would rather get their laughter than their tears. No, that man died that day with each tear they cried for me.

What it was, though, was my sweetest friend.

I almost didn't recognize him dressed in a perfectly pressed and tailored black suit. Dress shoes shiny from a fresh polish moving through the marked graveyard with a precision that shouldn't shock me from him. Not once did he look away from the casket. He was there for one thing only, and it was clear in each determined step that he took. It was the buzzed hair that gave me pause. Gone was the flamboyant man who got as much pleasure in teasing me as I did in acting like I hated it. Gone was the man who couldn't ever be brought down from the high of life he was riding. I had never, not once in the years I'd known him, seen that stoic look on his face. His mocha skin etched in stone, he remain focused on the box I wasn't in.

He didn't stay long, but it was long enough that a mark on my soul would forever be an inch deep and never heal … constantly reopening. He left what he needed to with the moments he bowed his head and then turned and walked the way he had come. But I didn't need anything more to know that my "death" would mark him just as deeply.

With a deep sigh that I feel in my gut, I turn from the brilliant water over the harbor and turn into my condo. So different from the life I left behind, the one that I live as a ghost here in Boston. The bottle of bourbon goes back to my mouth, and I take another heavy pull, my eyes already trained on the object I want across the room, center shelf, with nothing else sharing the wooden surface.

The ribbon isn't bright anymore. It's tarnished and dirt soaked, just like me. The glass doesn't shine like it did the day it was pulled from its packaging. It wouldn't, seeing that I find myself right in front of it almost like clockwork each week. But inside, each one of the flecks of gold glitter still shines just as bright as they did over two decades ago.

I take another pull from the bottle and manipulate the glass in my hand, watching those pieces of glitter dance inside their space, and smile. It's a twisted as fuck smile. One made of grief but also the love and happiness that this jar represents. I'm sure I look like a monster every time from the lack of smiling over the years.

Goddamn Sway.

Goddamn Sway and his fucking glitter.

And goddamn me for taking a life sentence worse than death.

But thank fucking God for this jar—my only connection to the life I had—because without it, I would have killed myself a long time ago. After all, what's the point of continuing to live when you're already a dead man?

I place the jar back on the shelf where that part of me belongs and force myself away from it. It takes another five healthy swallows before I'm able to tuck Zeke Cooper back where he belongs, in the ground six feet under. The whole walk through my condo to the office I have in the back of my space gives me time to get my shit together. To forget the ghosts of the past and focus on the reality of my present.

I boot my computer up and place the bottle on the desk, looking over my notes on the next man my team was in charge of killing. The next piece of shit the world would be better without. There's a reason they wanted me "dead." There's a reason I could be wiped clean from the earth and start over a million miles away, completely untraceable. There wasn't a person out there better to lead this team from the shadows than me. And after approaching me for years, it was a perfect storm when the shit stains of the earth were pushing in on their target—my family—and me getting shot. They didn't waste a second pushing through the recovery room, having already stood like sentries when I was in surgery, I'm told, to explain the situation. They needed me, and if they didn't have me, they couldn't guarantee they could keep those important to me alive. Fewer than ten people in the government know about the men I work for. The nation's boogeyman killers, that's what we are. All three men who work with me are "dead," the same as I am.

What better man to hunt the vile creatures of this earth than a man who's already dead, after all.

With that sick thought, I grab the bottle and continue to drink while I plan the best way to murder this next son of a bitch.

Life wouldn't be too bad if only everything that made my very alive heart beat didn't hurt as painfully as it did—especially knowing that it would never be any different for an alive dead man.

CHAPTER 6

Olivia

"SOMEONE'S SOMEONE" BY MONSTA X

"He's out there again," Ella whisper-yells into my ear.

Of course, it wasn't a necessary warning, seeing that Riley's been out there with him talking up a storm for the past half hour, so I already knew he was there. Without fail, he's there propped up against the brick at the corner of my building each day like clockwork. She's done the same thing every day when we're about to leave, and he arrives. She joins his silent watch from his relaxed post at the corner of Olde Mug.

Just like every morning when I leave my home and find him there, too.

Silently waiting, like it's the most normal thing in the whole world.

My questioning became more persistent when he showed up at my home.

When I walked out and saw him standing just outside the building's front gate, I just knew something was going on. However, having that gut feeling doesn't mean a thing when I can't get the man to talk.

It never works.

I'll give him credit. His stubbornness is one heck of a strong iron shield.

I'm pretty sure he could withstand any kind of torture and never crack.

I stopped questioning him a week in.

A solid week of him walking with Riley on his shoulders and me locked in my head trying to figure out what the hell was going on. All the while, he stayed silent.

I still tried asking every now and then, but really, I've all but stopped doing that. Somewhere around the two weeks mark, I just accepted his silence. Almost looked forward to it. But at the random moments when I did ask, there was still silence. He just looked at me, eyes calm, and cocked that damn brow. So I stopped wasting my time trying.

"You get it out of him yet?" Ella continues.

"I stopped trying," I reply with a shrug. "I wasn't getting anywhere."

"What the hell have you been doing for the past two weeks, then?"

I shrug again, drying the teal deep-set coffee mug with swirling lavender vines on it with a towel. "Walking home. Just silently walking home with Riley's chatter filling the air."

"And he still just leaves when you get inside?"

"Yup." I nod.

Thinking back over each night he's silently walked with Riley on his shoulders while she does all the talking for us, I noticed three days in that he was answering her with slight squeezes of her ankles with his hands. One hand for no and both for yes. I will never know how she knew what that meant, but it's just another one of those things I stopped questioning.

"This is seriously so strange, Liv."

"You don't think I know that," I snap, then sigh when I realize my tone is too sharp. "I'm sorry. I just have no idea what the hell is going on, and it's driving me insane. When he ignored my questioning of it for so long, I just figured whatever. It wasn't worth my mental sanity while I tried to figure it out on my own. He's been coming in here for so long, it doesn't feel like he's a stranger, but maybe it should feel weirder than it does. It just *is*. At first, it was awkward. Now it's just like … I don't know? Maybe comfortable?" I lift my arms in sync with my shoulders as I shrug, sigh, and drop them heavily at my sides.

"Oh boy." She sighs, her eyes wide, staring at me as if I have two heads.

"What?" I question, turning my head toward the front window, thinking that he was coming in. When I see him and Riley in the same position, her still talking with her animated movements and him just looking at her with all of his attention, I look back at Ella. "What?" I ask again, a little firmer.

"You like him."

"What?" I gasp, my head snapping back like she had slapped me.

"You like *like* him, like him."

"I do not!"

"Oh yeah, you do."

"I'm just confused by him. I do not *like* him. He's a puzzle."

She scoffs. "He isn't a puzzle. You're frustrated that you can't just jump his bones."

I narrow my eyes. "Would you keep your voice down?"

She tosses her head back and laughs loudly.

I look around the room and see we've gained the attention of a handful of customers. I look back at the window, seeing Riley laughing with her whole body, jumping on her toes. When my gaze moves to Drew, I see his gaze on her, but his normally stoic face looks relaxed and almost boyish.

I've had a lot of time to study him during our silence. As his attention is always on Riley, I take in as much as I can from the corner of my eye. Much more time than I've had over the years of him coming into Olde Mug. I knew he was older, but I had assumed he was, at most, five years older than my thirty-five. But when I get a good look at those sandy locks during our walks home, I've seen more silver in them when the sun hits his head. He hides them well, just as he hides the faint signs of him being older in his face. If I had to guess, he's closer to fifty than forty. However, when he's with Riley, a side of him comes out that looks a little more relaxed, giving him an air of something so contradictory to the harshness I've grown so accustomed to.

The wrinkles at the corners of his eyes give him away. I don't know what happened to him, but I have no doubt that Drew wasn't always this closed-off, hard man.

"Yeah, you definitely *like* him," Ella continues, snorting out a laugh and walking away from me when a customer approaches the counter.

I take my time with my thoughts, looking around the room at the four employees working on inventory on the merchandise shelves, restocking the milk and sugar stations, and tidying up the main floor. All younger college-age kids, all at the beginning of their lives, and always joking around and laughing with each other, keeping the atmosphere here light, happy, and relaxed.

Is this what Drew has always been like?

Was there a time when he gave his words away for free?

And if he did, what happened?

He's such a paradox.

A handsome one, but nonetheless confusing.

"Crap," I mutter.

"Ding, ding! She got it!" Ella exclaims from the espresso machine.

I grumble under my breath but don't argue. She's right. Something about him has always called to me, but now having spent this much time with him outside of his visits to the shop—even though he's silent—there is no doubt that I'm drawn to him in a way that is all about attraction.

"Crap," I repeat.

Her laughter echoes around the room, floating over the hissing sounds of the steam. I turn, walk around the side of the bar, and head toward my office.

"Hey," she calls out, causing me to turn my head. "At least, can you please try a little harder to figure out what's going on? Make up an excuse to get him upstairs and wait for Riley to be distracted and freaking figure it out, Liv."

I take a deep breath and hold it for a beat before letting it go in a slow exhale. I hold her gaze, knowing she's right, but I just don't know if I'll have the guts to do that. But instead of arguing or making an excuse, I just nod.

One way or the other, I'll figure out what's going on.

————

I pull the door of the coffee shop closed, trying to shield my frustrations over the situation behind my smile—one that I hope looks a little more convincing than it feels. I see Riley performing a song from *Frozen* for

Drew while twirling and dancing on the sidewalk in front of Olde Mug. Drew's in his normal position but more alert than relaxed, just as he is every time he has Riley near. She isn't even the slightest bit distracted by the people moving around her or the passing cars on the street. She's in her own world, one that is all about making "her giant" smile. I don't know how she knows, but somehow she knows this man wouldn't let anything happen to her. I'm sure that's why she's more at ease with him than most people, and that's saying a lot since she's the most carefree people person I have ever met.

I try to keep my focus on Riley. However, I'd be lying if I refused to at least admit to myself that my intrigue for the silent beast wasn't intensifying way past the curiosities and baseline lust I've had over time for him.

The lust, I never understood.

Sure, he's beyond good looking, and his stature is just flat-out huge. Not just because he's super tall, but even his aura puts off this dominating energy that makes him seem even larger than life.

His silence makes him all the more untouchable and mysterious … and makes me want even more to get under that shell and find out what makes him tick. He's a curious mix of hard laced with the signs of a past that tells me he hasn't always been that way. I see it in his eyes, but especially the lines on his face that tell me, at one time, this man laughed and laughed hard.

Aside from all of that, I'm not quite sure what it is about Drew that makes me feel more toward him than just a coffee shop owner and her customer. My body reacts the second he's near—it always has—but it's becoming such a powerful reaction that I almost fall to my knees. Or butt. It's intensifying the more time we spend together, and when he's near, I find it harder and harder to hide that immense power behind polite words and great customer service etiquette outside of the coffee shop.

This need in the pit of my stomach drives me to uncover what's beneath the surface of this silent man. I want so badly to figure out what pushed him to start being our bodyguard over the past few weeks, but it's more than that. I need to understand *him*. I've racked my brain for the possibilities that would drive him to escort us to and from home every day. So far, I've come up with a whole bunch of nothing that seems even slightly rational or relevant. Since he's clearly not going to explain it to me, I've decided it's either time to resign myself to the possibility that I may never know, fully accept that it is what it is, or force him to tell me. Something tells me no one forces this man to do anything, though. I'm just not sure I can keep the current course without knowing. I feel like I'm coming out of my skin.

Daily walks escorted by the silent beast, known as my bean's giant, will drive me to the nuthouse. I just know it.

I come out of my musing when I see Riley finish her sidewalk performance, taking a bow in front of Drew. If you weren't looking for a reaction from him as I was, you'd completely miss the slight tip of his lip. It might not seem like much, but it's the world to Riley, which makes it the world to me. Their connection is a mystery of a different sort, that's for sure, but one that I'm very fond of watching them nurture into something that grows stronger each day. It amazes me how much they can communicate between themselves without verbal responses, but their language is certainly their own and would be impossible for anyone to decode or understand. However, it *can* be felt, that's for sure. It's how I know without a doubt that she's safe with him.

I learned over the years that my girl has the greatest intuition when it comes to people. She's like some weird morality detector. She can say hello to someone and instantly know if they're a good or bad egg. That holds a big part of why I trust him with her, if I'm honest. She became so attached to Drew without a second thought and lacking any doubt. You can practically feel the attachment coming from both of them.

No matter his reasons for doing all this, he's given her so much joy over the weeks, I almost don't even care to find out his motives for that alone.

Almost.

"Are you ready to go home now, Livi? The BTS World Tour concert is waiting for me to watch—the new one from San Pablo. You remember, you promised that I could watch it today and we could have pizza for dinner! Right?" Riley finishes and takes a huge gulp of air, practically coming out of her skin. I actually had forgotten that we pre-ordered the San Pablo concert when it was digitally released. She's already watched their New York and European ones so many times, I know the whole set list of their shows by heart. "It came this morning! I already tracked the package!" She's bouncing on her tiny little feet with excitement, her adorable hands folded in front of her chest.

"You tracked it?" I ask, dumbfounded.

"Of course I did."

"Are you sure you're only five years old?"

She rolls her beautiful eyes and does something that is so Drew, I almost laugh … her tiny little brow comes up in question instead of asking me again.

"Well, in that case … since you made sure to keep such a close eye on the delivery, it would be a shame for us not to rush home this very second and get it turned on for you. Clearly, you're more responsible than I am." I wink, and she giggles. "What do you say we get home, get some comfy clothes on, and order that pizza so we can get to watching?"

Riley shrieks with joy, twisting her little body to look at Drew. "Hurry, giant! We're going to have to walk with bigger steps today. Don't worry, Auntie can keep up. We've got a show to watch! Kay?"

His eyes appear to be very confused by what she's talking about, but he doesn't pause as he scoops her up in the well-practiced way he does, effortlessly placing her on his shoulders and securing her with his big hands in a light grasp on her tiny ankles, keeping her steady.

"Hey, giant?!" she calls from her perch, poking him in the head like she's so fond of doing. "You're going to come in and see it too, right?"

My heart stops. This is the first time she's asked him to come inside, but it also stops because this is my chance to get him in my home and question him about what's going on. I don't even realize I'm holding my breath until my chest burns, and I let it out slowly so he doesn't catch on.

His eyes meet mine and lock. For a split second, I think I see something new. Or maybe it's something that's always been there, but I just missed seeing it before now. However, almost as soon as I see that small glimmer, it's gone before I can decipher what it actually means. He tips his head with a slight nod and then begins to walk hesitantly until our steps are in sync.

"Yay! Off we go to watch BTS awesomeness, giant! Onward!" Riley screams, pointing down the street. A few people around us smile, but I can't even react to her adorable behavior because I'm still trapped by his gaze.

I struggle to even attempt to stay engaged in their one-sided, all Riley bean conversation because all I can think about is that look. It was there and then gone so fast, but … it was different. Not calm, not stormy, but there was still a burning in those depths that didn't make much sense.

Almost like … hope?

After a few minutes of obsessing, I attempt to shake it off and focus on anything else that can take my mind off that little glimmer of hope.

Riley is explaining, in great detail, the members of BTS. Even going as far as telling him their real names so he "knows" who they really are. She tries the best that her little mind can to explain to him the platform of BTS and what they stand for, in a sense, but I can tell it doesn't really compute.

"They are really a big force in encouraging people to love themselves as they are and to speak their truths, without fear and worry of prejudice," I add, gaining his attention *and* Riley's.

"That's what I said, Auntie."

"Of course it is, bean. Of course it is."

She goes off on a tangent about how he needs to make sure to get his own membership into the BTS Army because he can't have hers, and it came with all sorts of fun stuff that he will like. Oh boy, this kid. The confusion on his face is unmistakable as she keeps going. Educating such a manly man on all things BTS—from a five-year-old's viewpoint— really might be the most comical thing I've ever witnessed. I have to admit, it's nice to be able to recognize his emotions for once without guessing.

We continue our walk, and I smile while she continues telling him how V, or Kim Taehyung as she told him it is important to note his real name, is her bias. Another word for k-pop fans to label their favorite person. To my complete horror, she then tells him how her auntie's favorite is Jimin. My goodness, I thought I hid that better. Instead of looking at Drew to see what his reaction is to that little nugget, I let my mind wander and tune them out.

Riley's birthday is just around the corner. In a couple of weeks, my girl will be six, and just like every birthday, I want to make sure she has the best day. This year, I hope to have a few surprises for her. If I can pull them off, that is. You would think she would have a mile-long list of things she wants at her age, but not Riley. She rarely asks for things, and her birthday is no exception. Not that it's a bad thing to have a child who isn't always asking for things, but it sure does make gifting on holidays and her birthday quite challenging. It's the only time I ever wish she was a little obsessed with something—anything—material or some hyped-up toy. She's never known a life where money was an issue, so I count myself lucky that she didn't turn into the bratty, entitled child that usually comes from a high-society culture. Those kids grow to thrive off their material possessions and not a single thing else. The children I grew up with only knew how to find joy from what they had, not what they could do. Riley, on the other hand, doesn't care about things. She cares about time spent with those she loves and being present to enjoy every one of the experiences that will fill her memories for the rest of her days. She thrives on being near others. Their happiness is one of the biggest joy givers in her day. That being said, she can also be extremely sentimental, and when she's given a gift, she cherishes it to the max. Even cards. Maybe more so because they have messages reminding her how very loved she is.

I glance at Drew quickly before looking away. All these thoughts about her birthday and what matters to her remind me that I need to find a way to get "her giant" there. We have a tradition of having a little celebration at the Olde Mug with everyone who cares about her. Regulars come to spend the day with her outside of their regular drop-in times and fill the day with lots of laughter. It doesn't hurt that pizza and cake are free-flowing. Even though she is never without tons of people coming by on her special day, something tells me nothing I could get her would mean more than having her giant attend this year.

He might say no, but if I've learned nothing else, I will never underestimate the power and spell my Riley bean has on her giant.

It should unnerve me, but instead … it gives me peace.

CHAPTER 7

Drew

"DISAPPEAR" BY ELI.

Riley runs off the second we clear the threshold of their lavish two-story condo. She couldn't stop talking about some alphabet letter group who had a concert she just *had* to watch on the TV. From what I gathered from Olivia's sigh, this was normal for her to ask for. It was all just a bunch of stuff I couldn't understand, so I stopped trying and just nodded when Riley expected it from me. Having no clue as to what I agreed to only makes me slightly apprehensive.

I'm not sure what compelled me to accept Riley's offer of coming up, but no way did I have the power to say no, not to her … or her aunt, for that matter. I watch Olivia move to the table a few feet from the elevator door and place her purse and keys in the middle. I take a moment to look around the opulent space.

Plush gray rug over white marble flooring.

Twin white chairs that look like they cost a mint on either side of the table.

Artwork lines the bright white walls with lighting in the ceiling placed perfectly to showcase what I'm sure are costly prints.

It screams expensive.

I knew she had money. After I realized who she was, I pulled all the shit I could on her. Knowing it and seeing it, though … I damn sure wasn't picturing this. Beacon Street isn't an area to sneeze at; she must pay close to fifty grand a month here. Again, knew she was loaded, but seeing it was different from knowing it.

This was all supposed to be simple.

Get close to the girl, wait for that slimy shit I'm hunting to make contact, and then move on to the next target after we take him out.

What it wasn't supposed to be is whatever this is.

What I wasn't supposed to do was grow attached to the beautiful coffee shop owner and her niece.

That, definitely, wasn't supposed to happen.

Not that it's not allowed to have relationships, but because I can't imagine how I could ever tell Olivia who I am … who I *really* am.

I look down at the top of her head. She avoids looking at me, something she does a lot, but usually, it comes with sideway glances she doesn't think I see.

Oh, Olivia Elizabeth Kelley, I fucking see you.

Every time her gaze is on me in any capacity, I *feel* it.

It drives me to the brink of insanity.

I can't afford even the littlest distraction, and here I am with the biggest one I could have stumbled on.

It's not because it will take me off the hunt. Nothing takes me off the hunt.

No, I can't afford *this* distraction because it makes me want things I can't have.

Why can't you have them?

Fuck. The "old me" has been a chatty fuck these past two weeks.

Logically, nothing keeps me from getting this tiny little thing naked and fucking this attraction out of my system. When I became the "new me," no rules said I had to become a fucking monk. All I have to give someone is secrets and lies, so why bother? Lies of omission and lies big bold and bad. The day I "died," I knew anything good I had left in me to give someone was a thing of the past.

Including fucking sexy, petite coffee shop owners.

It doesn't stop me from wanting her, though.

"Why are you doing this, Drew?"

It's not the first time she's asked me. She asked me the whole way to her place every day for the first week. She's just never asked me with that expression on her face. One that screams unsure and fearful.

Fuck me. Another punch to my resolve. I want to make sure that look never crosses that angelic face again. Consequences be damned.

I look toward the staircase that, I assume, leads to the main level of her house and acts as a separator from this entryway.

"She won't be back down here for a bit. She's watching her favorite group, and they suck her attention up, so stop avoiding the question…" She pauses. "Please? I've gone over and over it. You clearly have a reason." She clears her throat as color rises on her cheeks. The burn in my throat makes me want to give her more than anyone outside my team has gotten in over twenty years … me.

"I know men like you," she continues, making me pause. "My parents hired men like you. You're always alert. You make sure to keep Riley close. You even make sure to shield *me* when we come around alleyways low in foot traffic. Always looking for a threat. Always have your guard up and in place. So yes, I know men like you. What I need to know is why are you protecting my niece and me?"

Well, fuck.

"I'm an outstanding citizen. I donate heavily to charities. I make sure I check the pulse of the world I left behind on a regular basis. The upper crust of this world doesn't care about me, nor do they care I left their fold. I have no enemies, Drew. None. Riley is practically a baby, so I know she doesn't have any. So what could possibly make you think you need to be here to protect us? I can't for the life of me figure you out. We've managed just fine on our own for three years, you know."

She takes a huge gulp of air and drops the hands she had been fidgeting together in front of her to her sides. With one more hefty inhale, she blows the air out slowly, seemingly getting a decent hold over her nerves.

"Please, Drew."

I have to hide the wince. I fucking hate when she calls me Drew.

"I can deal with a lot," she continues. "I've lived a life that means I can handle it, whatever *it* is. What I can't handle is this constant state of unknown. I'm a planner. I need to plan. It calms me. Please … I need to

45

know what has you acting as a shadow whenever we step outside of my home."

I open my mouth to answer but close it when I hear Riley's voice coming from deep in the house, yelling in … no way … "She speaks Korean?"

Olivia rolls her eyes. "You're silent for years. Coming into the shop without so much as a peep. Sprinkle in a few grunts and a handful of single-syllable words, but for the most part, you," she huffs and pokes my chest, "are silent. Silent during this new development of you becoming my shadow to and from work. And *that* is what gets you to finally talk?"

I shrug. What can I really say that she will understand? The kid is cool. Try as I might to stay indifferent to her, she makes me feel like I'm back at home. Though, all those kids are a long way away from the little kid that Riley is. Regardless, she reminds me of this awesome little guy I knew in a different life. I often wonder how he is, how all of them are, but Riley's made me miss that part of the old me a lot more than I ever have. No, that's not right … Riley *and Olivia* have made me miss that part of my old life.

"She sings in Korean. Big difference."

"Still speakin' it."

"Drew," she softly complains, her temper showing. And I like it. I like it way too much.

"Dangerous city." Even to my own ears, it sounds like bullshit.

"I've lived here my whole life. I know better than most how dangerous it can be. That being said, I also know how to be safe in this dangerous city. Try again, mister."

Goddammit.

I should have just done this from a distance from the beginning. Had I not let my dick lead, she wouldn't be any wiser. For Christ's sake, she wouldn't even know she was being watched. I could have done all this while keeping a distance and jumping through the shadows. That's not how it went, though, because just as she's drawn me to her shop every day since she opened the doors, she drew me in when I meant to just watch her. There was no other option. I needed to be right where I was with a force driving me that I still couldn't understand.

I shrug, not knowing what to say. The thought of lying to her doesn't sit right with me. However, I also can't tell her what I'm doing. There aren't rules to what I do, sure. The government didn't help "kill" me just to put me under someone's thumb to control. The only rule they have is to kill the threats using whatever means necessary without jeopardizing the public's safety. Something I had started doing long before the day I was shot during an altercation not connected to my job for them. It came at the perfect time, too, because I had become reckless with my life. My face—the one I had then—was known by way too many people. The kind of people who would love to use the people I loved against me. My death meant they would never be used as a pawn against me. They would forever be safe with my death. Those people who would have used them had nothing to gain from it without me alive. Age helped, but I'm no longer that carefree and jovial boy next door.

That is, until Riley's infectious happiness started cracking at my walls. Letting Olivia's light just burst inside.

So I could tell her the truth if I knew she was someone who would be in my life for good, but I won't. Something tells me that she will be long gone when she finds out about the threat she doesn't even know is coming.

It's my job not only to take that piece of shit out but also to make sure he doesn't touch this life Olivia and Riley have built together.

"I'm going to need more than that, Drew. I'm starting to feel like I'm not safe. I don't like that feeling."

Her voice breaks through my turbulent thoughts, and I jerk my head back as if she's struck me.

"Unsafe?"

"Oh yeah."

"From me?" I question, pointing my finger at my chest.

She gives a giant huff, turning from where she had been standing in front of me—close enough that I could smell the scent of her floral perfume—and she starts pacing. It's adorable. She's a tiny little thing. Well under a foot shorter than me. Petite with just enough curves. Every time she turns to stomp back in the other direction, that shiny brown hair spins around with her and fans around her shoulders, landing to rest just above her tits. For such a small girl, she's got a good solid handful.

I feel myself stir and bring my attention back to her face and away from her sexy body. Not the time to get hard. Not the time at all.

"You come in to Olde Mug. Every single day for years, Drew. You never so much as give me a clue that you notice me for anyone other than your barista. A grunted thanks, or at least I think it's thanks that you would say. Sometimes you won't even look me in the eyes. No, scratch that … almost every time. Your friends, now I could make sense of it a little more if those guys started standing outside my business and home every day. They engage in conversation. They even reciprocate that conversation, so it's not like I would be shocked. But you? You are just as silent as usual. Acting like we're walking through an active war zone and not Boston. You're *that* alert, Drew. So please, tell me what's going on."

"Like the kid."

"She's easy to like. That's not it. Try again."

I need to change the subject. I have to change this conversation's path. So I do the only thing I know how to do. I use my looks—and the attraction I know she's felt for me—to distract her mind. It takes me two steps, and I have her pushed into the wall, my body covering her small one as I hold her up with my hands on her ass. My mouth hits hers the instant I have her in my arms in a kiss so deep, it steals my breath.

Fuck me.

Bad idea.

Colossally bad idea.

Now, now I know I'm well and truly fucked when it comes to Olivia Kelley.

Her legs wrap around my hips, her core burning me through my jeans. My cock is straining against my zipper. Her hands go to my hair, pushing into the thick locks and massaging my scalp. I suck her tongue into my mouth when she uses her nails against my oversensitive head. Our kiss grows hungrier and hungrier as we feed each other with our desire.

I push my length against her, and her mouth opens wider, allowing me to swallow her gasp.

Fifty-two years old and I'm about to come in my goddamn pants.

I'm no stranger to sex … well, no, it seems like I am. I was careless with my body when I was younger. All I cared about was how to get a woman naked and my cock inside her in the quickest way possible. We both always knew what was happening, not that it makes it better. I used them. And to be fair, they used me just as much. I made sure no one was confused. I only had sex. They would never get more from me. I made sure the women I was with were just as carefree about relationships as I was.

With this woman, though? The one who's currently feasting on my mouth like she's drunk for a drink only I can give her … she makes me want to break all the rules.

Turning my head slightly, I take her mouth harder, our tongues dancing together as if we've been doing this with each other for years. It doesn't feel like a first kiss, there is no hesitancy or awkward moments between us. Just two people who finally put the last piece in a long hunt to finish their puzzle.

In a way, maybe we have.

If it wasn't necessary to be watching her and Riley, I'm not sure I would have been able to feel what is in my arms right now. I lived by letting the cogs turn the wheel and only oiling it when necessary. I woke, worked, ate, and slept. One kiss from Olivia, and I feel like I have everything. Everything I had given up when I left my old life behind made me want them for the first time in over twenty years. Only everything I gave up then was for a good reason. The greater good, I guess you could say. I knew then I would never have a true connection with a woman. I would never have the kids I always thought I would have. It was a hard pill to swallow, but I did so with each passing year.

Until Olivia.

Olivia makes me want to change all the rules. Tear down all the walls left that her light hasn't finished crumbling. She makes me want to live again.

Her moan breaks through my thoughts and slams into my gut.

At that moment, I know that my tactic for distracting her just backfired.

The only thing I managed to do was distract myself because there is no damn way I'll be able to stop now.

I've had a taste of heaven.

And I never want to give it up.

Olivia lifts her head back, knocking the shit out of herself on the wall. She doesn't even seem to notice hitting her head, though. She's breathless, dazed, and gorgeous. Those pale-green eyes look into mine with a million more questions than she had before. Color high on her cheeks, her tits heaving against my chest. She might as well have a bright-red arrow pointing at her, announcing how turned on she is.

All from a few minutes of giving me that sweet mouth? That's all it took.

"YAY! It's climb the giant-stalk time!" Riley screams, her little voice breaking the haze of lust Olivia and I had created. I hear her running down toward us, closer. Still, Olivia doesn't move. She just holds my gaze. "Auntie, you got high! You got it wrong, though. It's okay if you're nervous. It's not that scary when you're up there. You're supposed to sit on his head!"

Olivia's eyes widen, and her cheeks get even redder than they had been, the blush spreading into her shirt, and my imagination can't help but picture that blush on her tits. For the first time in a long damn time, I feel the need to laugh. Of course, I don't, but it feels good to feel that freedom again.

Riley keeps climbing up my body, pulling herself up using fists of my shirt and digging her feet into the backs of my legs. She gets to where Olivia's legs are and uses them to get to where she wants to be. I reach back to help Riley and press my crotch into Olivia's hot center to support my hold on her in the process. The move both tortures and pleasures. Riley's hands go to my hair, her feet hook behind my back, and she lets out the sweetest giggle.

"I win!"

Her aunt, who only a second ago looked like she was about to explode—and not from anger—smiles sweetly up at her. I've watched them enough to know that she loves that little girl as much as she would if she was her own biological kid. Being this close to her and seeing her face light with that love for her niece hits me right in my chest like a punch. It immediately feels like a defibrillator has shocked the life back into my dead heart. Visions that I haven't let myself come close to imagining rush into my mind. Visions that died the day I did. Visions of seeing this expression for a long damn time.

"I don't think I could do that, little bean." Olivia laughs up at Riley. Again, I get another shock to the center of my chest.

"Sure, you can. You just have to grab on and get up."

"Wise words." Olivia chuckles.

"Hey," Riley calls down, tapping me on the head with her fingertip harder than a five-year-old should be able to poke someone. Every damn time she wants my attention, I think she's about to reach my brain with that little finger.

I keep her aunt's gaze and grunt, letting the little fireball of energy know I got the message … and the sore spot. My grunt must have moved my body some. I love the hell out of the way Olivia's eyes flash. I cock my brow, and she narrows her eyes.

"You're still going to stay for movie night, right?"

I don't even think. Not about the need to get the hell out of here before Olivia keeps asking questions I don't know how to answer without knowing *her* better. Not about how much I would like to slide into this sexy body and fuck her until we're both passed out from exhaustion. Not even about why I'm actually here right now.

I open my mouth, and for the first time in a lifetime, I don't even think about anything but this feeling of being alive.

"Yeah."

CHAPTER 8

Olivia

"PLAY IT COOL" BY MONSTA X FT. STEVE AOKI

The whole walk through my house, I keep thinking I'm in a dream or something. There is no reality that I could have dreamed up where this man would be inside my house right now, so it has to be a dream. I've clearly had an accident on the way home today, and I'm stuck in some coma or something and now in some coma-induced dreamscape.

I don't date. Riley is used to being around other people but never men inside our house. Yet here she is, acting like this is the most normal thing to invite a man for movie night. A man who, in reality, I honestly don't know well enough to be inviting into my house.

I know he's safe. That's all I truly know.

Ella found out a few years ago that he and his friends worked for the government. She saw their badges, so I know he's at least as safe as that would make someone. He's also been coming into Olde Mug for years. So what if today is the most he's ever spoken to me?

Now here he is, walking with Riley high on his shoulders, into our movie theater room like it's the most normal thing in the world. I look around the theater room—which is really just a big bonus area that I had renovated and blacked out with a wall-sized screen put in for the top-of-the-line projector—and try to see it through his eyes. The room is decent in size, but not one of our largest, so to save space and allow for the snack bar, fridge, and popcorn machine, we settled on two round cuddle couches in the center instead of rows of seats. They're, hands down, the most comfortable things I have ever sat my butt on, and they fit like perfection in this room. It's a cozy room, but it still screams money. Being used to that having a negative impact on new people, assuming I'm someone I'm not, I waited to see the look in his eyes. The one that tells me they think I'm a rich bitch, and they'll put up with me for what my money can give them. Only that's not what I see. Instead, I only see warmth.

"Down, giant," Riley commands, and Drew breaks eye contact with me to do her bidding. He swings her away from his shoulders with his hands on her waist, twisting his hold and giving her a little toss in the air before effortlessly catching her. She lands face-to-face with him holding her away from his body. Her little legs dangle in the air, and she wears a huge smile on her face.

She laughs softer than the loud twill he had gotten from her seconds before and reaches out to lightly poke his nose ring. Only then does he softly place her feet to the cushion. Like that little boop was the down button on her new elevator ride. She moves around the round seat cushion before settling her little body into the thickly pillowed back of the couch.

I watch in horror as she pats the cushion right next to her and looks up at Drew.

"Come on, giant. You *always* have to cuddle when it's movie night."

He looks over his shoulder and down at me, that damn sexy brow of his up in a silent question.

Well, crap.

I didn't think about this.

It's always Riley and me when we have movie night. Sometimes Ella will join us, but she just curls up on her own seat and tells Riley she only cuddles for chocolate. On a rare occasion, when she can get time away, Grace joins us. There's never been a man the likes of Drew—or any man for that matter—join us. I look from the couch, up to Drew, and back again to the couch. If he sits down where she wants, there's no way I can avoid making this awkward. I glance to my left and eye the second cuddle couch. The one that never gets used by anyone but Ella and Grace.

I could just go sit there.

"No," Drew's deep voice rumbles, breaking my musing and I know he's got to be watching me pretty closely.

"Riley, baby … there isn't a whole lot of room on there. What if we have game night instead and save movie night for tomorrow? We could all sit at the table and be cozy."

"I don't want to play games. I want to watch a movie with my giant."

"How about you sit with your giant, and I'll just sit over there on the other couch?" I ask, pointing at the second sofa.

"No," Drew repeats more forcefully.

"No," Riley parrots, mimicking his hard tone to perfection.

"There's just not that much—" I squeal when I'm moving through the air a second later, my words stolen from my mouth with the quick movement.

One second, I'm standing there, and the next, my back is against the couch with my side pressed close to Drew's. Riley lifts her head to look up at me and giggles over his chest.

The chest that's moving slightly, like he's … laughing?

I whip my head up and see a twinkle in his eye. But no other outward sign that he was, in fact, laughing.

"Do you ever laugh?"

He doesn't react.

"What about smile?"

Nothing.

"Do you do anything other than silently brood?"

"What's brood, Auntie?"

"Your giant. He's a brood."

"That's silly. He's a giant, not a brood."

This time, it's me that raises a brow at him. "Do you own any clothing that isn't black or dark?"

"His jeans are blue, Auntie," Riley informs me, pride in her voice for noticing.

"Dark blue," I mutter under my breath.

"Giant, do you want to pick the movie?"

He shakes his head. Of course he does. Because saying the word no would just be too much.

"Auntie, can I watch—" I cut her off with a shake of my head. "Please?" she continues.

"Absolutely not. You've gotten your way the past three movie nights, Riley. I'm sick of that one. I know you want to watch the San Pablo show over and over tomorrow, too. Let's take a small break from BTS tonight and watch an actual movie, okay?"

"But my giant hasn't seen my friends."

"Pick something else. There's only so much BTS I can take in one day." Which is a lie, I could probably listen to them on repeat. They're good, but I'm not admitting that to Riley. If I do, they'll always be on.

Riley scampers off the couch to go grab the remote. I use her absence to push up on the couch and look down at Drew.

"What are you doing?" I hiss.

His brow goes up.

I reach toward him and poke his chest. He grabs my wrist and pulls me back down to his side. Only now he's holding my hand captive, and he just places it on his chest like this isn't a big deal. Meanwhile, my body is on fire, and I'm about to hyperventilate.

"Drew," I complain.

"Hush." His tone gives me pause.

Each time I've heard him speak, he's had a gruff voice. One that I'm reasonably sure is from lack of use, seeing that he can talk but just decides not to, but this was not his normal tone. That was *hard,* with no room to argue. Sure, I could, but he knows I won't with Riley in the room. I do the only thing that I can do. I lie back down and grab the remote when Riley tosses it on the couch, almost getting Drew right between the legs. He grunts, his whole body tensing as it braces for impact. I whip my hand out and catch the device just in time. Just not quick enough to avoid feeling the thick ridge of his cock against the back of my hand.

This time, it's me that makes the sound deep in my throat.

"Snacks!" Riley screams and moves farther away, down the side of the room.

Drew's body moves as he crunches his abs and lifts up slightly from his position. His beard tickles my forehead as he leans closer. "You on the snack menu?" he asks, shocking me completely.

I jerk, elbow digging into the couch, and gape my mouth at him. This time, he not only shocks me but stops my heart completely.

Because Drew can *smile*.

His eyes hold so much in them. Not only has the storm remained gone while he's been with us, but that calm has been replaced with a burn so bright it can't be mistaken as anything other than what it is … lust. I think about his question. Does it really matter why he's been walking us home? Sure, but does it *really*? I know he's safe in the general sense, but what do I really know about him? Then again, it's been close to eight years since I've scratched my itch, and I imagine Drew knows what he's doing.

Deciding to throw caution to the wind and just roll with it, at least until I can get some answers out of him, I relax back into his side.

"It's a secret menu, but I'll let you take a look later."

His chest moves as he chuckles, and I smile to myself. Nothing wrong with a little fun, but with a mystery like him, I have a feeling this might be a little more like an adventure.

Riley returns a second later, climbing back in and dumping tons of candies and treats on Drew's stomach. He doesn't even move, just lets her use him as her sorting table. She doesn't lie back down because she's taking up so much room perusing through her loot. She looks up from her contemplation of Skittles or Twizzlers and smirks at me.

"The circus one, Auntie."

"Oh yeah?"

"Yup," she responds, the p loud in the silent room.

"If that's what you want." I point the remote toward the control center and start looking for *The Greatest Show*. It's one of our favorites, but something tells me that Drew isn't going to like the musical at all. He doesn't exactly seem like the type of man who sits at home watching musicals and singing along, like Riley and I do. Poor guy, he has no idea what he's gotten himself into.

The opening song starts playing, and Riley finally makes her selection. Then she points her face to the ceiling and screams, "Alexa, turn my movie room lights off!"

Drew's chest moves again with his soundless laughter.

I didn't even make it thirty minutes before my eyes drew heavy, and I let the safety I felt with Drew's arm around my shoulders and his warm chest lull me to sleep. The last thought I remember thinking was how much trouble I might be in where this man is concerned.

And I'm not sure I mind it one bit.

CHAPTER 9

Olivia

"HOLD BACK THE RIVER" BY JAMES BAY

I feel the heavy weight of a deep sleep coming off my body in slow degrees. Everything takes a sluggish pace to turn back on, my brain being the last to plug back in. I try to remember the last thing I could before falling into such a blissful slumber, but everything is just blank. All I feel is content peacefulness. Something I don't think I've felt in a long time.

That's when I feel something on my arm.

Something that sets fire to my skin as well as adds more of that peacefulness to my soul. So strange, the two of those feelings dancing together. It's when the touch reaches my neck, my hair sliding off my face a little from where it had fallen. The touch traces my hairline, tucking the hair behind my ear before following the trail of my jaw. When I lose it, it's like a jolt to my mind that finally pushes awareness to the forefront.

My eyes snap open, and I gasp when I see Drew sitting on the edge of the cuddle couch, looking down at me with something akin to reverence in his gaze. I move quicker than he expected because the top of my head cracks against his chin. I hear him grunt, but I'm too busy looking around the room to worry about the dull ache on the top of my head.

"Where's bean?"

"Bed."

"I'm sorry?"

He clears his throat. "You both fell asleep. Took her to bed, tucked her in, then came back to wake you up."

"You … tucked her in?"

He nods.

"You know how to tuck someone in?"

That damn brow. I shrug, not feeling bad at all for questioning him.

"It's not rocket science, Olivia."

"Do you know rocket science, too?"

"Are you always this stubborn when you wake up?"

"Drew," I start, but stop when he looks at me with a harshness that steals my words. "What?"

He shakes his head. It isn't until now that I realize he's not holding his words from me. There was actual communication that didn't involve nods and grunts.

"You're talking," I gasp, shifting so I'm kneeling. My knees dig into his thighs as I get a little closer and search his troubled eyes.

He lets out a burst of air so harsh, I can practically feel the weight of the world on his shoulders.

"Please, don't stop."

"It's not that easy, Livi."

"What isn't?" I ask, desperate to keep him from shutting me out. Proud that my voice doesn't get all weird when the butterflies kick up at the shortening of my name.

"You make me want things that I gave up wanting a long time ago."

I frown. This man, he's such a mystery to me.

"You make me want things I told myself I would never consider. So I guess we're both even there."

"You have no idea what you're talking about."

"You want to talk about stubborn. Hey pot, my name is kettle."

He sighs, then leans against the arm of the couch and looks at me. Really looks at me. In a way that makes me think he can read my very thoughts, see my whole past, and know what lurks in every corner that I keep shadowed for a reason.

"What keeps you single? Riley said you've never had a boyfriend."

"My parents weren't good parents," I answer.

"It's a lot more than that."

"You're right. Not only were they not good parents but they were never here. My sister and I were raised by a revolving door of staff that didn't stick around for long because my parents were even worse humans to them than they were parents to us. I learned a long time ago that it was best to live alone—now with Riley—because I haven't had a single healthy example of a relationship."

"So you just decided to never even try?"

I nod. "Yeah. I don't need a man to make me happy. I'm happy with Riley, Olde Mug, and my friends."

His eyes sharpen, his attention fully on me, but it's his breathing I notice. He isn't unaffected. So I do what feels right, I keep going. Giving him more than anyone has ever gotten from me.

"My sister, Emma"—I sigh—"was the dreamer. Where I just wanted to have my coffee shop and live a simple life outside of the social circles we had been forced into … she didn't have the same thoughts. She thought she needed a man to save her. She was convinced the first one who gave her a second glance was perfect."

"What happened?" he questions, something scratchy in his tone.

"You really want to know?"

"I wouldn't ask if I didn't."

"He ended up killing her instead of loving her." I know I sound detached, I can hear it in my own ears as well as see it in his features. I learned years ago that I have to be withdrawn or the pain of how I lost Emma would rip me in two, and I needed to be whole *and* healed from the sadness in order to be the guardian Riley deserves. Not only that, but I want Riley to see nothing but the love I have for her mom when I'm talking about Emma.

"Liv," he breathes.

"It's okay, Drew. I miss her every day, but I have Riley. She gives me a purpose."

"Riley mentioned her dad, too. What's she know about him?"

"Ray?"

"If that's the guy, then yeah."

"Nothing. I told her he died before she was born and that's all."

"You know she thinks he was a good man?"

I nod.

"You do?"

"Yeah." I sigh, looking away and down at my hands. "She lost her mom, someone who loved her with all her being, because of him. She was too young to know, and I didn't think she needed to have that kind of pain. So I told her that her mom was in an accident, and her dad was gone before she was born."

"She's romanticized the idea of him."

"What did she say?"

He swallows, holding my gaze, and I know I won't like it.

"That she wishes her dad was here. She said it was nice to have me here because she knew her auntie felt safe. She said you never sleep like that. You only sleep when she's asleep."

"Shit," I mutter. My beautiful yet way too smart niece.

"What happened to him? Her dad."

My exhale is loud. Fills the room with the sound and the heaviness of the memories of that asshole.

"Emma was five years younger than me. We were thick as thieves our whole lives. She didn't see the world like I did, but she also accepted that we both saw things differently and didn't try to change me to fit her views. She just wanted to be loved, while I was content with just loving myself. When she met Ray, he said all the right things, showered her with gifts, and made her think she'd hit the jackpot. He got her pregnant a month after meeting her, but Emma didn't care. She just wanted the family we never had. And she thought Ray was the saint that could give that to her." I glance up at Drew, seeing his expression getting softer as he lets me finish. "I didn't realize what type of man he was until it was too late. He always rubbed me the wrong way, but I thought it was just because he had a tendency to say inappropriate things."

"You don't have to tell me more. Not if it's hard."

"It's not that, I'm just trying to remember what it was that clued me in on how bad he was. I think it was when Riley was around one and I saw him talking to a man who is well known for being tied up in a lot of bad stuff. He didn't see me, but I saw enough to know he knew this man well. I mentioned it to Emma. I didn't hear from her for a week, and when I did, it was to ask me to watch Riley. The day she came to get Riley, I saw the bruises. I begged her to let me help her, but she wouldn't hear of it and didn't talk to me for close to six months."

"Fuck," he mutters, pulling me closer.

"Things were strained after that, but when she called me the night he killed her, she told me she was getting out. He was out of town, and she would go get her stuff out. She brought Riley to me, and we made plans to get her out of town. That was the last time I saw her."

He doesn't speak, but he doesn't need to. His arms come out and pull me into his warm body a second later. My cheek hits his chest, and I feel the rapid beating of his heart against it. His breathing is calm, but his heart is giving him away. This man isn't as unaffected by life as he pretends to be. Or maybe he just can't fool me. For whatever reason, I have a feeling the connection I've felt toward him from the first time I made eye contact is much more than sexual.

"What happened to him? Riley's father?"

"Died. Car accident."

Drew goes solid, and I lift off his chest to look up at his face. But, as normal, there is nothing to be read on his features.

"What is it?"

"When did this happen?"

I ignore his question. "What was that reaction about?"

He looks down, and I gasp when I see the heat in his eyes. Anger.

"When did he die?"

"The night he killed her. He was on the way to a small airport outside of the city. I only know that his plane never left, and his car was burned to bits. There was nothing left but a few teeth to identify him with."

"There's a lot of skeletons in my closet, Liv," he oddly says, his voice deeper with his anger very present.

"Okay," I hedge, not understanding where he's coming from.

"You just gave me all of your sister, but I can't give you all of those skeletons. I'm not sure I can ever give them all to you. There's going to come a day that you might find out something about me that will make you wish you didn't let me in."

I feel my brow furrow and look at him, studying the intensity in his face.

"But I can promise you that there will never be a moment to fear me for as long as I'm in your life. Men like Ray, they're the reason that I gave my life up for this career. As long as I'm here, you two won't ever have to worry."

"I don't fear you." I didn't expect him to react so strongly, but it's true. I don't fear him.

He grunts. "Maybe you should, but I swear I won't hurt you or Riley."

"I know that."

He goes silent and I rest my head against his chest, content despite the heaviness of what I just shared.

"Drew?"

"Hmm?"

"You don't need to tell me about those skeletons, not unless you want to or you need to. I do need to know what's going on that's making you stick close to us, though. If you want a sample from my snack menu, you're going to have to let me in on that before I let you in on me."

"Fuck," he hisses, one thickly muscled arm coming down to adjust the bulge in his pants, which just makes me lick my lips.

"I know you feel whatever this is between us. I feel it. I'm not asking for your secrets, but I am asking to be clued in if those secrets involve me or Riley."

"Yeah, Liv. I feel it. First time in two fucking decades I've been alive again. Trust me, babe. I *feel* it."

"I know the feeling. I didn't realize I wasn't content with what I had until you came along and started grunting your way into my life."

His chest moves, but he doesn't let the laugh out.

"Then tell me what's going on, Drew. Tell me what's going on and let's just take this a day at a time and feel alive while we do it."

"It's not easy for me to let people in, Liv. It's not easy for me to share this part of me with anyone outside of my team. To tell you what started me sticking close, I have to let you in."

"If you're worried I'm going to judge you—"

He cuts me off with a finger over my lips.

"I know you aren't that person."

I keep silent and let him work out his thoughts. I can tell he's doing just that because the silence is full of his energy. I'm not sure what I thought he would say, but it wasn't what I got.

"I work for the government, though you'll never find any record of my employment. I'm essentially their ghost. The guys and I. We do what they can't in the eyes of the law. That said, a man I'm hunting will be making contact close to you. I couldn't take a chance that something could happen to you or Riley, so I decided to keep watch on you and the threat."

"What? You didn't even know us, Drew. Someone is going to contact me? What does that even mean?"

"Didn't have to *know* you to know I wanted to know you. That's all I can tell you right now. Please trust me enough to let me keep you two safe, and when the job is over, I'll tell you more. I'm not keeping it from you to be a dick. I'm keeping it from you to keep you safe."

"That doesn't make me feel safe."

"I know. Doesn't feel right to keep keeping it from you. Just not sure how to explain it without making you scared."

"Why can't you tell me?"

"Been working on this case for a while, Liv. I can't risk you having knowledge of it and it messing anything up." He holds up his hands. "I don't mean that in a slight, but I need you acting like life is normal."

She's quiet, holding my gaze and mulling over what I've told her.

"It's scary to trust blindly. Thank you for sharing that with me. So what happens now? I just pretend someone isn't out there looking for me and wait until you tell me more?"

"Yeah, babe. Trust isn't the easiest thing to earn, I know that. Thanks for sharing with me, too. Now we continue as normal, and you let me get to know you in the process. How does that sound?"

"Scary. Riley's already attached to Drew. Don't say stuff like that unless you plan to be around for a while. I'll admit, I would like that, but we can still dance in the fire that burns whenever we're near without involving her. Not to mention the big unknown 'someone.'"

"Too late for that, Olivia. Way too late for that."

I shift, moving so that I'm looking into his brilliant eyes. "Yeah, I think you might be right. Guess she isn't the only one hooked on a giant."

His smile comes out of nowhere. It shocks me to the point that I gasp loudly, only making him smile even bigger. My God, I knew he was handsome, but I wasn't expecting *this*. He looks so much younger than when he's so serious. Almost boyish, in that all American way. I bet if he shaved his beard, he would look the part. Perfectly straight, bright white teeth, and those lines that I just *knew* proved a past of much laughter are all on display.

"Okay, Drew. I'm going to trust you. Please don't make me regret this."

His smile grows, and I feel lightheaded by the sight.

"I think I'd like to show you my snack menu now," I mumble, still looking at his mouth, transfixed by his handsomeness.

Right before I lose sight of his smile, he growls deep in his throat and crushes his mouth to mine.

Holy shit.

Alive, indeed.

Time to trust and let life happen.

CHAPTER 10

Drew

"BAD INTENTIONS" BY NIYKEE HEATON

I shift our bodies, taking me to my back with her on top of me. Just like earlier, I can feel her heat against my cock, burning me through our clothing. Her breasts heavy against my chest. She shifts when we roll, spreading her legs wider, dipping her arms so that her weight is resting on her forearms with her elbows digging into the couch ... her hands going into my hair. Something I've noticed about her, she definitely likes my hair. I never imagined it would feel this good having her fingers tangled in those annoyingly long strands. I don't give a fuck if I've hated this hair for years, and it no longer matters that it was only grown to help disguise me. I'm thankful as fuck for it now.

She moans into my mouth, deepening our kiss and rocking her hips slowly.

That's when I realized there was no stopping this.

My hands trail from her back, where I had been holding her to my body, to her sides. My thumbs feel the swell of her tits, but I keep going even though I want nothing more than to take those heavy globes into my hand. I don't stop until my hands are pushed into her back pockets and I'm pushing her down while thrusting my hips up. She makes a low and desperate sound, clenching her thighs and shaking with her whole body.

Jesus, this woman will ignite the second I touch her. I can feel it, her being that close to coming undone, and I haven't so much as moved more than an inch.

It's not lost on me, while I feel Olivia's hips doing a slow rock against mine, that this isn't something I should be doing until she knows the whole truth. I might have been living my life as a ghost for over twenty years, but I didn't live it stupidly. I know that by her giving herself to me, when she finds out what I'm keeping from her—as well as the truth about me in reality—it could end us catastrophically.

But just like the first time I saw her across the street walking into her shop, I'm powerless to stop the draw that she has on me.

I've never felt anything like this.

I watched my brothers, the ones from my old life, meet their partners and knew instantly when they met someone meant for them. It took one look for some of them. One damn look and they just knew. A few took the stubborn road and ignored that look or had to fight for a love they thought they had lost, but the common theme was … *they knew*. At that point in my life, and the past I had with an unhealthy view of women, I thought it was all a bunch of bullshit. I fucked my way through life back then, thinking it was the way to find a connection. The problem was, I was fucking easy women who had no desire to want me past what I could make them feel with my cock. Looking back, I now know I did it because I was scared to give more of myself to someone who could mean something.

I was blind.

I was naive.

I didn't believe.

Plain and simple, I didn't believe.

Now, I don't miss the irony. I was scared to give more of myself to someone then because it would make me vulnerable. I had a vulnerable childhood, so I didn't want that shit as an adult. Now that I've found someone I know means something more, I'm scared to give myself for different reasons. They all boil down to the same thing—me having to make myself vulnerable for someone else.

"I want you," she gasps, pulling me out of my thoughts and back to the present. The present where I have a live wire of a beautiful woman

67

looking down at me with a lazy haze in her eyes, drunk on the feeling of our kiss while she uses the friction of our bodies to climb high as hell up the peak of arousal.

"I fuck … Olivia, I'm not sure I can give you up."

She tips her head to the side and ponders my words. My gaze roams over her face, seeing the color high on her cheeks, her hair a mess from going wild on top of me, and her lips swollen from our kiss.

Yeah, I'm not sure I can ever give her up.

"I'm not sure I want you to, Drew."

Fuck. That goddamn name.

"Call me Coop, please. When we're alone, especially like this, you call me Coop. Middle name, but babe, don't call me Drew anymore. Not when it's just you and me. I can't explain more, but I'm Coop in your arms."

She looks confused, but still she nods before she licks her lips, and for the first time in this life of a ghost, I feel like I'm alive again when she opens her mouth.

"Okay … Coop," she breathes, the sound of my name on her lips wrapping around me.

"Okay," I echo, proud as hell that I kept the emotion out of that one word. I lift my head off the couch as my hands push into the silk of her hair, palms to her ears, and I pull her face back to mine and kiss her.

Our kiss is tender, but there's a fire burning there that makes it carnal and so fucking intimate, I can't help myself but keep taking. I'm powerless to do anything but. My body moves, flipping her to her back with a squeak. Her hands roam all over my body, and it takes me a second to realize that I need her skin. I lift my head and look around the room.

"Are we safe in here, or do we need to move somewhere where the door can be locked?"

"We're good. She won't wake up, not if she was asleep when you left her."

"Snoring," I grunt, looking at the skin at her stomach peeking from her shirt riding up. My eyes going from that and up the buttons in front of her blouse to her tits. Those tits that have made my mouth water every single day for way too fucking long.

"She won't wake up. We're safe," she repeats. She wiggles and tightens her thighs, but can't get far with my body between her. I watch her, desperate for my touch, and feel a smile curl at my lips, one that has nothing but promise in it. She groans and shocks the shit out of me when her hands come up, and she lifts her body to rub one dainty as fuck hand against the erection straining my jeans. "Please … Coop."

Hearing that name, *MY* name coming from her makes me come alive as quick as someone lighting a goddamn fuse. I lick my lips, then reach up and pull my shirt over my head. I hear her gasp, knowing it's either from the tattoos covering every inch of my torso or the unmistakable pucker scar from a bullet tearing through someone's skin. I ignore it and just as the shirt clears my head, I feel a rumble of appreciation come from deep in my gut when she curls those little fingers into the openings between her buttons and rips off her blouse. Buttons flying and the fabric opening instantly. Her white lace bra does nothing to hide her dusty rose and hard nipples from my view.

"Goddamn beautiful," I rasp, bending down and closing my mouth over the lace and sucking a hard peak deep into my mouth. My other hand comes up to play with her other breast. She goes wild the second the heat from my mouth hits her skin.

"Oh my God!" she exclaims when I start moving my erection against her core. "I need to feel more. I need more of your skin."

I ignore her, moving my mouth to the other nipple, pulling the cup down so there isn't anything between us anymore. I suck hard and then use my teeth until she alternates between pulling my hair to move me away and pushing me down to keep me on her nipple.

Wild.

I knew she would be wild.

"Please, Coop." My name comes easier the more she uses it. I love it.

I'm off her in a second, my hands going to the buttons on her pants and pulling them and her panties off in the same second. She lifts up and removes the rest of her shirt and bra before falling back on to the cushion. I wasn't expecting what happened next, but as I stood there with my pants unbuttoned and thumbs hooked in the waistband, I watch as the prim and proper coffee shop owner who has become my obsession turns into a wild woman.

69

Her hand travels down her stomach, her legs widen, and she pushes two fingers into her wet pussy, rocking her hips as she pumps them in and out.

My pants are gone in seconds. My cock springs free, and then I drop to the floor. My knees hit the hard marble floor, and my hands reach out to pull her hips to the edge. My growl is nothing short of primal when her scent hits me.

"Move it," I demand.

"Make me," she smarts.

"Fuck."

I snatch her hand out of her pussy, taking those two wet fingers and placing them in my mouth. She mewls loudly as my tongue swirls and sucks them clean. Not taking my eyes off hers, I release her fingers from my mouth and drop her hand to her side … then I drop my mouth to her pretty pussy.

The second her flavor hits my mouth, I'm a starved man getting his first meal in years.

I've been a fool.

I wasn't a saint before I was a ghost. I was a whore who used my body in the search of something I never could find because I had no respect for myself. In the years that I've spent hunting, I've not allowed myself a single slip back into the old me. The only time I've allowed myself a release was when it was with someone who made it clear they only wanted to use me. There were never emotions. No intimacy aside from heavy petting, a hard fuck, and a silent goodbye after. I knew I had nothing to offer someone, and they made it clear I was being used in the first place. I was okay with it because fuck me, twenty-plus years without any human touch to make you feel like you weren't actually dead is a long time.

Oh, how I was a fool.

I've been living my death this whole time like it was real. Going through the motions of the hunt I had committed my new life to, never letting myself feel alive. I knew what it was like to lose everything, and I couldn't do that again.

So I kept myself dead.

Until I saw this beautiful woman from across the street that fateful day and made it my mission to visit her coffee shop every morning for just a taste of that alive feeling she gave me. I didn't realize it then. Now, with her coming unglued as my mouth and tongue slaving at her pussy … I realize I never knew what feeling alive actually meant.

Even before I "died."

I suck her clit deep, taking a little bite of the sensitive skin with a nip of my teeth. Her cry of pleasure echoes around the room. My tongue comes out, lapping up the wetness dripping from her. I lick, nibble, suck, and devour her. The whole time my cock gets so hard, I'm not sure if I'll be able to stop myself from coming.

Her hands go to my hair, using the long length to keep my mouth where it is. I keep sucking at her clit, loving the noises she's making. I can feel her wetness through my bearded skin. I lift one hand from her hip and move myself back as much as I can without losing her pussy on my mouth, and push one thick finger inside her core.

Fuck, she's tight.

I slide my finger in and out, loving how she grips my digit each time I pull back, trying to keep me inside her. She's just as hungry for me as I am for her. All it takes is one more pass of my tongue on her clit, then I close my mouth and suck. I curl my finger deep inside her and look up her body. Her eyes watch me feast on her for a second before her head drops to the couch, the walls of her core tightening around me, and a rush of wetness leaves her as she cries out her release. Instead of stopping, I keep going until the last whimper leaves her mouth, and her body stops clenching around me. When my finger comes out, she gives a throaty whine but doesn't move.

"Look at me," I demand.

She shakes her head, a small smile on her lips, but she doesn't open her eyes. She's still spread wide, arms at her side, legs open, and her wetness glistening on her pussy lips. Even the couch has a wet spot. I don't give a fuck. I'll buy her a new one and put this one at my place so I never forget this moment.

"Look at me now, Olivia."

Her eyes open slightly, and she peeks through heavy and very sated eyes.

"I'm going to fuck you now."

Her face heats but not from embarrassment.

"What if I want to fuck you?" she challenges, her brazenness making my cock twitch.

"You'll fuck me when I want you to."

"Is that right?"

"You ever come like that before?"

She shakes her head.

"You're gonna let me fuck you the way I want to fuck you, then you can answer that again when I'm done with you."

"I already know there will be no comparisons when you take me. You make me come alive."

Fucking hell.

"You have no idea, Olivia. No idea at all."

I lean over and grab my wallet, tagging a condom from the back and sheathing myself in quick succession. When my body covers hers, her hands roam up and then slowly down my back, not stopping until she has my ass under her palms. Her hair wild around her head, her breasts begging for my mouth, and those lips still red and swollen from our kisses. She looks stunning. I keep hold of her gaze and start rocking my hips against hers. Sliding my heavy cock between her lips, I coat myself with her wetness. She meets every move with one of her own, us in sync completely. I watch the color rise on her chest, knowing she's already close to coming again just by feeling my cock against her clit.

"I don't do slow, Olivia."

"I don't want slow."

"I don't want to hurt you," I continue, lifting my hips slightly so my tip is at her entrance.

"I want to feel that pain," she gasps when I feed an inch of me into her tight heat.

"You don't know what you're saying. I'm a rough man. I don't want to hurt you."

She lifts her head and looks directly into my eyes, holding my gaze so I see the truth behind her words.

"I *want* your rough. You make me feel things I thought were forever gone for me. Fuck me hard and make me feel alive."

Alive.

Make me feel alive.

She has no way of knowing the power her words ring through me. The truth slams home in my heart.

Her words light the fire, and I thrust the rest of my cock into her body. I pause, letting her get used to me, and wait so I can breathe through the incredible feeling of being buried deep inside her.

"Take me … please. Coop, take me."

My cock twitches, and my heart slams inside my chest.

"Say that again," I demand, pulling out slightly.

"Take me," she says.

"No. Say my name."

Her wild eyes fill with something I can't place, but she gives me what I need, and I'm done for. Completely fucking done for.

"Coop," she says on a breath. "Please, Coop."

"Fuck," I breathe.

Then I take her. I fuck her so hard that I know it has to hurt, but she doesn't act like it does. She is just as lost in me as I am in her. She continues to say my name over and over, begging me not to stop. Like I even could. It would take a miracle for me to stop. I've never felt anything better than being inside this woman. Her skin slides against mine, our sweat mingling. I take her mouth and pour everything I wish I could say into that kiss. Keeping her fevered screams down my throat, I swear to everything there is that I can feel them reach my balls, curling around me and gripping tight. I power through, feeling her pussy ripple against my cock. When she sucks my lip between hers and bites down as she comes, I'm done for.

I thrust deep and lift my mouth off hers and bury my head in her neck, kissing my way to her shoulder. My mouth opens right over her shoulder, and my teeth bite down as I groan out my own release. I come so hard, I'm not even sure if the condom did any good. It feels too good. She's so wet, it very well could have been worthless.

I can't find it in me to give a shit.

"Wow," she breathes, coming down. "Can we do that again?"

I lift my head, look into her eyes, and for the second time in years … I smile.

"Yeah, babe. We're going to do that again."

Her smile is lazy, her whole body relaxed. "Can we do that a lot more?"

My lips keep turning up, smiling like I used to … like I didn't have a care in the world.

"Yeah, we'll do that a lot more." I move my softening cock inside her, and her eyes heat.

"I could get used to this, and that scares me," she admits with a soft cry when I slip from her body.

I look down between us and see that the condom isn't even attached to my cock anymore.

Lifting up, I look down at her red pussy lips to see the condom hanging out of her. I hook a finger and pull it out, looking into her eyes as I hold it up.

"This doesn't scare me, so what's that tell you?"

Her eyes widen, but she just opens and closes her mouth.

"Any other woman and I would have been close to losing my mind. Don't be afraid of me, Olivia. Don't be afraid of what you feel. Because if this doesn't scare *me*, then I can honestly tell you that you don't need to be feeling a damn bit of fear where I'm concerned."

"I'm not on the pill, but the timing should be okay."

"I wouldn't give a shit even if it wasn't. Give me your hand."

She listens instantly, and I place her palm against my chest.

"Not once in over twenty years have I felt like this worthless piece of shit was still working. Not once. We move at whatever pace works for us, but don't let fear into it. Not when you just brought me back from the dead, Olivia. It's only everything I've ever wanted but never let myself believe I could have."

Her eyes tear up, but she nods.

"You gonna ride this out with me?"

"Yeah, Coop. I'm going to ride this out with you. I understand you. It's only everything I gave up the dream of having."

"You gonna let me inside that body again tonight?"

She blinks, the wetness leaving her gaze, then smirks. "I think I might just do that."

After cleaning up our mess in the theater room, she leads me to the large master bedroom, and I spend the rest of the night with her breathing life back into my soul. It feels like I'm coming back to life, over and over again.

I didn't lie. She's only everything I ever mourned when I gave up my life to live in the shadows. But I'm also not stupid. There's a chance I'll lose her when she finds out what I'm keeping from her. I know I have to tell her, but right now, all I can think about is how good it feels to be fucking alive.

Tomorrow. Tomorrow, I'll tell her.

Maybe.

CHAPTER 11

Olivia

"OCEAN" BY LADY A

The morning hasn't even slightly gone as planned from the moment Riley woke up until now. It's just been one hot mess after another.

We're in a hurry.

And I hate being in a hurry.

There's always the anxiety that comes along with being late, too. Something I go through great lengths to avoid. Will you be making other people late? Will you forget something in the haste to get out of the house? Will you, worse, forget something like turning off the oven, and then poof, the house is gone? Then, because it wouldn't be a freak-out without thinking that you're messing up the natural order of events the day would bring if you *were* on time, ensuring that you would end with some *Final Destination* bang. It makes no rational sense. I know the world keeps spinning, even if I'm a couple of minutes late. I know there won't be some disaster because of it. But still … it's one of my worst features, for sure.

Riley, however? She's the total opposite. The sun rises with her smile, and it sets only when she sleeps. That's my bean, always bouncing and always happy.

Currently, she's booking it like a race horse to get to the front of our building. The whole way down the elevator, she taps her tiny feet in an impatient rhythm for it to hurry. The second the doors open, her little legs can't move fast enough. I have to pull back a giggle when I take in how awkward her rushed steps make her look. Her whole body leans forward, legs powering through as quickly as they can, while her tiny arms pump in time with her legs. She's a little tornado with a one-track mind.

I grab the handle and push the door open, holding back my laughter even more when she starts pushing herself through the opening well before it was wide enough for her tiny little body. And then she was off, racing to where she knew he would be waiting. The happy giggles echo around her when she reaches him and acts as if she hasn't seen him in years … when, in reality, he tucked the little monster in last night.

Last night, she pitched one mammoth fit. One so big, it had me wondering if he would book it right out the front door. It was that bad. They don't often happen—her fits—but when they do, whoa boy.

She wanted to stay up and wasn't happy with me when I told her she couldn't, especially not to watch her BTS DVD … again. It had been much later than I ever let her stay up as it was, and I knew she was exhausted from the excitement of the day, adding fuel to the fire of the tantrum that followed. She tried every trick in the book to stay up, despite the exhaustion I could see etched on her little face. The only thing that worked was when Drew—her giant—calmly injected himself and offered to tuck her in with a bedtime story.

Riley in overly tired whiny mode never seems to flow with me being grumpy and impatient. It's a recipe for disaster, even though it wasn't her fault that I was functioning on battery-saving mode at the time. I didn't handle it as well as I normally would—her being whiny and overtired—and I know a lot of it had to do with worrying about how Drew would handle a tantrum. I think I had been functioning with a shorter fuse anyway, with the worry over how he would handle it.

Drew thought he was just coming over for a relaxing night of TV and some DoorDash delivery for dinner. What he got, instead, was one heck of a view of the shit show that comes with Riley in meltdown mode. Not that it was really *that* bad, but tough days are just that … tough … and last night was just that. Tough.

There he is. The sole reason for her little legs to be rushing about, waiting for her right where she knew he would be.

Drew stands at the end of the walkway into our complex, nestled between two rows of perfectly manicured shrubs. It always reminded me of the entry to a grand garden. So much greenery, flowers, and thought was put into the space between the street side gate and the entrance into the condo's lobby. A juxtaposition to the crazy busy life that continues on the busy streets beyond with the lush haven inside.

The second Drew spots Riley, he crouches down and waits until she collides with him. He wraps his arms around her with zero hesitation to give her a welcomed hug. I stop in my tracks and just soak in the sight of such a strong, big, rough-around-the-edges man being so sweet with my girly girl.

I never had any real expectations for what this would be or become between us. That was before last night. And I guess a little more just now —watching this big strong man love on Riley as if she was his own. So much care written all over his rugged face I would put money on the fact he doesn't even realize he's doing it. It's such a difference from his normal stoic expressions. It's something that he started giving her well before he started giving me parts of himself. The bond they have, while it came about almost instantly, has grown into something I know will be unbreakable.

I think it's fair to say, after last night's meltdown and anxiety-driven overthinking, what the future will be like between us has been on my mind a lot. It was supposed to be just sex, but something about him screams to me that this is so much more than just sex could ever be.

I continue to watch, giving them their moment and letting myself get lost in my thoughts. Sometimes I think there are two sides to him. The one that shows the world he's rough, tough, and everything dangerous you can think of in one human. That's the one I knew for years. Years of him silently coming in to the shop, waking me up with no real communication. I thought I knew him.

That is … until he showed me this side.

A side that I would bet my life not many people have seen. When it's just the three of us together, the rough edges of him start to soften. Little by little, those edges soften ever so much to let him peek out and show me there is so much more to this man than anyone realizes.

Even me.

Those moments drive home just how much I've been affected by his presence, as well. He's shown me time and time again that even though I'm capable of doing everything on my own, having some extra support isn't that bad, either. He gave me a taste of what it would be like to have a partner in my life, and I would be lying if I said I didn't love it. He gives Riley something she's been missing, too. He plays with her, and he really lets this boyish part inside him burst free.

At that moment, I know something big hurt him and caused him to hide who he really is under those sharp edges. When I get that part of him, I know it's a gift worth holding on to.

I have no doubt that I'll love it because of who that partner is, and that's all there is to that. There isn't another man who would awaken this much attraction, respect, and a connection that feels like we've had decades to perfect. It's something I never thought I would allow for myself, either. That dependency on another person to help navigate and handle your life with. I hadn't ever looked at it in a healthy way … until him. Even with two sides of him, I know neither of them would intentionally hurt us.

I smile and focus on the two of them as they finish their moment alone. Just a little world that belongs to the two of them. Riley adamantly whispers to him, and I know she'll be a little while longer. I walk over to the little bench just outside the entrance and sit, watching them while my heart fills up with a powerful thump even though it's already racing speed. My thoughts take me back to last night. To the moment I felt that shift from what had started between Drew and me to what I knew in my gut was building into something completely different.

I had been standing there just staring at Riley while her mood deteriorated. Drew came and took my shoulders in his big strong hands, and when I looked up at him, I saw the exact moment he noticed the tears of frustration hovering at the edge of my eyes, just waiting for me to blink before they fell over the edge. And once they start, it's hard to pull them back.

He cautiously ordered me to take a deep breath and go upstairs to soak in the bath.

To relax.

To have a moment alone, he said.

I blinked, those dang tears falling, and when he made a sound deep and low in his throat that sounded a whole lot like pain ... over my tears? I felt that sound hit my heart like a battering ram. He asked me to wait and I was shocked silly when he came toward me with a full glass of wine. He placed it in my hands, spun me softly by his hands at my shoulders and gave me a gentle push toward the stairs. I moved, ever so slowly, toward the master suite. I didn't see the stairs, I didn't even really recognize the path that took me to stand in front of the tub.

He found me not too long after, fast asleep in the tub. When he told me how he had put Riley to bed, the rest of my heart might as well have jumped out of my chest and into his hand.

Riley was tucked in with no trouble. He read her one story, and then she even got an extra one out of him. Right before he left her room, he said she told him that she was scared. Drew being the man he is, her giant, stood in the doorway to "watch out for those monsters" until she was asleep. He didn't move until her soft snores reached his ears.

Later, long after my bath, he spent a couple of hours making me feel more alive than I had ever felt in my life. Something magical started burning in those moments before I fell asleep in his arms. My whole dang heart might as well be his now.

He's stayed overnight a few times in the past few weeks, using his stealthy skills to sneak out just before Riley gets up in the morning. Those stolen moments are nothing short of magical. This, what we shared last night, though? That was next level.

Glancing at my watch, I realize how much time I let pass, pushing us even later. Something that should make me even more anxious, but looking at the two of them have their moment, I know I wouldn't care if we were hours late.

I stand, brush my hands over my black dress pants and start moving toward them, at a much more leisurely pace than Riley did earlier. Drew looks up over her head and smirks at me, causing my face to flush and my steps to get slightly wonky for a split second. I know how much he loves making me blush, so when that smirk ticks up a little more on his handsome face, I feel the heat grow. I take in his fresh clothes. He must have had more time than I thought to run home. He's freshly showered and changed and still on time. I'm fairly sure it didn't feel like a walk of shame for him because I imagine he doesn't care enough about what other people might think to actually be ashamed. Though, he knows my blush is one hundred percent because of him and not because of being embarrassed. No, my blush is all about my desire for him. And he loves it.

We both look away and down at Riley when she climbs up his body. Pretty normal for her morning, wanting to climb to the top of her very own giant. She makes it to the middle of his chest before she needs help to make it the rest of the way up. He hooks her under her arms, and before she can even get one full stream of giggles out, he has her placed on his shoulders with his hands around her ankles to keep her safe.

I hold back a laugh when she bends down over the top of his head, curling her little body around him until she can peek at him from her perch.

A crazy mess of brown curls, a big loopy smile and giggles that rain down on him.

"Morning, my giant," Riley says, parroting the almost curt tone that Drew uses on others. She's taken to mimicking his tone a lot lately, only she does it in a few different ways and always mixes them up to catch him off guard.

It never fails to make me laugh when I hear her trying to mimic his tone. She's been trying to echo the exact way he speaks for a while. It's probably the most adorable part of our day, hearing her try to be gruff and hard. Drew doesn't speak often, or say a lot. That is, outside of the walls of one of our homes. He chooses the words he says and delivers them, that's all there is to it. Those words he does say, well, you can guarantee they're important.

And those carefully chosen words that he gives us?

Those matter the most, to him and to us.

"Morning, bean," he replies in a low drawl. As a matter of fact, to the point, nothing else given. That's just him.

I can see her smile grow before she answers.

"Away we go, giant! Carry us onward! It's time for the quest for knowledge."

My head jerks slightly, not noticeable to Riley, but Drew catches it. He quirks his brow to give me a look that says it all. We both are two grown adults who rarely take orders from anyone. I would go as far as to say that he likely *never* takes orders. However, it isn't lost on me that both of us unquestioningly follow her marching orders when it comes to Riley. I give him a small shrug, a bigger smile, and we follow.

The breeze hits my skin, cooling off the heat that the sun had given me just moments before. The sun feels unusually bright today, giving a heat to my skin that is much-needed since the chill has started to move into the city's air. It's the time of year when there's a good bit of people out enjoying the nice weather. A little more than you would normally see during the hot days of summer. Everyone wants to soak up these remaining days before it's too cold to.

Bikes cycling, people running, and various activities going around the park. There isn't a time of day when you don't see picnics, various small groups playing sports, and people like us milling around. It won't be long before winter creeps its cold claws back into our bones, and the parks become hard to enjoy. Those cold days make walks like this harder to fit in, us switching over to my car. I soak in these days when I'm able to walk Riley to school—and the shop—instead of being stuck in a vehicle. There's nothing like walking the city of Boston when the weather cooperates.

Riley's little voice comes through my thoughts, and I give myself a little mental shake to snap out of these daydreams. When I hear her call the coffee shop her "work," I can't help my soft snort. Drew looks over, his eyes over where his leg is resting, hiding the smirk I know is there, and I can practically see the remark he wants to jest toward me dancing in his eyes.

"Don't you think, Livi?" Riley says.

I look up from his beautiful eyes and give her my attention, the heat growing on my cheeks. "What was that, bean?"

"You're silly," she starts, giving a bell of giggles after. "Don't you think my giant would be better at games than you?"

"Hey now!" I exclaim with mock shock.

She laughs harder.

"Why would he be better than me, little miss?"

"Because he's a boy. Lewis is a boy, and he's really good at Mario Kart. I bet Mr. W would be good too, even though he's real old."

"That's not nice, Riley."

"Why? He says it all the time."

"She's got you there," Drew adds, giving me a wink.

I narrow my eyes at him, and the two of them laugh.

"Well, just because he says it doesn't mean you need to repeat it, Riley."

"Okay," she chirps, then goes back to leaning over Drew's head. "Did you know I have a TV and some games at work? If you come early today, I can show you how to play, and you can play instead of Livi. She doesn't like games that much because she always loses. Did you play games when you were little like me?"

"Not the kind of games you have now. Didn't have much of that fun stuff when I was little."

"Why?"

"Grew up when there wasn't tons of those games you play. Most kids were playing outside with sticks and rocks, basketball and baseball. That kind of stuff."

She leans up and I watch her face as she ponders his words. She looks at me and gives me a wink. I swear, this girl.

"Well … we can teach you. You're a boy, and you'll be able to beat Livi real quick. She can do other stuff, and we can play. Lewis is my friend at work. He's really good at games, too. Sometimes, when there aren't a lot of people there, which is like never, I get to play with Lewis, and he teaches me tricks. Do you know Lewis? Cuz he's real nice."

"You always give me that much to digest, kid?"

"What is digest?"

We laugh, and she squints at me.

"I'll be there early today," Drew starts with a gruff grumble, drawing her attention back to him. She doesn't speak again, content with the fact she got what she wanted, and that's that. I, however, hear what he isn't saying. Something is on his mind, and it's clear as day.

The walk to her school is silent after that. Not uncomfortable, just the three of us being comfortable enough to afford that silence. The world keeps moving, traffic and sounds of people enjoying the weather whips around us with the gentle breeze.

"I see my school," Riley says, interrupting the silence. "My giant, did you know I didn't like my school at first? I like it now. Even though I want to be at work with Livi and Ella more. It's not more fun at school than work, but at least I get to do both."

"Gotta have balance, bean," he says.

"What's balance?"

He lifts her off his shoulders when we reach the edge of her school's property, just before the gate. When her legs clear his head, he gives a little push from his hold, and she's spinning in the air before he catches her—this time, facing him. He holds her out and away from his body and keeps her face level. She smiles, wonky and toothy full of love for him. He takes it in with a deep breath. The two of them just look at each other, and her little legs start swinging.

"Balance is knowing how to have what you love while doing what you have to do."

"Do you?"

"Do I what?"

"Do you get to do what you love, too?" she asks, so much innocence in her question. She doesn't realize her aunt is close to hyperventilating.

He looks over at me, just a beat, then back at her. "Hadn't for a real long time, bean. Hadn't until recently."

"Do you love what you have to do?"

"Not at all." This time, his answer is immediate. Not even a sliver of a second seemed to pass.

"Then you should probably stop doing what you have to do and fix your balance."

He grunts out a laugh, no humor in it at all.

"I'll have to look into that, little girl."

"You do that, giant."

He bends to place her gently on her feet and stands back one step, letting me know silently that he'll wait for me to walk her in.

"Ready?" I ask her, still looking in his eyes.

"Can my giant walk me up today, Auntie?" she asks, drawing my attention back just when the shock reaches his eyes.

"Of course, sweet girl. If it's okay with him, of course."

She leaps up in the air a little and claps her hand and reaches to my side, toward where he's standing. I hear him clear his throat before his hand enters my line of sight, and I watch his big mitt envelop her small hand. She turns around once on their short walk and blows me a kiss, which I catch before blowing one back for her to catch. She turns around right at the edge of the opening gate, where all the moms stand and let their little ones run the rest of the way. There is never a break to their ranks, and no mom from that group ever goes farther—almost like some sort of forcefield keeps them from walking the rest of the way.

This special treatment could be an issue when there's no longer any need for him to stick close to Riley and me. Riley will still be just as attached when that overprotective bear inside him can be soothed. It would worry me had I not seen how much he cares for her with my own eyes. It meant a lot to me that he was honest and told me what he could, enough information to settle my nerves. The person he was investigating was in proximity to us. It's only natural that it's made his already protective nature more primal. And I would be lying if I said I didn't like knowing he was close, and so was the safety that being near him gives me.

He's different than I expected. He might not be the type of man who would ever wear his heart on his sleeves, and honestly, sometimes I have no idea what he's thinking, but he's shown me in no time that I don't need all that to know he would do anything to protect those he cares about.

And there's no doubt that he cares for Riley and me.

I should be worried that when this threat he's investigating is gone, we won't share the same connection we do now. Or that it may not be what I think it is. The old me would have thought that, but now? I don't know how to explain it other than a feeling I have about him. He's been hurt, that's clear as day, but one thing he's never hidden from me behind that stoic mask he wears is his heart. It used to be that I could hardly see it shining. Whatever haunts him rides him so hard that it can't shine past the darkness. In the past few weeks, though, I've seen it and basked in that glow's glory. He might be rusty at this whole letting people in thing, but I have no doubt he's been loved and has loved right back. When he lets me see that side of him, I always see the wonderment that takes over him. Almost like he can't believe this is real, either.

I shift to see past the hoard of moms, no doubt not watching their children now that Drew's perfect self has walked into their sight. I have to get on my toes to get a clear view, and when I do, my heart melts at the two of them.

He's stopped just shy of the doorway and taken a knee directly in front of Riley. She's got the biggest smile as they move their hands in the space between their bodies. Pinkies linking, fingers dancing a tango together in this new secret handshake they made up a few weeks back. I can't hear them, but when their lips start moving, I know they're saying the little chant that goes with it. Riley always goes off on her own solo during that part, giving some more hand slaps before ending with something about a UFO.

When they drop their arms, she leaps toward him and hugs him. Once back on her feet, she turns, and I watch her look for me through the thirsty mom fan club. I get a little wave with one heck of a big smile before she runs through the door and into the school.

I glance back toward him, having missed when he stood during my goodbye to Riley, just in time to see him part the thirsty moms like the Red Sea. He doesn't break his stride. Whatever they see makes them scurry out of the way and create the path for him. His legs have him standing in front of me in no time, eyes never leaving mine the whole way.

"I'm going to hurt you, and when I do, it'll hurt her."

His eerie words hit me like a hammer. It takes a lot, but I don't let him see the hurt they inflict. There's a vow to his words that makes it seem like a premonition to come, not a worry due to something bothering him. Just as quickly as his words hit me, so does the resolve to make sure that never happens. I will not lose the magic this man has brought to my life.

"Seems simple enough then, honey," I whisper. "Don't."

CHAPTER 12

Olivia

"UNBELIEVABLE" BY WHY DON'T WE

"You know, I find it incredibly unfair that, since you and Drew started this weird thing, he still hardly talks to me. It's been almost three months, Liv. What do you guys do on the nights you stay at his place? Do you guys just sit around and look at each other when you're together? Or does Riley just run the show? Because, girlfriend, what is with that silence?"

I roll my eyes at Ella and smile at Grace across my kitchen table.

The girls came over to have our once-a-month gab session, which really means we sit around and chat about everything and nothing. It's one of my favorite days of the month. And they're even better now that I have Drew in my life.

He came to get Riley about an hour ago, taking her on a lunch date while the girls and I have some kid-free chatter time. As much as I love the ability to talk to my girls without worrying about her little ears hearing things she shouldn't, that's not my favorite part. The relationship that he's forming with Riley has brought so much joy to our lives. While he and I have been growing closer, so have they and it fills me with happiness.

Riley, as I expected, didn't even flinch when Drew and I started showing the change in our relationship. We started slow, hands being held as we walked together to and from school and work. The biggest change was when he started sticking around almost every night for her bedtime.

"He isn't silent with us," I answer Ella, loving the expression of doubt and shock on her face. "In fact, he's become a bit of a chatter bug."

"You're pulling my leg," she accuses, eyes narrowing as she squints her disbelief my way. "Do you believe this chick?" she adds toward Grace.

"I heard him the other day," Grace chimes in. "He actually was quite chatty with the two of them."

Ella, having been looking at me incredulously, slowly turns her head in Grace's direction, jaw dropping along the way, and glares at her.

"You lie!" she gasps.

"Nope. I tell no lies."

I laugh at my friends, lean back in my chair and sip my drink.

"He stood right outside of Mug and talked to me before they left, too." Grace continues to tease.

Ella's head turns back toward me and she narrows her eyes. "Where was I?"

I shrugged. "Probably inside. He was in there before we left talking to Mr. W. How did you miss that?"

"What day?" she barks, looking between us wildly.

"I don't know, I think it was late last week some time."

She blushes, and I know exactly why she missed it. I just wasn't going to call her on it. What she does on her break is her business. It's not what she does that's causing the blush. It's *who* she's been spending the time with.

"Yeah, that's what I thought," Grace jests with a laugh. "You can't get mad the guy doesn't talk to you when you're too busy sneaking off with one of his dudes and missing all the fun. You want to hear him get chatty you have to stop getting chatty with Mr. Tall Dark and Handsome."

Ella's face gets even redder.

"It really isn't that big of a deal, El."

"Not that big of a deal," she says. "I'm your best friend, and he doesn't speak to me."

"Do you speak to him?" I ask, knowing the answer.

"Well …"

"So you are upset that he doesn't talk to you, but you don't talk to him either. You can't have a tizzy over missing out. Maybe he thinks you don't like him."

"I never thought about it that way," she mulls.

Leave it to Grace to lay it out there for Ella with not a whole lot of room for her to argue more. Naturally, she finds a way. Silly girl.

"He's kind of scary, don't you think? I mean, if it wasn't for the fact that my best friend is enjoying the giant, silent man I would think he was pretty much incapable of opening up to anyone. It's been years that he and his friends have come in and he just now starts getting chatty? I don't get it. So yeah … he's kind of scary."

Ella's proclamations give me pause. Not for the first time I wonder what changed to make him open up to us. I like to think it was the connection I feel between us. A lot because of Riley, too. Maybe it's just how protective he is that made it grow. I'm not stupid. There's also that "something" that he's asked me to leave alone until he can tell me. I don't push, but the more time we spend together, I know I have to get to the bottom of this before it eats my overthinking heart alive. I've seen his shadows though and I don't want to hurt him by pushing him to open up. He's given me no reason not to trust him so I won't be starting today.

"He's a good man, El. We all have a past and he's gone through something that made him close up and get silent. In time, I'm sure I'll know all there is to know about how Andrew Shaw became to be the man he is, but right now I know I trust him and that's all I need. He doesn't have to give me his life story all at once. We're enjoying getting to know each other slowly."

I know Andrew isn't his real name, however, I also know I can't share the name he's given me to use. I still don't know why he hasn't given me the reason behind the name change, but I trust him and I have to trust that one day he'll feel like he can tell me.

She ponders over my words, looking me in the eyes the whole time she does. I love her to pieces, even when she tends to question everything more than she will just go with the flow. She's protective of me and Riley, so I know she means well.

"He fulfills something inside me," I continue. "Like there was a big piece missing for a lot of years and the pieces around it started to get weaker until they started to crumble away. He doesn't just fill up the space those pieces left behind. He makes the rest of the parts around the broken ones even stronger. It hasn't been that long and he opens up with me little by little. You don't need to understand it to just be supportive."

Before she can speak, I hear footsteps and the giggles of Riley. All three of us looking toward the doorway of the kitchen as Drew walks in with Riley on his shoulders. His eyes had already been scanning the room and come to rest, holding my gaze. Riley pats his head and I watch as he silently lifts his hands to hold hers as he lifts, does his infamous flip and spin to a laughing Riley as she comes down from her perch.

"Auntie, I fly!"

Looking away from him, I smile down at Riley right as she is placed on her feet. She takes off as she runs toward where I'm sitting. She grabs my face between her little hands and beams up at me.

"Guess what," she breathes.

"What's that, little one?"

"My giant has a surprise for us. He told me I had to wait for you before he could tell me all his secrets though. Then he taught me how to fly!"

"How to fly, huh?"

She giggles and turns, dropping the hold she had on my face. "Show her!" she demands, looking at Drew the whole time with her hands on her hips.

He doesn't pause, doesn't question, and instantly drops down to a hunch. A small smile playing at his full lips. He picks her up effortlessly and tosses her up. Thankfully, because of the vault in the ceiling, she is launched with no fear of the ceiling. Her giggles raining down on us and throughout the room, little bells of euphoria. Her brown curls swirling around her face in cute little waves. His hands hook under her arms and he swings her around and back on his shoulders. Then he reaches up and waits until her tiny little hands are in his. With a wink to me that has Ella clearing her throat. Then he has Riley moving again, this time swinging her over and giving her a toss-up. Her arms wide and her smile blinding, she looks up at the ceiling as she "flies" with the biggest smile on her face. He catches her with ease and places her firmly back on the ground.

"Your turn," she squeals at me.

"Oh no, honey. That's okay." I laugh awkwardly.

When I look from Riley and over toward Drew, I know I won't get out of it. He looks downright devilish. Swoon worthy, but devilish nonetheless. God, I love when he lets me see this playful side of him. I know the two at the table with me aren't unaffected, either. Both make little breathy "oh's" every so often.

He closes the distance, places his big hands on the armrest of my chair and leans down—nose to nose—and holds my gaze. His eyes light up. I'm so not getting out of this. He must have found what he was looking for because one corner of his beautiful lips tip up and his eyes start to crinkle at the edges.

I don't even have time to process how my butt left the chair before his hands are under my arms, pulling up at the hold on my pits and I'm in the air. He doesn't put me on his shoulders like he did Riley, no … he lets go and lets me fly before he catches me with a breathy grunt when my arms land around his shoulders and my legs start to wrap around his waist.

Front to front, I'm wrapped around him.

I hold on happily.

Especially when I feel his hardness brush against where my crotch is now nestled against his. I hold his gaze and when I feel him flex his hard length between that connection, my hands squeeze his shoulders.

His grin grows.

"Hey," I breathe, my mouth so close to his it wouldn't take but an inch to close the distance.

I watch him closely and just a moment later I get my reward. I feel his blindingly handsome smile hit me and my whole body gets warm. I know he's forgotten we aren't alone, too. I can count on my hand how many times he's given this side of himself to anyone other than Riley and me. It's never happened until right now. I soak it up. Just like the other times I alone have seen it, I map each line that forms when he lets himself free. This man used to laugh and he used to laugh a lot. I love every second of these moments, watching the hardness and time wash away from his face. In place you see a youthfulness that, despite his age, takes over. He looks like a completely different man. At least ten years younger. No shadows, just happiness. No hiding himself. My heart picks up speed and I know he feels it through our connection. His eyes close and he takes a breath. He nods as if he understands what I was thinking.

"Missed you," he says after a brief silence.

We don't break our gaze while those two words hit me and I soak up the importance of them. He hasn't been shy in letting me know he has deep feelings for me, but until now he's never said anything remotely close to that.

"I …" I clear my throat, the emotion just a little too thick. "I missed you, too," I continue on a whisper, uncurling my fingers from his shoulders to wrap them behind his neck to frame his face with my palms. I give him a shy smile before I lean forward and place a small kiss to his lips.

"Well, that's new," I hear Ella chime into the silence.

He lifts his lips away from mine and with a small squeeze to my butt, he helps me drop down to my feet.

I lean my body into his side and wrap my arm around his center without realizing I had done it. That is, until his arms snake around to shift me. My back to his front, arms around my body engulfing me in his scent and he pulls me a little harder against him. His very hard front pushing into me, making me shift as need takes over. I know they can't tell what's happening between us, but I'm practically coming undone just from feeling his hard cock against my back.

"That's *definitely* new," Ella continues, eyes as wide as her smile.

"No, it isn't," Riley sings, running over to Ella and giving her a hug before giving Grace the same treatment.

"What do you mean, little bouncy bean?" Ella asks, her eyes not leaving mine and Drew's direction.

"Auntie and my giant are special friends. You know, like the bestest of friends that hold hands and mouth kiss each other."

Grace has the decency to cover her laugh, but my best friend absolutely does not. She tosses her head back and laughs loud and long. Riley joins in, little giggles that tell me she has no idea what she's laughing at, she's just laughing because that's what kind of little angel she is. Loving life, that girl.

"Mouth kiss, huh?" Ella gasps when she finally stops laughing, reaching up to clutch her chest in mock shock. Playing this up for all it's worth, apparently.

"Yup. Those." Riley places her hand over her mouth and laughs a little harder. Her body moving with each one that escapes her adorableness.

"Wow, Riles ... that is quite the news. I can't believe you didn't tell me about this sooner. You holding out on me, girlfriend!"

She smirks and I should have braced while I could. I should have known she would manipulate Riley into more confessions.

"Auntie even got a spanking the other day. She wasn't giving him his ..." she looks over at us and oddly nods after a second. Just like Drew does when he's studying us for something only known to him. "Sweetness."

"Oh my gosh," I gasp.

Grace stops covering up her laughter up at this moment and joins Ella when she lets out even more loud giggles of her own.

"I don't think you should keep your sweetness from him, Auntie." Riley continues, to my horror. "Why would you not want to be sweet to my giant?" She glances back to Ella. "So you see, that's why she needed a spanking."

I open my mouth to shut this down at the same time that my back starts vibrating and the man pressed tight against it bellows out a deep, rich and smooth as honey laugh that is so spectacular to experience the whole room goes silent ... well, minus Riley, who is laughing with him and looking at him as if he was holding the moon out toward her in his arms. I wish I could see his face. When he laughs like that the man deep inside him that is rarely shown bursts forward. I close my eyes and picture how breathtakingly handsome he looks in these moments. Soaking in his velvety laughter, no longer as rusty as it was when we first started this thing between us. That youthfulness he rarely shows enveloping the room around us. I feel so much lighthearted excitement from just hearing his laugh, I have no doubt would be knocked flat on my tail if he wasn't holding me.

Ella's eyes meet mine and I see the shock in hers. I've been blessed with this man's laughter for almost three months now, she hasn't seen it once though. I know from experience how heart stopping it is to see his handsome face when he lets go like this for the first time so I completely understand her reaction.

"Well, I really didn't see that coming either," Ella whispers when he stops laughing.

"What?" Riley asks.

"Him," she responds, pointing at Drew.

"How did you not see him? He is right there, silly goose."

She reaches out to ruffle her curls. "Takes some people a little longer to see what's in front of them," she adds without looking away from Drew and me. Something tells me she's talking about a lot more than not seeing this side of Drew before.

Riley giggles, but doesn't spend any time mulling that over. She launches over to us, gives Drew a hug with me in the middle before taking off and running out of the room toward her playroom in the back.

"Don't mean to interrupt, but I was hoping to steal the rest of this woman's time today," Drew rumbles low toward Ella and Grace.

"Are you actually speaking?" Ella crazily asks.

"Uh," I start, but snap my mouth shut when he snickers low in his throat.

"I am."

"To me," she adds.

"You both, but yes."

She hums and slouches down so she is resting on the back of the chair.

"So … you do speak."

"When I have something to say,"

"Well, that's a relief. Now I can get this off my chest." She leans toward him and points toward his chest. "Hurt them and I'll be your worst nightmare." She lifts her finger and drags it across her throat.

"Ella!" I gasp.

94

THE LONG WAY HOME

"Noted," he says over me, nothing but the unmistakable promise in that one word.

"Good. Just so you know, I'm serious, mister. I know how to bring the hurt."

Grace snorts a low laugh. "You don't even kill flies."

"Flies don't make my best friend look like that."

He clears his throat. "I wouldn't expect less."

"Good, we understand each other," she responds after a beat of silence shared between them. "Alrighty, Grace ... stop taking up all their time and let's go."

I shake my head and smile at my best friend's crazy antics.

Grace rolls her eyes, but stands and starts moving around the room, collecting their things. Drew's phone starts ringing and he gives me a little squeeze before letting go and stepping out of the room to take his call. We make small talk as they both help me clean up our lunch mess before I walk them to the elevator to tell them goodbye.

I've got the biggest smile on my face when I turn from them and make my way back to the kitchen, just in time to see Drew coming in from the balcony. The expression on his face clears the second he sees me come into the room. I didn't miss it, though. He looked almost worried.

"I have a meeting tomorrow with the guys at my place. Are you and Riley okay with cutting our plans short a little?"

"Of course," I tell him, walking over and reaching up to frame his face with my palms on his cheeks. "Would it be easier if Riley and I come back here instead of staying at your place tonight?"

"Absolutely not. Want my girls with me."

I smile, having had this conversation with him a few times before.

"Well, in that case, why don't we go get packed up and head over there to drop our stuff off before you take us on this secret outing?"

His mouth presses a light kiss against mine before wrapping me in one of his delicious bear hugs. When he lifts his head back to look down at me, I see something moving in his eyes that I haven't seen before ... hope.

CHAPTER 13

Drew

"MERCY" BY SHAWN MENDES

What the hell am I doing?

This isn't me.

Or it *wasn't* me. Not the man I've become. He doesn't do things for fun. He does things to hunt.

Walking through these doors with these two females at my side, though? They are making me believe this is the me I can be—taking the shadows I've been living in and letting the light Olivia and Riley cast onto my days shine brightly with hope.

Not the first time my thoughts have led me down this path.

Not when I pulled up to pick them up earlier, deciding to dust off my Jeep to give them this experience. No damn way I was willing to trust someone else driving them around. Not even one of the men on my team that have always had my back. There isn't a single person I would trust with them. A thought that I wasn't willing to put too many questions on. Something was physically pushing me toward her, making my gut scream for me to listen. The biggest tell that this was something special was feeling that hard jerk—almost as if I had something tied to my spine giving a hard tug—pulling me back to the girls.

It started out so simple.

Stay close, watch them, and wait for Ray to make his move. I would never let him hurt them, but there was no other way for us to pull him out of hiding without continuing to watch them as I had originally planned. It wasn't supposed to get further than keeping them safe.

Now, though?

Now they have me feeling things a dead man like me shouldn't feel.

Keep the shadows from the brightness.

The thought slams into me as if each word was a physical punch.

Can I do that? Can I keep living in the shadows I've been in for two damn decades and keep them away from that light this woman casts?

"Drew! Look!"

Riley's excited gasp pulls me back to the present. She's pointing, everywhere and nowhere at the same time. Her eyes shine bright with excitement and wonder. The inside of the large tent set up almost identically to the movie they had me watch about circuses, the whole reason I brought them here. Her eyes had brightened when watching that movie. Her happiness got a little bigger with each song until it was a living beast.

I was high on the feeling of giving her this moment. The magic she's feeling rolls off her tiny body in waves.

Riley starts moving quicker, her legs are pumping so fast, she's pulling me with a strength a kid this little shouldn't have with her steady hold on my hand. I hear Olivia giggle behind us, the sound going right to my heart like a jolt of electricity.

Is she the reason I'm having all these thoughts?

Stupid fucking question.

Of course she is.

"Are you okay?" she asks after speed walking to stand next to us.

I grunt a sound I hope sounds like an affirmative, but I'm too busy watching this little girl lead me into a tent and the spell settle over us. Her excitement in seeing a made-up story come to life. Me ... well, mine with something real close to hope settling deep in my chest and taking root.

Hope that I never have to stop giving this little girl her dreams in real life ...

"Are you sure?"

I look down at her, letting Riley continue to pull me.

Damn, those eyes.

My heart jolts again.

Breathing life back into me.

Each pump of the organ that had been dead bringing me back to life.

Well, shit.

"Yeah, doll. I don't think I've ever been better."

And just like that, under the peaked top of a circus tent, I really believe that I can have this magic.

CHAPTER 14

Olivia

"HOLD MY HAND" BY LADY GAGA

"Who is that boy to you?"

"He's hardly a boy, Mr. W." I laugh, following his gaze to where Drew and Riley have their heads close together over the top of the table they've been sitting at for the past hour.

"You get my age and tell me that," he grumbles. "She seems smitten with him."

"She sure is," I agree, smiling when I see Riley knock over another chess piece before pumping her little fists in the air in victory. This is the third game in a row that she's won. Each time she made a move, a little frown line joined Drew's handsome face.

"She's also a shark."

"And who, pray tell, taught my little angel how to hustle in chess?" I laugh.

Mr. W has the decency to look sheepish.

"I thought we talked about teaching her to hustle anyway," I jest.

"I just taught her a few key plays." He holds up his hands, his bottle of Jameson winking at me from its spot next to his hip.

"What about when you taught her how to play poker? I vividly remember how you started showing her the right way to count cards without getting caught before you started, too."

His weathered face gets a familiar expression of mischief that never fails to spotlight how much life he still has in him. There's a little rascal inside of that old man, gained from a long life full of experiences and knowledge.

"Now you don't say," he grunts, taking a healthy pull of his drink.

"Don't you play coy with me, mister. She played for everyone that would entertain a five-year-old bringing the hustle, and at the end of the day, she had a pocket full of the coins she had won off the people she challenged."

He tosses his head back and lets out a deep belly laugh that shakes his whole body and has those around us looking over with smiles. His deep voice booms around us when he looks over at Riley just in time to see her take a dollar from Drew.

"That's my girl! Show no mercy," he bellows toward her.

She jerks her head up, her curls dancing around and over her face obstructing her view. She pushes them away with one hand, looking around until she meets his gaze and gives him a smile that has so much pride and joy in it. Of course, that's when she lifts her hand that had been under the table and shows off a bunch of bills clenched in her tiny fist.

"See," I grumble. "You've created a monster shark, mister."

He laughs even harder at that. I just shake my head.

"He's good with her," he remarks a few beats later, still watching the duo as they set up another game. Riley, my little shark, slaps her hand down next to the board, all of her cash (and it looks like a lot) in a messy pile, and points her finger at the money before moving it to point at Drew. I don't hear what she says, but her expression tells me she's being adorably sassy. Not unaffected by her cuteness, Drew looks over at me and gives me a small wink before pulling his wallet out of his back pocket and slapping a twenty down.

I look away with a snort and glance back at Mr. W. Mr. W who is now studying me with an intensity that I've not seen from him before. A seriousness takes over him. He peeks a quick beat over to where they're sitting before that concentration is right back on me again.

"I should have seen it before now. You're his person," he mumbles, voice low and eyes clear. "Might not realize it yet, but that man right there was meant to find you and that little princess." He leans forward, pushing his cup out of the way, and grabs my hand. "Lived a lot of years, sweet girl. Seen a lot, some more than I care to remember, but I mostly was blessed in this life. I had a damn good woman until the Lord took her home. I lived a happy life full of love that no other woman could ever replace the spot she held. She, my Rachel, found me when I was fresh out of the Army and had stopped seeing any good in the world." He steals another peek toward my girl and Drew. "When I look in that man's eyes ..." He leans forward even more. "When I see the same shadows dancing in there that had held me captive before her, I worry."

My heart pounds as I consider his words. Is Drew my person? He certainly feels like he is. Just the thought of being without him physically hurts. I look forward to our walks to Olde Mug in the mornings just as much as I do our nights spent getting to know each other, both physically and on an emotional level. Though, it's the mention of shadows that I had seen myself that gives me pause. Realizing he may very well be my person and knowing there's something that could shake that foundation is scary.

"He's going to hurt you," Mr. W continues, voice low and his eyes now glancing off into the distance, not seeing anything while at the same time seemingly seeing everything.

"He's not going to hurt me, honey," I respond, not sure if I believe my own words now that I'm saying them out loud. What I know, though, is that I feel what we have is worth fighting for, no matter what may come about. Life is never perfect.

"He's going to, but you'll sort him. That, my dear, I have no doubt in."

"Sort him? Mr. W ..." I stop talking when he holds up one weathered hand.

"I know what it looks like to look into someone's eyes and see a pain so deep it radiates with so much strength you almost feel their hurt yourself. I know what it's like to see that pain hidden, concealed, and locked away to fester over the years. I know, sweet girl, what it is like to have ghosts and nightmares chasing your coattails. When he gets around you and that precious girl, and you see hope trying real hard to douse the flames of those nightmares. You two soothe the pain behind there … just like my Rachel did for me."

I don't know what to say, stealing a glance at where Drew and Riley are. His hand's held over the board, ready to make his next move, but his eyes are on me. There's distance from where he's sitting by the front window and where we are closer to the counter, but I don't miss the very shadows that Mr. W talks about. They're never far from the surface. That is, unless he's with just Riley and me. He has no way of knowing what we're discussing, but nevertheless, it's almost as if he can sense the change in me from across the room. I give him a small smile, but it's enough for him to look back at Riley.

Goodness me.

That was intense.

I speechlessly look back into Mr. W's very knowing eyes.

"He wouldn't hurt me," I whisper.

"He wouldn't intentionally, you're right."

"He wouldn't hurt her," I continue.

"Now that, sweet girl, I have no doubt because you would shield her before he even had a chance."

Grace walks over and pulls out the seat. "What's going on? Are you okay?" She starts fussing over Mr. W before he can answer. He swats her hands away when she gets close to his hidden bottle. "I know it's there, you ridiculous man."

"Then you won't mind filling me up a refill," he replies instantly. "Might as well shake a tail feather."

"Oh, I'll shake something." She grabs his bottle and shakes her finger in his face. "You will make me gray before I'm old enough to be gray."

His deep rumble of laughter follows. "Hurry up, little one, so you can get your nosy self back to ask more questions."

She ignores him and looks over at me. "You okay? Looked like this was getting intense." She turns long enough to narrow her eyes at Mr. W before the concern returns to her face.

His words are still ping-ponging around my thoughts. I have seen the darkness drape over his eyes a few times in the past months. I have seen them a lot less than before he and I started … when he was just a silent customer I felt an instant connection to. I see the care and

102

compassion he has for Riley and me much more often than I see those shadows. Like every day he's with us, they're slayed a little more. I would be lying, though, if I said it didn't bother me. I just don't know what to do about it.

"I'm okay, really."

"You remember what I said?" he interjects.

"You know I do," I answered him, still looking at Grace.

"They're almost gone, sweet girl. Still there, but they're not as strong as they were. You have the power, just as my Rachel did over mine. I meant what I said, but that doesn't mean that you can't get through it, and you both be better for it. You can give him something strong enough to put an end to that pain. Just got to weather the storm, hold tight, and be the person he is for you, for him."

I have to blink quickly to keep the burn behind my eyes when I see the love behind his words, trying to keep them from turning into tears.

Goodness, I love this man.

He's the father I always wished I had.

"Pete," Grace says, using his first name to ensure she has his attention. "What are you up to?"

"Hush, you." He doesn't look away, not until I feel a presence directly behind me. His eyes go up from my face and don't look away from where they land for a heavy beat. I don't turn around, but when he looks back down at me, whatever he was about to say is gone. His expression changes, his eyes holding mine. "Yeah, you'll be good, sweet girl."

Riley skips over a second later and hugs him, breaking the moment. "Want to play chess with me?"

"Why?" he grumbles. "So you can take an old man's money?"

Her giggles break the moment, and it's only then do I turn to look up at Drew. The intensity in his eyes has a small gasp escaping my mouth before I can stop it. It's not loud enough to be audible to those around us, but I know he didn't miss it. I see the shadows Mr. W is referring to, but I also see something that looks a lot like love dancing in there with them, directed right at me.

I stand quietly and grab his hand. Riley sits in the other empty chair and works on setting up the chess board she brought with her from where she had been playing with Drew. A quick look at Grace tells me she's watching over the two of them. I give her a nod and a small smile, then start walking. He doesn't resist, falling in step behind me until we cross the threshold to my office and the door is shut.

We stand there, both of us breathing a little quicker than we should be after just walking a few feet. His gaze searches mine, and mine searches his. We don't close the distance as our hearts do the silent talking.

He moves first. His hands frame my face, eyes still dancing with questions. I reach up and place my hands on his waist.

Still, we don't speak.

I'm not even sure how we moved without me noticing it, too wrapped up in what his eyes are trying to tell me. I don't know that I've ever spent this much time just looking into his eyes, but it's because of our intense stare down that I notice something else. That and maybe the overhead lights.

"You wear contacts?" I whisper lamely.

I wasn't expecting the flash of panic to wash over his face, gone just as quickly as it was there.

He doesn't speak.

"Drew?"

Panic bleeding into pain flashes.

"What's wrong?" I try again.

"Why did you look like that when you were talking to him?" he says, not answering and changing the subject.

"Like what?" I ask sincerely, giving him that.

"Like you had just been punched in the gut."

My hands trail up his hard chest, and we shift to get a little closer. My fingers dance across the skin on his neck, and I glance down just in time to see the goose bumps before they fade.

I look back up and don't break eye contact again.

"It was nothing, honey. We were just chatting."

"He didn't look at me just then like it was nothing."

I sigh, dropping my gaze to his chest.

"What?" he tries again. "I can't fix it if you don't talk to me."

"Please don't hurt me," I mutter, and I feel those four words hit him, each one like a shot.

"Olivia, where is this coming from?" he asks, lifting my face up with a soft touch to my chin so he can look into my eyes.

"He's protective of us. He's also not stupid and can see there's something big growing between us. With everything he's done, lived, and survived, he was coming to me with his concerns and advice."

"And …" He starts, then pauses, and swallows thickly. "What did he say?"

"That you'll hurt me," I answer, seeing the words as if they physically slammed into him. He doesn't even try to keep how he's feeling from me. "Though, he said it wouldn't be intentional," I add, as if that would make it better.

"He doesn't know me well enough to be giving you those thoughts, Olivia."

"He sees your pain, honey," I mumble softly. "He thinks that I can ease that for you."

"You do," he answers immediately.

"He was coming from a good place. He's a good man."

"I have not one doubt about that, but it still wasn't his place to put those doubts in your head."

"He thinks I'm your person."

My eyes round when that comes out of my mouth. His face relaxes quickly, and I get the gift of seeing it change to a boyish expression with not one ounce of pain making it look hard.

"He isn't wrong."

"Drew," I breathe, blown away by his words and what he's showing me by looking at me that softly.

"You know I have a past, but I don't want you to doubt that I'm with you because of whatever was said. I've lived a long time alone, Liv. I've been a ghost. A shadow of myself that was hardly living. No sunlight has been able to touch me while I stayed living in those shadows. Just darkness and loneliness. You and Riley, though …" He stops, looks down at the floor, and shakes his head. "You have breathed life back in with the sunshine from both of you."

"Honey," I try again, my emotions crawling up my throat, making me blink back tears.

"Hurting you—hurting her—that is the last thing I ever want to do, babe. There will come a time that I unintentionally may and I …" He pauses, pulls me closer, and bends his head so I can see what's working behind his gaze. "I can't promise you that one day I might not hurt you, but it wouldn't be because I want to or deliberate. You've given me a reason to breathe again, Liv … I won't be stupid enough to give that up when I had stopped believing I would ever have the beauty of someone like you."

"I'm having a hard time not falling in love with you," I blurt out, telling him honestly what was in my heart after hearing his words.

He pulls me into his chest, arms wrapped around me, and I breathe in his scent. The comfort and safety I find within his arms tells me I'm full of crap … I'm already there.

"Ditto," he softly responds.

CHAPTER 15

Olivia

"FEELS LIKE THIS" BY MAISIE PETERS

Something shifted during those moments back in my office.

Something big.

Something so huge, it was as if the earth had shifted.

Even now, hours later, I can feel it.

Dinner was quick. We enjoyed an easy conversation that Riley led. We've been sitting on the couch watching her play in comfortable silence since cleaning up the dinner mess together. She loves being here at his place. The stark white space dances with an explosion of color with her toys scattered about. Her favorite corner of the vast room housing a makeshift bedroom for her American Girl doll might be the most colorful spot, though. Drew even went so far as going to the store and getting her a doll bed that she could keep at his place when we're here. Not just any bed, either. He must have spent a small fortune at the American Girl store because she's got a bed, a small dresser, and even a tiny doll-sized nightstand. When he pulled out new outfits, Riley clutched them to her chest and thanked him while happy feet danced all over the room.

She hasn't left the corner since, setting it up to perfection before she has to go to bed. Chattering softly to her doll as she goes.

"Drew," she calls from her spot across the room.

"Right here, little princess."

"Do you think she will be okay sleeping out here by herself," she questions in a serious tone. She points one small finger toward the huge windows that line his space. "It's a really, really long way down, Drew."

I feel his laughter silently against my side where I've been relaxing and reading.

"Is she not yours?" he asks strangely.

"Silly, of course she is." Naturally, she understood him when I didn't.

"Way I see it, she'll be more than okay since you're the bravest girl I know. How could she not be too? And, my girl, you love adventure, so I bet she does too."

At that moment, I watch with rapt fascination as Riley falls a little more in love with her giant. She looks at him with her all-knowing eyes, studying his silence and mulling over his words with a quiet of her own.

"You think I'm the bravest girl?" she questions a moment later, her tone full of wonder and amazement.

"Yeah, beanie, I do."

Her melodic giggles echo around the room, and I have to quench the urge to cry over the beauty of this moment. I love this for her, oh my how I love this.

"Thank you, giant."

She leaps from where she's standing and lands in his lap. He grunts and looks over at me, and for a moment, my heart hurts when I see the expression on his handsome face. He loves Riley, no doubt, but the fear that he isn't hiding from me squeezes my heart.

He's been hurt, and while I may not know the depths of that pain yet, I know that it had to have been really bad for it to affect him in the way it has and continues to.

His arms stay held out, but only for a beat, then he wraps them around her tiny frame and hugs her close. At that moment, I know my heart will forever belong to this man. His eyes close, his face relaxes, and he hugs my girl with so much tenderness, something he rarely gives without making sure no one is around. He's given it to me, but this is the first moment I've watched him give that to her.

It's absolutely breathtaking.

"Do you want to play with me?" she asks, leaning back and looking him in the eyes.

He grunts a sound that must have been enough for her because she looks over at me with the whole world shining in her beautiful eyes—so light-green they almost look clear full of a happiness that I haven't seen before. Which is saying something because my girl is one happy kid.

Content to watch this play out, I settle back in my seat and watch the giant and his bean.

My book forgotten at my side.

―――――

After tucking Riley into the guest room, we head back into the living room. It's not the first time that I've stayed over here. Riley and I have been here a few times a week for the past couple of months. I'm not even sure when it happened—that moment that told my heart it worked better when we were together. It could have been Riley and him, watching them bond, but I know it's more than that.

"Tell me about your family," I request, noticing the shutters coming down over him as soon as I finish speaking. "I don't want to pry, but honey … I want to know *you*."

He moves around the room, turning out the lights as he goes so the only thing that is shining is the city well below the windows we're sitting next to. His home may be white and almost sterile in its vast emptiness, but when those lights go out, we sit in the sitting area that he has behind the couches and living area. It was meant to be a spot to gaze out into the world beyond his high-rise. When he settles into the chair next to mine, I expect him to remain silent, but he shocks me stupid when he pulls my arm over to his lap and takes my hand in his.

"They're gone."

My chest hurts, knowing just how hard it is to lose a family member. I can't imagine what it would be like to have no one left. I squeeze his hand and wait for him to continue.

"It's been damn near two decades, and it still feels like I lost them yesterday."

"I'm so sorry, honey."

His shoulders come up as he silently shrugs. "Been a long time, babe."

"Might be so, but you haven't healed. You know you can talk to me, right?"

"Isn't that what we're doing?" he questions with a wink, one corner of his lush lips tipping up. There one second, gone the next, his face back to the stoic expression he had before. He takes a deep breath and holds it a beat before letting it out.

"You know what I mean."

He gives me the slightest of smiles.

"Some things are best left alone, Liv."

I pull my hand from his, not too gently, because he wasn't ready to let me go and stand. His eyes track my movements the whole time. My feet take a few steps to stand in front of the chair he's sitting in. His arms rest on the arms of the chair, head against the back, and his whole body's held tight. He doesn't even try to hide the pain in his eyes, not this time.

The driving need for me to ease his soul almost steals my breath.

I push my knee into the side of his seat, next to his thigh. His hands move to my hips just when my other leg joins in, and my butt hits his thighs. His breathing is harsh, but his touch tender. Reaching out, I dance my fingers across his cheeks until my palms rest against his bearded cheeks. I can feel the rapid beat of his heart from where my fingertips rest against his neck. The rest of him might as well be turning to stone.

"I know loss, honey. I know that life-changing feeling only comes when you've lost someone incredibly special. I look at you sometimes and see the same expression I had after losing my sister. Almost six months after I first met you all that time ago, I realized what I saw in your eyes. A pain so haunting that it consumes your soul. You continue to keep that inside, it will destroy you. I've watched it inside you for years. You don't have to carry it alone anymore."

He holds my gaze, not looking away as the pain slashes so bright and deep behind his.

"I had a great family," he begins, his voice low and deep. I hold my breath, not wanting him to stop talking. Only when he continues do I let it slowly out. "I had a great family. That was after a shit childhood when I didn't have that. I found my way to them. Had a great damn brother, too. Had him from the day I was born, and he protected me every one of those bad days when we were little. Even with a shitty mom, I had love because of him. It took me enlisting to find my real family, which damn sure wasn't what the woman who gave birth to us."

I move in the seat, my knees hitting the back of the chair, and try to pull myself closer to him. His hands at my hips flex before pulling me toward him the rest of the way. I stay silent though, letting him run the show. My hands move to his chest and I wait.

"I've seen a lot of dark shit in my fifty-two years, Liv. Seen a lot of stuff that would take a lesser man out at the knees and he would never get back up."

He glances away and I feel the loss of his eyes.

"I never thought that I would have this though," he whispers into the Boston skyline. "I never allowed myself to believe I had anything left to wake up for than whatever I had on my workload. I'm not the man I was before I lost them, Liv. The heartache of that doesn't go away."

"No, it doesn't," I agree emphatically. "I'm sorry for what you lost. I wouldn't wish losing family on anyone, but you didn't die, honey. You don't need to keep that hurt locked away anymore. You don't need to keep them locked up, not with me. I'm here and I want to help you carry that so it doesn't slash so deep into you."

"You do."

I smile sadly at him, my hands now resting on his chest don't miss the rapid pounding I feel.

"One day, you'll be able to remember them without pain," I vow.

"Hasn't happened yet, baby. Not sure it's possible."

"The first thing you have to do is let them out so their memory can bring you comfort and not pain. Think of all the good times you had, and you hold on to them with all you got in you. It won't happen overnight, but it does eventually get easier to remember them without it feeling as if your very breath is trapped."

"Ash, my brother," he starts and just those three words sound like it was hard to get out. "He would have loved you for me."

My smile draws his eyes and my heart picks up when I realize he won't stop.

"I had an incredible family at the end, Liv. It kills me not to have them anymore."

"They're always with you."

This time, his eyes come back up and he looks gutted. "No, no they aren't."

He moves us, standing with little effort despite the fact that I was in his lap. He helps me steady myself on my feet before he moves to stand at the window. Looking down at the city below us. I walk the few steps and to stand behind him and run my hands around his middle and press my face against his back. Silently giving him my support while he runs with his thoughts. He relaxes slightly when my head presses against his back but tenses up when my hands hit his abdomen. Not the first time he's done that. I feel the reason against my palm. The little bundle of scar tissue that I notice every time we're intimate.

"How did you get this scar?" I question, something I haven't done before now.

He places his hand over where mine is resting above his scar. His silence follows my question. I wait, seeing if he will answer me. I don't know what I was expecting. Well, that's a lie, I was expecting him to ignore my question and change the subject.

"I was shot."

With a gasp, I jump slightly, and he tightens his hold of my hand above his scar.

"It was the day that I lost everyone that I considered my family."

Oh my, this man. My heart breaks for the pain that he carries with him, especially knowing this. No wonder he wears that pain like he does.

"Honey," I breathe and he turns in my arms.

"It's been a long time, Liv."

"Yet you still have the pain of that riding you every day as if it was yesterday."

"I always will, babe. It's just the reality of it."

"You've let it change your life though. You've let it keep you from living."

His gruffly grunts. "They haven't kept me from living. I do what I do for them."

"What do you mean?"

"Never had someone other than the guys ask me to explain something I'm not able to explain. You know I work with the government, but it's all top secret stuff, Liv. I can't tell you more than that. Everything I do for them is in the name of the family I lost."

"I understand that's what you think, but you're not doing it for them if you've been stuck living half a life while you do your hush hush work. Do you think they would want you to have held yourself back from others all this time?"

"Might have been a good change of pace from the old me they knew."

"You're still that man, Drew."

His body jolts. "Coop. Don't … just, please. I can't right now."

I lift a brow. "You aren't naked, honey. Pretty sure the rule was 'only while your cock is out,' or something like that."

My heavens I love the heat that takes over his handsome face when I talk like that. There is no doubt in my mind that he loves getting me to talk dirty. A welcomed reprieve from the hard conversation we're having. His lip quirks at the corner and he leans down to press his forehead against mine.

"When my cock is out, I plan on doing my best to make you forget your name as well as mine long enough for you to call *my* name when you give me your sweetness."

"Coop," I breathe, leaning my weight into him.

"Yeah, baby. Your Coop."

We don't break eye contact, so much unspoken between us. He lowers his head to take my mouth in a deep kiss, and starts walking up toward his bedroom. I know the moment to continue this conversation is over. There's only so much pain from the past someone can handle at once.

One thing's for sure, I'm going to work my tail off to remove that pain from his heart.

CHAPTER 16

Drew

"BROKEN" BY SEETHER

"You're being fucking reckless. Are you even watching out for Ray's slimy ass anymore? Because there hasn't been a single sighting of him in weeks."

"You think I don't know what I'm doing?"

Saint leans in, his tan skin in stark contrast to the bright marble countertops he's resting his hands against. Then again, everything is a stark contrast in my condo. There is no color. The only time that I see color in this place is when Olivia and Riley are here.

I glance away from Saint to where Riley left her American Girl Doll. Complete with a mini fucking suitcase that had exploded all over the corner of the room. I haven't moved it in over a week, not since their last time here after I surprised them with our night out at the circus. There hasn't been much time for my two worlds to learn how to coexist lately. The one where I'm a ghost not sure how to tangle with the one that makes me feel as if I have a reason to breathe again. I've been struggling on how to handle my feelings for Olivia for a while now. The only thing I know with certainty is that this is something I'm not willing to give up. Which is what brought this conversation to a head when the guys got here for a briefing on our targets.

"I think that you're using your cock and not being logical about what'll happen here. You think it'll end well when you tell her that you got close to make sure you had the best chances to kill the kid's father? I bet she'll love that. She let that kid into your home and you're using her to kill her father."

"Hey, man. You know he's not using her. That's not fair," Evan, always the fucking peacekeeper, disagrees.

I groan in my throat a sound of pure threat. "Fucking watch it, Saint."

"I'm not going to fucking watch it, Drew. We all gave up a lot to be in the shoes we're in. You're jeopardizing it all just to get some pussy."

It takes every ounce of calm I can muster not to come over the island between us and strangle this fuck.

"You think this is about getting my dick wet?"

"What else is it? You get close to her, helps she's a hot piece and all, and you just happen to be where you need to be in order to take out Ray. You get the target and you get off the whole time. Doing that makes you reckless."

I cross my arms and level Saint with a cold glare.

He matches me and leans back in the barstool he's been sitting at for the past hour, in my kitchen, and throws that shit back at me.

I see Evan and Hunt shift uncomfortably, both of them silent after Saint said his peace.

"You got anything else to say, *brother?*" I grunt, not entirely in control of my anger.

"Said it all."

"Said too fucking much," I snap back.

He tosses his arms in the air and stands from the island and I hear the barstool crash on to the floor behind him. The sound echoing around the silent condo like a gunshot.

"What the fuck do you think will happen here? You going to let her know that you're a dead man who spent over twenty years killing people? How about, you going to give her a chance to freak the fuck out *after* she finds out and leads the very people you died to protect your family from right to your doorstep—or worse, theirs. You know damn well what happens when they find out that you aren't dead. That family you've spent all these years being dead for will become pawns. Oh, never mind, that'll make good bedtime stories for the little one while you're fucking her aunt, won't it?"

"Out of line," Hunt adds, sounding bored.

"Damn well not out of line and you know it," Saint shoots back. "You aren't the only one that has a stake in this game. I have people I 'died' to protect, too."

"There isn't a single chance of that happening and you fucking know it."

"Do I?"

"Every one of those people who could have hurt my family has been dead a long time. I made sure of it when the man I had sitting on my family told me he hadn't seen anyone in years. I stay gone because they're better off without me. And you fucking know nothing I do would jeopardize the people you left behind."

"Reckless."

"She makes me feel alive, brother," I add, tone still hard and spitting nails, but of all the things I can tell him to make him understand what Olivia makes me feel, that's it. That's all he'll ever understand. Because we've all been living and breathing as ghosts, not feeling a fucking thing since the day we became the men we are right now. "Not only does she make me feel alive, but that little girl gives me a sense of purpose that is more than just killing motherfuckers that make the world better when they are leaving this earth. I've lived feeling, seeing, tasting, nothing. Not a fucking thing. Look around you, Saint. I live in a box with no feeling. I've been existing, waiting for my real death. I've lost everything and never allowed myself to think that I could have more in this life. I was reckless and brought this to myself back then, but I'll never make the mistake of being that way again. I left to protect those that I love. Do you not think that, by finding someone who made all of that seem like it was worth even more, that I shouldn't hold the fuck on?"

Evan clears his throat and I move my eyes to him. He gets it. He's always been the one preaching that we didn't just leave our lives to protect those we love. He always swore there was a bigger picture to the sacrifices we made. He fucking gets it.

My eyes travel over to Hunt, seeing the normally unruffled man staring at me with so much written on his face, I don't know how I missed it before. He holds himself with an air of detachment, but not because he's unaffected ... but because he wants this. He wants what I'm feeling with Olivia. He wants to feel alive again.

"No shit?" he asks while my attention is on him.

"Heart started beating again the night I asked her to call me Coop in bed."

"You dumb fuck."

I snap my eyes back to Saint, leveling him with the coldest of glares.

"You're going to get us and everyone we left behind killed."

"No, I'm not."

"What do you think will happen the second she slips and calls you that when you aren't in private? You know just as well as the rest of us, if the right person hears and sees your ugly mug, there will be no going back. And the second they start digging into you, they start looking into us. The only reason we've been successful in staying fucking dead is because we keep ourselves in the shadows without attachments!"

"You think I would be that reckless with you three? Let alone the people who I loved and left? LET ALONE with Olivia and Riley!" I roar the last part, feeling all of the rage and pent-up frustration I've felt since we started this conversation rushes to the surface.

"I think you got a taste of sweet pussy and can't think straight."

I'm around the island with his neck in my hand, his back against the wall, and my face breathing down on his. He matches me almost inch for inch, but I have him on build. He won't get the best of me until I want him to move. So I hold his gaze, both of us with anger and frustration riding the surface of our skin like a cloak.

"I got a taste of fucking life again," I level out in a deadly calm. "I got a taste of a future that made my heart come back online for it. I held that woman in my arms while she drooled on my chest, her girl on my other side with her little feet digging their way into my gut, and I felt like I had finally found the reason that I gave up everything. It, for the first time in my life, didn't feel like I had sacrificed everything the day I left my home. It felt like I had been given a second chance, one that meant I did the right thing all those years ago when I let the people who meant the world to me believe I had died. It wasn't for just them, it was because *she* was waiting for me. You tell me how that isn't thinking straight?"

The heat in his eyes simmers and he just looks at me.

"That woman wouldn't so much as blink if I asked her to do that in private only. You know damn well she's a good woman. And if you would think about why you're really acting like this, you know you would do the same thing if you found someone who gave you the gift of life after being a dead man for so long."

I let him go and turn back to face the others. Both of them showing nothing but understanding in what I just shared.

"You ready to hear what I know about Ray now?"

"Dick," Saint mumbles, fixing his sweatshirt. "You have to push me against the hard-ass wall?"

"You have to be a fucking asshole about something that you didn't even take the time to ask about?"

He holds up his hands.

"Look, I'm sorry, but you can't blame me for questioning this. You've shown no interest in any woman since we started this unit."

"She isn't just any woman. Not sure what else I can give you to make you realize that."

"Man, you know we were told this was okay when they set us up here. Encouraged even," Evan states to Saint.

"Said we would hide better with a family," Hunt adds with a scoff.

"Yet none of you mother fuckers have a family and we're hiding just fine."

"Doesn't mean we haven't wanted one, brother," Evan continues. "Just because you're scared of finding more doesn't mean we haven't been waiting for the moment when we find someone worth living again for."

"Shit," Saint breathes, shame written all over his face. "I'm sorry. I didn't think."

Evan shrugs, but the pain is slashed on his face. He doesn't talk about it a lot, but his chance to disappear came when a car accident stole his wife and child at the same time he

"died." He left behind a large family who felt that loss a lot harder because it wasn't just him.

"Long time ago," he mutters, looking down at his hands.

"Still sorry."

"Can we talk about Ray?" Evan asks, clearly done with this conversation.

I move back to the other side of the island and toss them each over a folder. It's not thick, but it contains what we've been waiting for.

"Surveillance footage of Ray Graves leaving Schiphol Airport in Amsterdam a week ago. Confirmed from both facial recognition software and voice confirmation during his chat with the gate agent. From what we could gather, he was coming from a flight leaving Charles de Gaulle Airport, but he hasn't been staying in Paris or our contacts would have picked him up on CCTV already. Best we can tell is he's been jumping around Europe for the past month so much that we lost track of him. Staying under the radar well enough not to get picked up on camera. Mafia's after that fuck, so it's not us he's hiding from. He has no idea we're after him. But, it's clear he's trying to get back to get the money that he knows Olivia and Riley have, that will clear the path for him to start funneling guns back into the states and we can't let that happen. Last shipment ended up in a mass casualty gang war in Chicago."

"What's the plan when he makes contact on US soil?"

"The flight he boarded landed in Rome. He caught his tail ten minutes into his travel from the airport. We're watching, but the thought is that he's making his way back to Boston with a few distraction flights. I suspect he's looking for a private charter at this point. His money might be running out, but it's not all gone yet. He needs to get here, undetected, in order to make his move and get what he needs from Olivia."

"And," Hunt starts with a deep breath. "What exactly do you think he plans on doing with Olivia?"

I lean on the counter and look at each of the men who have made up my team. Men who I trust with my life, and in turn Olivia and Riley's. Men who I'm proud to have been living the life of dead men with.

"I think he's planning on taking Riley and forcing Olivia's hand with a ransom demand."

Equal heated words are grumbled on under of their breaths.

"Not anything we can do other than stick close. One of you at the shop every day. I'll stick close to Olivia and Riley. We do what we need to do to get Ray, and I do what I need to do to make sure the girls who restarted my heart aren't harmed."

We continue to make small talk for a bit, catching up on sports and the women who Hunt and Saint met at the bar the other night that turned their backs into a mess of scratch marks. Those two, not sure why, but enjoy sharing way too much. It isn't until I'm shutting the door on them that I realize what felt so wrong about my space this morning. Something that I didn't notice because I was too busy focusing on Riley's doll shit in the corner to see anything else.

I see it now though.

And it sends a chill through my veins.

"Jesus fucking Christ," I mutter, walking over to the bookshelves.

Right there in the center, where it's stayed for over twenty years, is the jar that meant the world to me: both the old and new me. The jar that I watched my family cry over as one of the most loving men I ever knew mourned his friend … me.

Only this isn't *that* jar.

That jar is moved a little farther back, but not to hide it. No, it was moved back so that another could take its place. Identical in every way. Only perfect and new, not handled with so many touches and too many years of deep rooted sadness.

Tentative steps take me to the shelf and I see the folded piece of paper in the space behind it, tucked between the old and new jar.

If you weren't so handsome, I would kill you for real.
Tomorrow. 2:00 pm, I'll be at your door.
Don't think of locking me out either, you hunk. You think Sway didn't learn a thing or two from you brooding alphas?
2:00 pm, Zeke Cooper.
You've got a lot to explain.
And I have a lot to get off my fabulous chest.
Secret's safe with me, for now. I'll see how I feel after you explain your actions.
Tata for now,
Sway

. . .

"Fuck," I hiss, my eyes burning at Sway's words.

Only he could put so much flamboyance into a letter like this. I know, if he knows I'm here, that he can't be feeling as carefree as it sounds. I just have to figure out what the hell he does knows and who he's told. How the fuck could he have even seen me to find me? He would have to know someone in my building to get in, but if he's learned from my old brothers, he could have scaled the fucking wall and no one would have noticed.

I picture Sway, short and round in his crossdressing ways, scaling my high-rise with his platform heels. His long blond wig dancing in the Boston breeze. Glitter blowing in the air as it passes him.

I check the clock and realize I have an hour before I come face-to-face with my past.

The guys were right to feel fear over what could happen if me being alive got out. I just have to pray that Sway will handle it well and understand why I did what I did.

Because if he doesn't, not only will I lose what I'm building with Olivia and Riley, but everyone I loved and lost will be in danger.

"Fuck," I echo, feeling like the weight of the world is on my shoulders.

That's when I recognize the emotion weighing me down the heaviest. One I haven't felt since I "died."

Fear.

CHAPTER 17

Drew

"HOW TO BREATHE" BY MATTHEW MAYFIELD

The heavy tick of the clock speeding the seconds closer to two o'clock are heavy in my empty condo. Each tick, each tock. They all sound like gunshots. I stand here, holding the note that Sway had left in one hand hung loosely at my side. A complete contradiction to the tenseness that has solidified my whole body. If it wasn't for the sound of my breathing, I would think I had truly died. Not even my heartbeat is allowed to race, held captive in the paralyzing fear that has a stranglehold on me.

He never should have been able to find me.

None of them should have ever been able to find me.

I was careful. I moved in a way that each step was planned and each second was calculated. I knew what was coming before I moved. Always. It's how I've stayed alive in my death.

I changed the way I looked in such an extreme way, you would have thought that I had surgery. The only thing that was left from the man I had been was my eyes, which I wore contacts to change the color of, and my smile. Something that I hadn't done in so long. Still rusty, but each time I gave that to Olivia and Riley, it becomes easier to recall.

If there ever was a man who would be able to spot me just by my gait though, it would be goddamn him.

Sway.

Dilbert Harrison, the third.

Hands down, one of the best men I've ever known.

He was one of the first—and only—men who I had encountered in my life that had no qualms about flirting with me. It never bothered me. I thought it was hilarious. That was, when he wasn't tossing glitter around like a goddamn fairy. Right before I "died," I asked him about it. All he said was, when he was forced to suppress who he really was, he used art—and glitter—to experience his happiness. He was a gay man, in the Deep South, with two southern Baptist preachers for parents. He was never allowed to be him and as a young kid, glitter gave him that. And his glitter gave me and my brothers that. I'll never forget the day he painted the sidewalk outside the office park his salon and the office our security firm were in. Not a single person questioned him … much. He was right though, it brought a smile every time I walked over it. He also had a fondness of keeping glitter in his skintight pants and tossing it on us as we walked by. Even though it took weeks to get that shit off, he did what he meant to and cleared any negative moods that we were in.

That's what compelled me to take the jar all those years ago.

Not only did I desperately need that happiness to carry me through my life as a ghost, but it was my lifeline that teethered me to the life I left behind.

And fuck me, I've missed that man.

With a heavy sigh and even heavier steps, I place the note back where I found it. One finger touches the glass of my new mason jar of happiness, and then I turn to walk over to the wet bar. I skip the glass completely and take a long pull from the bottle of Jack. The burn claiming my throat not even registering. My mind too busy spinning on the past. I haven't let myself think of them often. It hurt too much. But now, with ten minutes before Sway gets here, I'm powerless to do anything *but* think of them. I can't help it.

Axel Reid, Greg Cage, John Beckett, and Maddox Locke. All four of the men who had been at my side during our time in the Marines, but also past that when we were doing security. Cage had been in Georgia and the rest of us out in California after we got out. When we moved the firm to Georgia and became Corps Security, that was also when I hit my spiral.

Just as I said earlier to the guys, I remember how reckless I had been back then. The guys were falling in love, having kids, making families, and all the while, I was searching for *anything* that would make me feel loved. Sure, I had my brother, Asher, but his love for me was different. He protected me his whole life. It killed me when I "died" to know he would feel that deeply in his soul, but it was my turn to protect him. To repay him for all the years he protected me. It was because of my reckless search for something that made me fucking feel that he was in danger anyway. I fucked my way through women, I didn't give a shit about tossing myself into anything dangerous, and bottom line, I truly had a death wish.

A death, ultimately, I got.

I knew the second I had killed my last mark that I'd fucked up. I killed the right hand of one of the most predominant drug and gun runners in the Southeast. He, the man I killed, was in charge of running flesh for him. The night that I got him, I also saved sixty-three women who were about to be transported. I got on Dominic Murphy's radar and that's a place I couldn't afford to be. Not when I also shut down eight other organized crime operations that same night. There wasn't a single criminal that didn't know who I was.

So I did what I had to do.

I died.

And I've spent the past two decades and some change hiding from those criminals *and* my family. I faked my own death, but still lived a dead man's life. Until Olivia and Riley, I didn't give a shit when I was going to die for real. I was just going through the motions, ridding the world of the worst kind of evil as I continued to take out the most vile criminals.

I was smart, no one saw a ghost, but somehow … someone more dangerous than them found me anyway.

More dangerous because he has the power to ruin everything I sacrificed.

There would be too much pain for them if I came back. I've been a dead man walking for way too long.

I get three more swallows from the bottle before the knock comes from the direction of my door.

"Fuck," I mutter, looking down at my boots and rubbing the tension out of my neck with my free hand. I glance at the bottle of Jack, almost going for another drink, but then I hear him.

"You open this door right this darn tootin' second, mister!" he calls through the barrier.

Despite the situation, I can't help but feel a little ease at that.

Same old Sway.

I place the bottle back on the counter and move toward the front door. One hand wrapping around the cool metal knob and the other unlocking the bolt. When I pull the door open, I wasn't prepared to be hit full force. Sway gasps, does a little jump, and wraps his arms around my neck. His hug is so tight, I feel the air in my lungs protesting. I wrap my arms around him and give him a hug of my own, one that I know he feels with the impact of every year I was gone in. Just as I do.

He's a short guy, so I imagine we look hilarious with him hanging in the air as we hug. I notice as he pulls away that his blond wig is missing. His hair is also completely gone, the mocha skin shining bright under the lighting.

I step back from the threshold and usher him in. He's still wearing those damn heels and they click as he walks into the living area. The whole time, he's looking around.

"Guess this is as close to heaven as a dead man can get, hmm, sugar britches?" he states when the door clicks shut.

I snort, but follow him into the living room. I glance around, seeing the opulence around me, and admit he isn't wrong. Even colorless, it's stunning. "How'd you find me?"

His hand goes to his chest, covered tightly in a dark maroon v-neck shirt. "My heavens above, richer with time, but that voice is still all you."

I don't speak. Uncomfortable.

His head tips as he studies me, tears falling down his cheeks.

The silence and that goddamn clock's tick continue around us.

I dig my fists into my eyes when I feel the wetness collecting in my lids, taking a second to compose myself.

"You tell anyone?"

He looks offended in a second, but thank God the tears stop. "I'm not stupid, Zeke Cooper. I know damn well you had to have a big reason for what you did the second I saw you strut that fine ass into the lobby of this building."

I frown. "When did you see me?"

"Walked right past me, honey pie. I'm in town for a hair show, and a friend of mine lives on the first floor. Right on past Sway and there I was with my jaw on the floor like I had just seen, well … a ghost. You didn't have eyes for me. Not with that stunning creature at your side and that precious little angel in your arms. Had it not been for that sleepy little baby, I would probably have brushed it off as a coincidence. But you held that little angel just like you used to cart Cohen and Nate around. I knew right then and there you were my Cooper."

"Name's Andrew now, Sway. Or Drew. But don't use that name. That's not me anymore."

His hand comes out and grabs mine. I look down, his dark skin slightly wrinkled with age holding the heavily tattooed one of mine. I feel the emotion of the life I left bubbling up, but I swallow thickly.

"You'll always be my Coop."

"Not me anymore, Sway."

I hold his gaze while he studies whatever the fuck he sees in my eyes. It doesn't take long for him to nod.

"Want to tell me how you got into my house?"

He tosses his head back and laughs. "I've been watching those fine-ass men walk around for way too long, darlin'. I know how to pick a lock, disarm a system, avoid cameras, you name it. Which, now I know why you weren't the install man because your system is hands down to the ground garbage."

"Best there is," I lament.

"No, darlin' man, you just forgot your roots."

Damn. I don't say anything. He isn't wrong. It's the best system there is, but I hardly use all the features. What's the point? I was a ghost, and nothing I owned mattered to me.

"Been a long time, my friend. Help me understand why you led everyone to believe you were dead."

A humorless sound comes out of my mouth.

"Don't you dare think you can keep it from me. I know you're alive,

Co—Drew. I know. Now, you want me to keep this from them, I'm going to need more than that."

"You have to keep it from them, Sway."

"Then help me understand."

I lean back against the chair and look at him. He's relaxed, his purse on the table between us. Legs crossed proper as fuck. One red high as fuck heeled booted foot bouncing in the air. His face calm, and his eyes full of confusion and love. Even in this situation, he practically radiates happiness.

Same damn Sway.

Same. Damn. Sway.

"Made a lot of enemies over the years, Sway. I was in some shit that there was just no going back from because I was so irresponsible in my quest to find some meaning in my life. I put everyone back home in the crosshairs. With me gone, you were all safe. It wasn't even a question."

He hums, nods his head, but continues his silence.

"I spent the first five years trying to hunt down everyone that knew who I had been. Changed the way I looked, got a team, survived in the shadows and took out as many of those threats as I could. It was another five years when I realized I would never rid the world of all the people and organizations that could harm my family. It took another eight for me to come to terms with that, still trying to get all of the motherfuckers. The rest of that time, I've resigned myself to this life. I do what's needed of me and I stay away and hidden. I make sure the family I left doesn't feel any pain from the shitstorms I had created."

"You didn't trust them to keep you safe during this?"

I suck in a breath.

"I know damn well what you all are in to. I know you also were badass hunks running around doing badass stuff when you were all enlisted. I know, just as you know damn well, you should have given them the choice."

"Not that easy, man."

"You're wrong."

"Do you know what kind of men these were? The kind that peddle flesh, hand out drugs and guns to kids, have no trouble raping a woman in broad daylight. They were everywhere. There was no fucking way that

127

they could have been kept safe when the enemies after *me* were larger than anything we had ever seen. And Sway, that includes our time fighting for our goddamn lives in war. Not enough eyes in the world could have watched all the angles these fucks would have attacked. You think I didn't think this through?"

"I know you did. That's the problem."

"Explain."

He leans back, picks up his hand and checks his polish. "You didn't give them a chance to know you were still breathing because *you* assumed the only way to protect was to disappear and never say so much as boo. You, by the way, might still be a fine-ass hunk of love but you make a terrible ghost, darlin'. Did you ever think that you could have had both? The shadows and the connection to your old life?"

"Do you not think, if there was a chance, I wouldn't have taken it!" I stand from my seat and start pacing. "I almost reached out, but that was when I discovered everyone was being watched, fucking stalked, and as good as my guys were, they didn't even see it. From the shadows, where filth lives, they watched and waited. They weren't stupid. In the underbelly of the world, faking a death isn't uncommon. Seventeen years they watched. I know because the man I had on everyone reported that back to me. He stayed there in Hope Town, getting regular cuts at your salon, and had one job—watch and protect. He knew who was getting close and when. I knew of no fewer than three men who were on each person I left behind—including you!"

Sway gasps, but I keep going.

"Sean, the man I had on the town, had to kill a man about fifteen years after I left. Fifteen fucking years and those motherfuckers still thought I was out there. Sean got to this one before he could grab her, but that was the day that Emmy almost died. No one was the wiser, not a fucking one of you guys, because I made sure to keep the shadows from the brightness you all got to live in. That was the day I felt like I really died, knowing there would never be a time I could get close."

"My heavens above," he gasps, the tears coming back instantly.

"Spent every year since taking people out, some ordered and some not, to ensure that never happened. There isn't a single one left but I can't go back after all this time. At this point, I'm better off dead."

"You are never better off dead. Not to me and not to them."

"Yeah, Sway … I am."

"Are there …" He gulps. "Are there still people watching?"

"Sean is still there, but he hasn't reported seeing anyone in about six years. Not after I took out one of the largest crime networks in the nation. I hunted them all, Sway. Sean stayed because he made a life for himself in Hope Town, but he still keeps an eye because I asked him to never stop."

"Then why can't you come back?"

I drop my head and look at the floor. "There's been too much time, Sway. Time for them to heal that would only cause pain if I came back now. For so long, it was because I couldn't be sure there weren't still people out there. Then it was because so much time passed while I picked them all off, it became too late. They aren't just a group of men with nothing to lose anymore. From what I was told the one time I asked, you all have families."

Something moves across his face that I can't place, but whatever I saw, everything inside me screams to brace.

Fucking brace.

"Yes. We all have families." He takes a second, then leans over to pat the chair I had left. "I think you need to sit down, honey love."

129

CHAPTER 18

Olivia

"SHALLOW" BY BRADLEY COOPER AND LADY GAGA

What a day.

I lean over the counter and place the last folded shirt of Riley's on the kitchen island and think about how the morning had gone.

It was shocking, first thing this morning when Riley and I were headed out, not seeing the man who had been a daily constant for our walks. I had been so used to that routine we were creating, never once having him miss a day, that I hadn't been able to shake the concern that hit me like a battering ram. It felt wrong seeing Evan standing there where Drew should have been.

Evan hadn't given me anything, but he knew I was shocked when I saw him standing outside of my gate today and not Drew. I don't like the feeling that I had when I looked out there and didn't see our guy leaning against his normal perch in the alcove to the gated entryway. It felt wrong. Like I was missing something vital.

I asked, but he brushed my question off to focus on Riley instead. If she noticed anything was awry, she did a great job of hiding it.

He was polite, but what I saw working behind his eyes told me that I was right to worry.

Ever since that night I stood with Drew and he opened up some, we have been getting closer and closer. He hasn't talked more about the family he lost. He started letting his guard down more and more, letting me see glimpses of him carefree.

What he hasn't done, however, is missed a single day. He's never ignored a text. He's never not taken my call. His silence, while it's something he gives everyone else, hasn't been given back to me since he and I started growing closer. Since we became *us*.

Luckily, today was so busy I didn't have a single moment to let my thoughts run away with me. I had been spending less time at Olde Mug than I normally would, and more time with Drew, so a busy day wasn't surprising. It was welcome to keep my thoughts from overrunning me with fret and worry.

Once I got done with payroll, it seemed like I was putting out a million different fires all day. Great for not thinking about the man who's stealing all your thoughts, but not so great when you know something is wrong with said man and you're powerless to help.

"I don't like this," I whisper to the empty room.

I drop the last item I had folded into the basket full of her laundry and move over to where I left my bag earlier. I knew there wouldn't be anything from him, but not seeing the screen light up without any calls or texts from him amped up my concern to a whole new level. I had tried, of course, to reach him. Before today, he didn't ever ignore my calls. Another thing that makes me know something is wrong. My thumbs make quick work, and despite the hour, Ella's response comes right away.

Me: Hey—you got a second?

   Ella: How goes it, girlfriend?

Me: Are you busy? I need to run out, and Riley is sleeping.

   Ella: I'll be there in two shakes.

That's my best friend for you. Never even questioning, always there when needed, and God, do I love her even more for it. She may act like she doesn't care too much about anything, but I know better. She lives for Riley and is more of a sister to me than just a friend, if I'm being real.

Knowing I have at least twenty minutes before she arrives, I rush around gathering up the spilled items in my purse and dropping the laundry basket off on Riley's dresser. I walk over to her bed and look down at her peaceful face. She was worried about Drew, too, but it does my heart good knowing that her youthful innocence will still allow her to stay somewhat ignorant to the real adult emotions around her.

With a kiss to her temple, I head to my room to put my shoes on so I can leave when Ella gets here.

My room feels nothing short of depressingly empty when I walk in. Not that Drew had been here often, but he was here often enough that my space was starting to feel wrong when he wasn't in it.

Empty and cold.

Which was the complete antithesis to what my room should feel like.

When I moved in, I made sure the large space was as inviting as possible. One wall holds nothing but windows, then my bed across from it.

I drop my butt in the chair across from the large mirror and start to pull my tennis shoes on. When I glance at my reflection, it doesn't take a mind reader to see the concern and worry written all over my face. My work clothes long since changed into yoga pants and a tight tank. My hair pulled into a bun on the top of my head and my face free of makeup. I never leave the house like this. I always make sure I'm put together. I always have, and I know it's probably the one thing I did take from my childhood after I got out of that life.

People will judge you less, at least to your face, when you don't give them something to tear apart. For me, it was to always give the best presentation of myself.

Right now, I couldn't care less.

The color on my cheeks is the only thing that covers my pale skin. My eyes more mossy than their normal green because of the little crying fit I had earlier. I've always been one to cry when I get too overwhelmed with things, which thankfully tonight has given me enough color that I don't look so pale.

I run my eyes down as I stand and take in the rest of me. He's never seen me in something so tight. I mean, sure, he's seen me naked, but

THE LONG WAY HOME

never dressed with something that is more like a second skin. If it wasn't for that nagging feeling in my gut telling me that he needs me, I would take the time to change.

"Hey," Ella whispers in the silence, making me jump.

"When did you get here?" I ask, walking over to give her a hug.

"Just now. I didn't want to be loud and wake up the munchkin."

I nod, and I feel my chin starting to quiver.

"Hey now, what's this about?" she questions with concern high in her tone.

"I don't know how to explain it, but I feel like he needs me. You saw he wasn't there this morning or when I left work. He hasn't called, nothing. When I asked Evan about it, I'm telling you, El, there was something working behind his eyes that all but confirmed my concern. I felt like he didn't want to betray his friend by outright saying anything, but it was there. I know it. He needs me."

"Maybe it's not that, hon. Maybe he's just busy?"

"He hasn't ever been too busy for us. Not in months, El."

"Evan did mention something about him earlier, but I didn't even think twice. It was right when the rush had come in, and we were too swamped for me to pry."

"What did he say?" I ask, squeezing her hand before dropping it and moving around her to leave the bedroom.

"It was weird. They had left his place earlier and nothing was wrong. He hasn't been able to get ahold of him since."

"I'm really worried about him, El."

"I know, girlfriend. I know."

"Thank you for coming to stay with bean. I'll try to get back quickly."

She laughs without any humor. "You won't do anything of the sort. Get over there and make sure your man is okay. If he is, enjoy the night and be as loud as you want without little ears around. If he isn't, well … I know my girl's got this covered, and the last thing I would want you to do is cut some of that healing love you're so good at giving short. I'll take care of bean and get her off to school in the morning."

"I'm lucky to have you."

"Yeah, you totally are," she jests. "Now go. Check in, though, okay?"

I give her a hug and promise to let her know what's going on. Knowing Riley is in good hands is one less stress on my shoulders, but the concern for the man who is quickly starting to own my heart isn't doused in the slightest.

———

I climb out of the Uber and close the door, stepping up on the curb to look up at the building where his place is. Even though I can't see anything—the windows are designed to keep people from seeing in—I can sense him. He's up there, I know it.

My sweaty palms remind me to get it together, and I wipe them on my pants before reaching out and pulling the door open. I smile when I see Stanley, the night guard, behind the desk. Thankfully, I shouldn't have any trouble getting up.

"Hello, Stanley," I call out, walking across the expanse of the lobby to stand in front of his desk. I notice his book and ignore all the security monitors. "Looks like a real steamy one you have today."

His laughter is immediate. "Wife has them all over the place. Never thought I would get into this chick stuff, but damn if they can't write a catchy little story. Would you believe that this one even has some mystery in it, too. They're not all throbbing members these days."

I laugh at his joke. "You don't have to tell me twice. I love a good hot romance read."

"Now don't go letting my secret out, you hear?"

"Secret is safe with me," I vow, bringing my hand up to mock lock my lips sealed. "As long as you tell me which book you're reading."

He winks, his mocha skin without any wrinkles despite him being close to seventy, and turns the book so I can read the cover.

"What can I do for you, sweet girl?" he asks a moment later.

"I'm just here to see my man. I have a night without the little one and figured I would surprise him." I point at his book. "You know what I mean. Spicy romance and all."

This time, he leans his stocky body back in the chair and laughs. "You go on up. You know the code for his floor, right?"

"I do. Thank you, Stan."

I start walking, but turn back to him when he calls my name.

"Known Drew for close to fifteen years. Since the day I started working here. Not once has he added someone to his guest list. Not until you. It's really good to see him like this. Happy, I mean. Whatever you're doing, you keep doing it."

"That's my plan, Stan." I wink and turn to walk over to the elevators. His words warm my soul.

The doors close almost the second I enter the elevator, and not for the first time, I marvel at the security of his building. Each floor has two apartments except for the top two, and you need a code to get the elevator moving for those. I press the six digits quickly, and the door slides open before I have time to wipe my hands again. I walk the small space between the elevator and his doorway and punch in the code to unlock his door, walking into the foyer of his place.

Not a single light on.

All the windows covered with the thick panels that come down from the ceiling to keep the sun out. The only light that is on is the one that lights up the bookshelf in his living area. It's enough light, though. The glow from them has my feet rushing forward the second I see his still form across the couch in what looks like the most uncomfortable position I have ever seen. That's saying something since the little girl who I left sleeping to come here can fold herself up in all sorts of ways when she's tired enough.

This, though … this is more than just tired.

This is something much worse.

I step over the beer cans, moving silently through the reminders of how he came to rest like that scattered all around him. An empty liquor bottle is still in his hand as it dangles from the couch. His hair a tangled mess around his face. One leg hanging off the couch and the other hooked over the back. His clothes from the other day when I left his place not changed.

He looks terrible.

I want to wake him and demand answers to what is wrong. I know he needs something different right now, though. I don't know how I know that. Maybe it's because there is some kind of sadness hanging thick in the air that tells me I'm right. One thing I know with complete certainty though is that I need to be his support and not judge whatever state he has gotten himself into.

It takes one hell of a herculean effort to walk away from where he is, but my feet carry me to the kitchen anyway. I don't bother with the lights, knowing right where his trash bags are and wanting to remove this mess he made before I wake him. It doesn't take me too long to clean up all the evidence of his pain. The trash bag is full before I even realize it. I keep moving around the room, tidying as I go. I'm quiet but not silent, so when I hear him mumble my name, I drop what I was wiping the coffee table off with and shuffle on my knees the few steps toward him.

"Hey," I whisper, reaching out to brush my fingers over his forehead to get the hair out of his face.

"You're really here?"

"You tell me."

"You're really here." He lets out a long, painfully heavy breath. I notice immediately how clear his voice is. There's no way he had recently drank everything I cleaned from the room. He doesn't sound the least bit intoxicated.

He does, however, sound broken, and that rips through my heart like a knife.

"Honey, what's going on?"

"Found me."

"Who found you?"

"I was careful. How did he find me?"

"Sweetheart, I don't understand what you're saying."

He turns his head, no longer talking to the empty space above him. His eyes haunted.

"I needed to stay dead."

I gasp and feel the tears welling up. "Baby ... you don't mean that."

He sits up, shifts his body so his elbows are resting on his knees, and drops his head down in his hands.

"Every one of them," he whispers. "I died for them."

"You aren't dead, honey," I exhale, feeling a desperation I hadn't before crawling up my throat.

"Been a dead man for more than half my life."

"You aren't making any sense. I don't understand what you're saying, honey."

"Fuck!"

I jump when his bellow rips through the quiet room—bringing his attention back to me. It's too dark to read what's on his face, though. Instead, I wait for him to talk again with my heart pounding in my chest.

"Didn't think it was possible to find you, though." He lifts his head, and I feel his gaze burn across my skin.

"Honey..."

"Gotta let me get this out, Liv."

His words stop me. I don't even take a breath, reaching out and pulling one of his hands into mine, kneeling in front of him.

And I wait. I wait, silently, so he knows that this is his time, and I'm listening.

"Don't know where to start."

"Drew," I exhale.

"I know, sure as shit, I never want to hear that name out of your mouth again, though."

I feel myself blush, embarrassed I had forgotten. "Coop, shoot, I'm sorry. It's new for me and slipped my mind."

He pulls his frame up and takes his hand from mine, reaching out to turn on the lamp behind my shoulder. When the warm light hits the darkness around us, it takes me a second to adjust. I blink a few times before I'm able to focus on him.

When I do, I gasp.

Gone are the eyes that I've grown to love over the past few months. I had questioned him before, but never had any confirmation from him about it. Well, I do now. His eyes are blue now. Completely different from the dark green I had seen every day for so long. Seeing such a vibrant color is a shock, but it's the changes to his whole face that have me so stunned. They're like a stormy sea in the clearest of waters. He doesn't look away as I study him. He doesn't even seem to be breathing, just waiting for me to get a good look.

"I was born Zachariah Cooper. There hasn't been a single day since the one when I became Andrew Shaw that I haven't wished I could be

Zeke Cooper again. When I died, I knew that void would remain a giant hole inside me. They were my past, and a dead man can't go backways, no matter how much I wanted to or missed the family that I left. I knew when I told you about my family, you believed them to be dead, but it was me who died to them.

"I had someone from that past visit me the other day," he continues, rumbling softly, the words sounding painful. "He shouldn't have been able to find me, but there he was, and it was like twenty-plus years hadn't even passed. He stood right over there and, just like you, had more questions than I knew how to answer. One thing he did manage to do is remind me how much I've lost just by standing in my apartment. I have no business wanting them all back in my life, but that's all I can think about."

Not wanting him to stop, I keep my lips pressed together and bite the inside my cheek so I don't get the urge to interrupt. My heart feels like it might rip through my chest with its frantic pounding.

"They all think I'm dead, Liv. I made sure of that. I turned my back on my family and let them mourn for a man who wasn't really dead. Just living like he was from that day on. They moved on eventually, thank God. I heard from the person I had in town that they were all breathing easy, alive and well. I know I did what was right back then, but now? Now, I'm not even a little sure I did." He holds my gaze, so much working behind those beautiful *blue* eyes. "When I was shot, I made it my life's mission to wipe the earth clean of the scum that had threatened my family. I knew I had one choice and that was to let them think I was dead so I could ensure the threat that got me would never touch them. I just had to make sure I stayed a dead man, stayed in the shadows and hunted. All of the people responsible for that bullet I took—the bullet I took to stop it from hurting my family—they're where they belong. Didn't matter, though. They took that life from me, and I have been living like the dead man they all thought I was. It didn't matter what I did, I had to live with the choice I made to keep them safe. Dead men don't come back."

He stops talking and then he blows a long exhale. Somehow, I know in my gut that exhale tells me I should brace silently before he continues.

He tells me about the men he was enlisted with, the years they spent together before moving to Georgia. His whole demeanor changes as he tells me about his family. He continues as I learn about the people who he says he left behind when he took a bullet meant for someone else. The whole time he speaks, his voice is low, and sadness hangs on each syllable. I never in my wildest dreams would have guessed that the family he said was gone was gone because he made them believe he was dead.

"There's more …" He pauses, and I start to think he won't keep talking until he opens his mouth and shocks me stupid. "I … I have a son."

My mind swirls as his confessions continue. I hurt for the pain he's lived through. The tears burning behind my eyes begging to flow. Sadness for what this man has sacrificed and lived without.

"I have a son I didn't know existed until a day ago. I have a son. A man now. I have a son who I don't even know a thing about. A son my brother has raised. Only thing that doesn't hurt is knowing how loved my boy has to be having my brother as his father. As much as that news has thrown me, knowing he has my brother is more comfort than you can imagine."

"Honey," I hiccup, blinking the tears from my eyes. "I don't know where to start."

"I don't know where to start either."

"You faked your death?"

He nods, not looking away and letting me see that he's completely open to giving me all of him. There's nothing holding him back, no walls built up or shadows hiding behind his eyes. His bright-blue eyes I still can't get over.

My beautiful man needs me. No matter how shocked I am, he *needs* me.

"I know you think that you have to stay gone because of all this, but you have to know if there was even a small chance to have someone you love back, it's taken. There isn't an amount of time that could pass that I wouldn't welcome my sister back. It sounds like they loved you, honey. Don't you think they would want to know you're alive?"

"Back then, Liv, the cases I was on put some unwanted attention on me and, in retrospect, them. The only way to keep them safe was to become a ghost."

"And now? After all this time?"

He leans back, and I miss the heat of having him close to me. He takes a deep breath, studying me while he does.

"The men who I had gained a big spotlight from, they were part of an even bigger network. I couldn't. Not for too many years. By the time I had made sure they were no longer able to hurt them, it had been damn near fifteen years. After that long? How do I walk back into that life, into the shoes of a man who they have spent over two decades mourning!"

"I guess by taking one step at a time."

"Olivia, I have a grown-ass man son. What kind of fucked-up shit would he have to deal with because of me popping up in his life and saying surprise, not really dead after all?"

"Well, I wouldn't go about it quite so dramatically. Maybe start with your brother and then … I guess then you just take one step at a time."

"And if I go back and just bring more danger to their door?"

"And if you go back and just bring love and healing?"

"I'm not the man they knew anymore."

"They likely aren't the same people you left behind, either."

"You make it sound so easy."

"This is your family, Zachariah Cooper." He jerks when I use his real name, but I can tell it wasn't because of something negative. I'm speaking to him … the real "Drew" I've seen this whole time, just didn't understand what I was seeing glimpses of. I'm speaking to *him,* and he's hearing me. "These are the people who made you who you are and then stayed with you from a distance while you made yourself all over again … alone, but never really when the memory of that kind of love is with you. I promise you, and I don't need to know these people personally, a loved one would do anything to have someone they lost back. It doesn't matter what the how's are or what the whys may be. You take what they have to give and you let them heal while they heal you."

"How are you not pissed I kept something this big from you?"

"You didn't keep it from me because you were trying to hurt me. You don't just wake up after all this time and spill to the woman you are with. The one you just really started something with. Trust comes with time, and I'm thankful that you feel like you can trust me enough now to share your pain with me. I'm not mad, honey. Gosh no. My heart hurts for what you have lost and lived without, but it doesn't have to continue to cause you pain."

"I don't deserve you."

"Yes, you do."

"That simple?"

I give him a small smile. His eyes watch my lips move.

"There's more," he tells me after holding my gaze for a couple of minutes. "You know I work for the government, but it's more complicated than that. The reason they're safe is because I made it so none of those men would ever touch them. That side of me? It changed me just as much as living as a dead man for all these years has. Please don't ask me to explain the details of the job because I can't, and it's not to keep things from you; it's to keep you safe from that world."

"You kill people," I softly say, watching those beautiful blue eyes flash brightly when I guess correctly. "These people, the ones that give you orders ... are they safe?"

"Some might say that they're the safest men on the planet. They're good, but they're dangerous to the underbelly scum. I've done my part, though. I'm done."

"Done?"

"Two nights ago, I made sure that the last three men who could hurt my family just for knowing who I am are gone. The team? Saint, Evan, and Hunt? I need to ensure they know what's going on and will continue. Fieldwork, though? Done. I can't be a ghost when I know what I know now."

We're both quiet for a second. I can tell something is still on his mind, but I don't press him on it. Tonight has been a night of revelations, and he's fragile enough. I'm sure whatever else there is for him to tell me will come in time.

"I can't go back to that life alone. I need you," he softly says.

"You have me."

"I still don't understand why you aren't mad."

I move, shifting so that I'm on his lap.

"You don't get mad because someone needed to learn how to let go of pain first in order to let you in. You don't get mad at the person you're with, especially when it's very clear that it wasn't done in malice or to deceive, but because it was the life you lived long before you met me. I had to earn your trust, and I would never be mad because you needed that before you gave me all of you." I stop talking, mulling over the rest before I give it to him. The heck with it. "You damn sure don't get mad when the person you love is hurting. You stay by their side and help however you can to heal that pain."

CHAPTER 19

Drew

"CUZ I LOVE YOU" BY LIZZO

"You damn sure don't get mad when the person you love is hurting. You stay by their side and help however you can to heal that pain."

Her words ping around in my mind, this woman … she never gives me what I expect. The women that I knew in the past, they would have lost their shit if I had kept this from them. Something this huge … a second life, a kid … but her? I had expected her to run. To take that beauty that I found with her, my second chance at a real life, and never look back. My turbulent thoughts are doused just as quickly as they came, though, my heart pounding uncontrollably in my chest as I realize what else she said while I had been too focused on the rest to process.

"What did you say?"

"Which part?"

I hold her gaze. I see her lip quirk up at the corner in the most adorable way. How can she make me feel this good after what I've been feeling since Sway's visit?

I know how.

Hearing her repeat it though is something I need more at this moment than anything else.

"You love me?"

She blushes, and damn if I don't feel that right in my gut. She brought me back to life, and every second I'm in her presence, I'm reminded that life is worth living. Hell, she makes me *want* to live. To fight my way through this pain and find a way to face what I need to in order to have that sweet life she promises me with each adoring gaze.

"Are you going to say it again?" I ask when she doesn't speak.

"This moment isn't about me, honey." Her soft voice is a balm to my turbulent soul. "Right now, it's about making sure you're okay. Only then will I give you an answer."

I sigh. Well played. Well played, indeed.

"I don't know how to go back, Liv," I tell her after a breath of silence, having to work real hard not to push her on those three words. "If they don't forgive me … God, I don't know if I'll survive that."

She exhales and gets closer, shifting so she can rest her head on my chest and curl in close. There isn't a part of her that isn't touching me.

I love this.

I *need* this.

"You go back, and you give them the gift of you. The pain will be calmed by the joy they feel by the miracle of seeing you in the flesh before them. You aren't the only one who's lost something. They *all* lost *you*. In their shoes, even in this little time that I've had you? Nothing and no reason would stop me from accepting the gift of you back with open arms."

"My son?"

"I hurt for the years you've lost, but any man who's even a sliver of you would fight for a second chance to have you back in their life. He might not have known you personally, but do you think your brother would keep you from still being 'there' in memories?"

My breaths come fast, deep and rough. The emotion I'm fighting winning the battle. I'm not sure I deserve her words or the acceptance and love she's giving me. I lied to her and still she sits in my arms making me feel better. How the fuck did I get this lucky? And worse, what will I do if she finds out about the rest? About Ray and the real reason I started staying close.

Worries for another fucking day.

"You need to heal, too, honey." She continues when I keep my silence.

I lean my head back against the couch. She moves with me, not lifting her head and offering her silent support. She has no idea how much her presence has eased the pain a little. She's got no clue how much she means to me, either. Not yet. I tighten my arms around her and bring my head down to kiss her shoulder. She shifts, and I loosen my arms enough for her to push up and look down at me. Her hands move to brush her fingers through my hair with one hand, the other cupping my jaw the way she loves to. I know she's right. I need to do this. But not just for the reasons she mentioned. I need to make peace with that part of me in order to give her what she deserves.

Only everything I held out believing I could ever have is right here.

The man I've kept locked away for far too long and the woman who loves him.

I move quickly, shifting so I frame her beautiful face in my hands and bring us so close that when I speak my lips dance across hers.

"If I do this …" I drop my forehead to hers and breathe in her scent. "I can't do this alone."

"Tell me what you need, honey."

"You."

"That, you've got."

"It's not going to be pretty."

"Healing never is, my sweet Zeke."

Hearing her call me by that name, part of the old me that fits the man I am now. Now that she knows the real me, I don't think I want to hear anything but that. Even though that doesn't feel like me anymore, Coop is still a close second. Before I can stop myself, I tell her just that, earning me the blush I've come to crave.

"Do you think you can get away? I don't want this to touch Riley, Liv. I don't want her ever to know that kind of pain in her life. She can know them, and I want her to, but not yet."

"You tell me when, and I'll make it happen. Riley loves sleepovers with Ella, and Grace will also be on hand to help."

"We have to travel. Are you sure you'll be okay leaving her?"

She gives me a small kiss. "You're just as important to me as you are to her. Your happiness is on the line, honey. She, my little bean, she's got so much of that inside her she will be excited for our adventure without needing to know more. She likes the people she loves to be happy."

That's the second time she's given that to me. A clue to where her heart is. She hasn't said it. Hasn't answered me from when I asked earlier. She was serious that she wanted to be there for what was hurting me before making it about something else. I still feel it, though.

"You ready to tell me yet?"

She winks, sassy thing. "Make me."

The fear that fell from my shoulders just moments before when she said she would be by my side through this is replaced with the red-hot need to get this woman—my damn woman—naked and show her without words what she means to me.

Our mouths meet a moment later, and I swallow the groan that comes from her. The sound goes directly to my cock. Her scent fills my senses and makes me hungrier for her. Hands under her ass, I effortlessly stand from where we were sitting and start moving us toward the wall. When her back softly presses against the cool surface, she gasps, and I lose her mouth. Works out perfectly, though. My hands move from her ass, supporting her body with my own when I trail them around her body and up toward her tits. Her head hits the wall when I graze her nipples through her shirt.

"No bra?"

"I was in a hurry," she confesses with a small shrug and blush to her cheeks.

"This shirt important to you?"

Little frown lines form between her eyes as she looks down at the baggy plain black shirt covered in splotches and bleach stains.

"Uh, no? It's just …" She stops talking and lets out a gasp when I reach up and rip the cotton right down the center. Her full tits bare for me, making my mouth water as they jiggle and move in sync with her rapid breathing.

I grab her hands and place them on my shoulders, moving my own back to her ass. With a wink, I press against her and push her up the wall. Understanding what I want, she uses her hold on me to push up … putting those delicious tits right where my mouth wants them.

"Oh yes," she mews when my mouth covers one pointed nipple,

drawing it deep and sucking her the way I know she likes. Deep pulls and lots of suction. She goes wild, just like she always does, loving my mouth on those sensitive nubs.

My mouth pulls deep before I lift up just enough to be able to talk against her tit and drive her a little crazy while I do.

"You ready to say it yet?"

"Hmm?" she whines, trying to push me back on her tit with one of her hands moving behind my head.

"You ready to tell me?"

"I don't know what you're talking about," she responds smartly, looking down at me and smirking.

That's fine.

I've waited this long to be on the receiving end of those words again. I don't mind working for them a little longer. My heart feels like it's beating wildly at the thought of what I know is coming. I want those words from her more than I can express. It feels like I won't be able to get a full breath until I have them, but having her *and* getting them at the same time? That sounds like something worth a little pain to get.

Turning quickly, I hold her to me as I walk into my bedroom. Before she can blink, I have her in the air, landing softly in the middle of the mattress. She squeals adorably when she flies. When she lands, her shirt flaps fall perfectly to the side, letting me see her tits bounce. She reaches one hand up and pushes her hair out of her face, watching me as I start to strip down. No doubt my expression contains raw hunger. She adjusts, getting cozy, and continues to watch while I undress.

I jerk when my pants and briefs drop, and the cool air hits my fevered skin. My hard cock springs free and points right toward her. I rip my shirt over my head and stand tall for her to continue her lazy feast of my body.

"Pants off, Liv," I demand, loving how her eyes get brighter and a little wild when she's turned on.

"Make me," she retorts.

Well, fuck me, that mouth is hot when she talks back like that.

My hands are in the waistband of her pants, hooking her panties at the same time, and they go flying over my shoulder in one swift movement. Her shirt still lays open and forgotten under her body. Not in my way, but something I plan on using. My hands go to her hips, and I flip her before she can react. She lands on her stomach. I grab the shirt and start to slide the material down her arm, but stop shy of freeing her from the ruined top. I move quickly, and when it hits her wrists, I wrap it around her so she can't get free yet.

My lips go to her ear, and I softly bite her lobe before licking the spot. "How about now?"

She wiggles but doesn't speak.

Fuck me—she likes this.

When she lets out a low moan, I smile a little bigger.

I was wrong.

She doesn't just like it ... she loves it.

"Give it to me, Olivia," I demand.

"You," she pants, rubbing her legs together. "You ... give it to me." Her words slam into me, and any plans I had at drawing this out are long gone.

I rip the shirt from her body and toss it behind me. Hands to her hips, I flip her and move to my knees between her legs. My eyes roam over her body, my cock throbbing painfully to be inside her. When I reach her eyes, I see the same hungry need that she must see in mine.

"I should make you work for it, but I can't wait," I tell her.

Her feet go to my back, and she pulls me toward her waiting body. "Make love to me, Zeke," she says, again with that word.

Those words, in that tone, *with* my name, though?

Nope.

I'm powerless to stop now.

I enter her, my cock enveloped in her heat, and we both cry out when I hit that magic fucking spot deep inside. Our mouths move, tongues tangling, and I start to move. The feeling of her wet heat around me makes my balls draw tight. It won't be long. Not when I'm this close to the edge. We move together, her rocking against me as I thrust into her. My mouth takes turns sucking her tits and feasting on her mouth. When she rips her mouth from mine to jerk her head back, I know I'm about to feel her come around me.

I shift, moving so I'm kneeling again, and pull her up. She screams out, her pussy clamping even tighter around my cock as she rides her last orgasm into another. I feel wetness start to roll down my balls, and I groan when she rocks forward and bites down on my shoulder. With one push inside her, I move us back to the mattress.

One arm goes to the mattress, elbow going deep, and the other grabs her hips while I start moving rapidly in and out of her. Her eyes hold mine, her sounds of pleasure mingling with my own.

She reaches up, one hand to my cheek, and continues to come alive under my touch.

"I love you, Zachariah Cooper."

"Oh shit," I groan, her words like a fire set ablaze inside me. I don't even get a full thrust in before I'm coming long and hard.

"Olivia," I breathe, still feeling my cock jerk with aftershocks.

"Every part of who you *are* and who you *were*. I love *you*." She continues, her words breathy from exertion.

I pull her into me and hold her tight with my mouth at her shoulder. She holds me back just as tight.

"Every part of who I am and who I was?"

She hums but doesn't say anything else. Not that it's needed. Just having her accept that part of me, the part that lied to her about who I really was, slams into me with so much certainty that I'm in the right place ... home.

"I love you, too, Olivia."

We shift, and I pull the comforter over our bodies. We settle in, her body pressed against mine and her leg hooked over my thigh. She runs her fingers through the hair on my chest, content in the silence.

I can do this. Go back to the life I left. But only if she's with me. It's the only way. Having her there to ease the pain in my soul while it's being torn to bits. I'm starting to think she's the only one who could ever piece it back together.

"Can you be ready in a few days? We'll fly so we aren't gone long."

"I can be ready tomorrow," she answers instantly.

"This is going to be hard," I tell her softly. Something I'm sure she knows without me telling her.

"It will," she agrees. "And then it won't be. It won't feel like this forever."

"I don't know how to make this hurt any less for my brother or … my son."

She lifts her head and looks up at me from where she was resting on my chest. She studies my face and smiles softly.

"You do that by living, honey."

Well, damn.

CHAPTER 20

Olivia

"ANYONE" BY DEMI LOVATO

"Do you have everything you need?" I ask Riley for the hundredth time today.

She laughs and nods her head. Luckily, she loves me enough that she doesn't mind my constant reassurance that she is okay. I never imagined how hard it would be to leave someone until she came into my life. She might not be my biological child, but she is my blood, and I love her just as if she was my own.

"I'm just a call away, you know that, right? No matter what you need or what time—I'm just a call away."

"Okay, little bean … tell your auntie goodbye so she can get to the plane on time and stop fretting."

Riley gives me a big hug and that toothy smile I love so much. I ruffle her curls a little with my fingers before I stand to hug Ella as well.

She didn't so much as blink when I asked her if she would keep Riley and handle the shop by herself. I know she has help and isn't completely alone. Grace will help with Riley, and she has Lewis at the shop. This isn't the first time she's had to cover by herself. I know the nerves about the trip have me the most on edge, not actually the ability she has to cover the shop on her own. She could do it all with her eyes closed.

I'm not really worried about her or even Riley. It's how he'll handle the fallout after our trip and the reunion. I'm worried these people will make it harder than it already is for him. I don't know them, so I can only pray that they'll handle it okay. Mostly, though, I just worry about him.

"You'll let me know if you need me to come home early, right?" I ask Ella.

"I won't need you to come back early. I might not know everything that's going on, but I know it's something important to you. That's all I need to know right now, girlfriend. We've got it covered, and we'll have a great time."

"One of the guys will walk you two to her school and the shop. Please make sure and use one of the numbers I gave you if you plan on leaving the condo," Drew adds.

"Yes, sir," she smarts, saluting.

He shakes his head, but I see a hint of a smile on his lips.

"Come here, beanie," he says softly to Riley.

She moves to stand in front of him with the grace of a dancer, twirling on her toes. He drops to his knee, taking her hand in his and earning her giggles.

"Gonna miss our mornings and bedtime stories, little girl."

"Me too, giant. Will you read bedtime stories to Auntie? That will help you not miss me as much."

"You bet he will," Ella jokes under her breath.

"Not any of the good ones I save for you, though," he says, ignoring Ella.

"You'll come home to me, though? Right?"

"You can count on that."

My eyes get wet, and I know I'm going to cry soon. To witness seeing how much those two love each other is something so beautiful. They have a bond, one that no one else can touch. Something about that bond, giving her something she's been missing her whole life, I can't help but hope this never fades for them … or us.

She smirks, hugging his neck before taking Ella's hand again. They stand at the curb by her car and wave as we grab our suitcases and start walking into the airport.

It's been three days since that night at his place, when he let me in and we made the plans to travel to Georgia—where his family is clueless to what is about to arrive on their doorsteps. He's so nervous and so unlike the man I've come to love.

It doesn't take long for us to check our bags and make our way to the gate. We still have some time to spare, so we settle in and wait for them to call our flight. I had grabbed some food and drinks for us as we walked through the airport, but nothing too exciting. Candy and chips from the news stand and two bagels from the café near our gate. It's enough to keep him distracted at least.

"I don't want it to be a surprise when he gets there, but the man I told you found me? He's going to come by the hotel and help me clean up. I need to get a haircut, probably a shave. Years might have passed, but how I look right now is nothing like the man they said goodbye to. It would be less shocking for them to become less of the man I am now."

I blink up at him, not too sure how to respond. He never put his contacts back in after that night at his place, letting his beautiful and stunning blue eyes shine bright. If anyone else noticed, they didn't say anything. This is big, though. His hair is long, his facial hair is plentiful, and while I know he'll be just as handsome any way he looks … it's a lot of change in a short time when he's already struggling so much, especially with the emotional reunion to come. So many changes can't be easy to handle at one time.

"It's been like this out of necessity, not because I like it. It's a good change, babe. Promise."

His eyes are clear—no shadows and no pain.

"I'm not sure I can handle you getting more handsome, honey."

He laughs softly. "I might look like an ogre …. You never know. Been a long time since I looked in the mirror and saw any parts of the man I was before."

"You could never look like an ogre."

"Tell me that later after Sway gets his hands on me."

"Sway?"

"Yeah, the one I told you about. You'll love him. One of the best men I've ever known. Just watch out for him if he gets his hands on glitter," he adds oddly with the most serious of expressions on his face.

"No glitter, got it."

"You'll like him, Liv, and he is going to love you."

"I can't wait to meet him," I tell him honestly.

He smiles, and I'm relieved to see some of the stress over our trip is gone from his face. I know it's still lingering below the surface, but he doesn't appear as nervous as he had been. We continue our wait, snacking and talking about a whole bunch of nothing, passing our time comfortably together. When they call our flight, I know he's getting nervous again. It's coming off him in waves, but he's also gone silent.

I take his hand and squeeze it.

"I'm here with you every step of the way," I promise.

He gives me a quick kiss just when our section is called, and we make our way on the plane, anxious energy coming off us both now.

I say a little prayer when we take off that this won't hurt him more than he's already hurting. That his family welcomes the shock of him coming back into their lives.

One thing I know for sure, this is going to be a trip to remember.

————

One thing's for sure about Georgia.

Georgia is hot.

Even this late in the year, the heat feels like a living beast burning its way down your throat only to steal the air straight from your lungs.

It feels like you turned the blow dryer directly to your face while trying to breathe normally.

This is no joke kind of sticky heat.

I've always heard stories about the humidity in the South, but this is my first time experiencing the Peach State, and I already can't wait to run back to Boston. Shouldn't it be cooler here this time of year? My goodness, how do people live in the South?

I glance at Zeke—what I've come to call him solely. He told me the other night that I was the only person who called him that, even before, making it special to him, too. I still call him Drew in public. Until he's ready, that's how it will be. I know I could call him Zeke always, but these baby steps will take us to when he's ready to let that part of him go.

154

Now that he's shown me who he really is, I never want to put him back in a box again.

Zachariah Cooper deserves to live.

He will always be a little of Drew, I suppose. That's the person who he became for over twenty years. Drew is just as much a part of him as Zeke Cooper is. We haven't talked about which of the two men will remain "him" back home in the future, but I have hopes that this trip will give him what he needs to be himself.

The closer we get to the baggage claim, I can feel him getting nervous. His hand slightly tightens around mine, not painful, just enough that I know he's struggling to be back home. Knowing what's to come and the pain that will be brought to the surface are daunting.

We just cleared the impossibly high climb up the escalators that feed up from the tram system below and up to the level where baggage claim is.

"Yoohooo! Over here, you big stud, you!"

My head jerks up at the voice screaming above the low hum of activity inside Hartsfield-Jackson Airport. Even though this place is huge —I'm talking *huge*—and there are so many people around, I have no trouble finding the person who just yelled over the crowd.

Just off to the side of where we entered from the escalators—leading us from the transit system that moves passengers around the large airport —is a neat roped-off section filled with people watching those arriving. Each of them holds different expressions of expectations. Some with signs, iPads with names displayed, and (the cutest) little kids with smiles as big as the balloons they're holding. I'm distracted briefly when I see one of the kids break away and run toward the people arriving, stopping when she gets scooped up with a smile by the older gentleman in front of us. I glance away from the happy reunion when I hear the voice again … then I see him.

The man who has to be Zeke's Sway. No question, I know in my gut that it's him.

He's bouncing in place adorably, full of excitement that would rival any little kid that just reunited with their own loved ones. He's got a pair of black slacks on, tight and molded to his thick thighs, but when I see what shoes he has on, I can't help but giggle. Yes, Zeke described him

155

well. Standing in a pair of stunning gold heels—that make me feel slightly self-conscious of the designer sneakers I decided to wear for our day of travel—he looks as if he was born to wear them. The gold flowy top that fits him to perfection has me making a mental note to ask him where he does his shopping.

Sway has class.

Class with a capital C.

Somehow seeing him in person, I feel a little of the stress and tension leave my body, and when I reach his face, I see his eyes trained right on me.

His smile huge, his chocolate skin absolutely flawless and radiating happiness under the bright lights above him. He reaches up, rubs the top of his bald head once before letting his hand fall. His eyes travel to where my hand is joined with Zeke's, and his smile grows so big and so blinding that I swear it has to hurt his face.

I steal a glance at Zeke to see his face awash with so much emotion. I know he's seen this man recently, but this moment is hard for him, and I'm so glad he has someone in his corner.

I squeeze his hand, and he looks down at me.

"Go," I softly encourage.

His eyes flash brightly, and his hand jerks in mine.

People move around us … the two people just stopped in the middle of a busy crowd rushing about, and not one of them seems to notice us having this monumental moment.

"Go, baby," I try again when he doesn't move.

This time, when I see his eyes flash, I know he's *heard* me. He bends down, presses the softest of kisses to my lips, and I lose hold of his hand when he starts walking.

I move to the side, getting out of the crowd's way, and watch. I'm close enough that he could reach out and get me easily, but just enough distance to allow them to have their moment privately. When he reaches his friend, I watch them both struggle to compose themselves before they reach out at the same time. Arms around each other, they hug tightly. I lose the fight with my tears when I see Sway shed a few. Blinking them away, I notice for the first time the man standing next to Sway.

He's beautiful. Tall, blond hair that looks more gray than the blond it was before, and the most stunning eyes. You can tell he smiles often, laugh lines sprinkled around his strong features, and the brightest smile pointed directly at me.

He steps toward me, away from the two men still embracing. His arms open immediately, and I walk into them without hesitation but feel slightly awkward about hugging a man who I've never met before. His hug, however, lacks any signs that he's feeling the same awkwardness. You would think we've known each other for years.

He takes a step back, holding me with his hands at my shoulders and studying me intensely.

"I'm Davey," he says after a moment.

"Olivia," I respond, not sure what else to do.

"Thank you for bringing him home. A lot of people love this man of yours."

I glance over at the two men. They aren't hugging anymore, but you can tell they're still lost in their moment.

"That guy is mine." His words continue as if I hadn't looked away. "One might say, had your guy not done what he did, I would never have him. We wouldn't have our sweet Stella, either." I glance back, giving him my attention while he speaks, seeing the admiration in his gaze. "That day changed us all. If this meeting was this emotional, I imagine the storm is just getting started. This will be hard, but you seem like the kind of girl who can weather it."

"I'm from Boston, of course I can," I respond with a smirk and nod, trying to add some lightness to the mood. What else do you say? He's spot-on. It will be one hell of an emotional trip, and some of those emotions might be harder to handle than the rest. We both know I understand what he's saying. "In all seriousness, Davey, it doesn't matter how turbulent the sea may get. I'm not leaving my post."

He smiles, and if anything, he gets more handsome.

"You're going to fit in just fine."

"Uh," I begin, but stop when Zeke's arm goes around my shoulders.

"Oh, my sweet heavens above. Get out of my way, you big hunk of yummy, and let me get my eyes on this tiny little thing."

Before I know what's happening, I'm being spun by the man I can only assume is Sway. He gives me a few extra twirls with my hand held above my head before he stops and dramatically wipes his forehead.

"Tell me I can get my hands on that hair, girly pop."

"Uh …" I lamely say.

"Goodness me, look at you," he continues, ignoring my inability to form words, looking behind him at Zeke. "You did good. A fact that doesn't surprise me, though. All you hunk-a-hunks find equally beautiful women. I tell you what, girly, when you're blessed with a body like that, you show it off. What are you wearing this big sweater for? This is Georgia."

"It was cold on the flight?"

"Who're you asking?"

Zeke, the big goof, at least has the decency to try to cover up his laugh. He doesn't succeed, but he tries.

"What do you have on under that?" he asks, cocking his hip and appraising me again.

"A shirt."

He nods, pulls the most fabulous crossbody bag over his head, and hands it to his husband. Before I can so much as blink, my hand is in Sway's, and I'm rushing to keep up with his steps.

How on earth does he move so well in those tall heels?

Hand in hand, or I guess more like hand dragging hand, he pulls me into the bathroom. I get fluffed, buffed, and stripped of my sweater in no time. When he spins me around to face the bathroom mirror, even in the harsh lighting, I'm amazed. How did he make me look like I hadn't just been up all night and then traveling for half the day? The dark strands of my hair look like I just spent hours with a hot tool: waves, body, and so much shine. My sweatshirt now tied at my waist, my jeans a stark contrast to the light-green material. I should have thought about what shirt I had on a little better when I answered him. Though how would I have guessed this was what he had in mind. The crop top tee leaves a good two inches of my belly showing where the crop top ends. It's just a baggy shirt that had been designed like that, but still … it's a lot more skin than I was showing.

"Sneakers will do but only because they're Gucci. Girly has good taste, I see."

"Are you talking about just my shoes or the man?"

He winks. "I think I'm going to like you."

I give myself one more glance before meeting his dark eyes, matching his smile with one of my own.

"Right back at you."

"How is he?" Sway asks as I pull my bag back on my shoulder.

"He's struggling," I answer after a beat. "I do think he's doing okay, all things considered. I think he's scared of hurting them more."

He nods, humming softly. "He has no idea how much he's loved. He didn't back then either. Not one person who he left hasn't wished for a day with him back in it." His eyes start to fill with tears, and his jaw starts working as he pulls himself together. "Thank you for bringing him home."

"I didn't do anything. All I did was tell him I would be by his side. He did the rest."

"All you did? Honey pie, no way he would have been able to do it without you. I've watched each of these big strong men who he left fall in love over the years. Each one of those hunks as alpha as it comes. Independent, strong willed, okay with being alone, and some of the baddest of bad asses you'll ever meet. However, when it comes to their women? They're better with them than without. Just because they're manly men doesn't mean they don't need their person—the one meant for them—before they can become the best version of themselves."

"That's really sweet of you to say, but I'm not sure you're correct."

"Sometimes all you need is a second for your life to change, darlin'. Just one second and you feel the winds start to pick up, giving you a hug while pushing you toward what you deserve."

He gives me a smile, his whole face transforming, making him even more handsome than he already is. I nod, but don't argue with him. I certainly know I'm a better version of myself when Zeke is around. When we clear the hall of the bathroom, seeing the men standing just outside leaning against a little glass wall, I watch the man I love relax a little the second he sees me. That tiny movement might as well back up the words his friend just told me.

Well, what do you know?

"I told you," Sway says, leaning into me so he can speak quietly and just for me.

I loop my arm in his and smile at him, making his face soften. "Yeah, you sure did."

CHAPTER 21

Drew

"YOU" BY LOUYAH

Liv is fretting.

I know she's worried about what is coming, and I would be lying if I said I wasn't as well.

The closer we get to the hotel and see how much Hope Town has changed since I left, the tighter my chest becomes. It feels like someone has reached into my chest and started squeezing.

That feeling hasn't let up once since, either.

Davey left a little while ago and took Liv with him to get some provisions for the room—snacks, drinks, and a few toiletries we left behind. In reality, I needed her to go out so Sway could work his magic and take me the final step back to the man I was. Or as close as I can get. I've changed a lot over the years, but not enough that I won't look pretty close to the man I was with some careful help of his hair tools. Older, harder, and weathered with the pain I've experienced in the time I've been gone has changed me. I wore my hair and my beard as a mask. A mask I need to shed not just for this reunion but also to be myself for the woman who owns me.

It wasn't that I didn't want her here. I seem to always want her with me. This, though, I needed to do alone. I've told myself it was because I didn't want to turn her fretting into a full-blown worry session, but I know the truth now. Watching him through the mirror, I need this moment with my old friend just as much as I'm betting he does. I needed to face the past, myself, and be able to let him go.

"You sure about this, handsome?" Sway asks for the fifth time, still brushing his comb through my long hair. He's been playing with it a lot more than he's been brushing it, though.

"Needs to be done, Sway."

"You know … " He starts, trailing off while reaching to grab his scissors from where they had been resting on the tall cart that Davey rolled in for him when they arrived earlier. The silence ticked by. The whole time, he kept running his hands through my hair. Would have been weird, but damn, if it wasn't relaxing.

I give him the time he needs and look over at the cart again. Sway says it holds everything he might ever need, but I'd put money on it holding a bunch of glitter in half the drawers.

"For so long, I couldn't wait to get my hands on you. In the platonic sense, you dog." He laughs when I look at him funny in the mirror he set up in this makeshift salon in the corner of the room. "Don't you get old Sway wrong, you hunks are still oh-so hunky. Only now I have a hunky man of my own, and honey child, no way would I stray from my man no matter how hard you tried to get me." He tosses his head back and hoots loudly at his own joke.

"Tell me about your husband. How did you meet?" I ask, too full of nervous energy to join in his hilarity but also genuinely wanting to know about his life now. I'm not touching the flirting bait he always loved to toss at myself or one of my former friends. Shameless. That's just who Sway is. It's oddly refreshing to know that hasn't changed in the years that I've been away.

He keeps cutting my hair, not speaking. I watch as the long length falls with each snip.

Brush. *Snip.*

A blond piece falls to the floor.

Brush. *Snip.*

Pieces of the man I have become fall away to the floor with each bit of hair he releases to the floor.

Brush. *Snip.*

Pieces of the man I had been before fall into place with each cut he makes.

I was transfixed as I watched each piece he cut and the dance with the man I was and am warring out in the mirror. Each piece flutters to the floor, his pink-tipped fingernails twinkling all the while he is unaware of how mammoth this moment is. Who am I kidding … he knows. Hence the silence.

"He took Emmy's place at Corps Security, honey buns," Sway says softly. He doesn't stop cutting and I look away from myself to focus on him and his dreary tone. I have just a moment to try to recall if I had ever heard him sound so … normal when he speaks again. "When you … well, when you died, honey." He stops, dropping his arms to his sides and looking at me in the mirror.

Half my hair is still long on one side.

The other just looks like a mess.

Doesn't matter, though. I can already see the change in my face.

Jesus.

What a mind fuck.

"After that, Emmy didn't handle the aftermath that well. Most everyone will say that is the understatement of the millennium, but I digress. It was hard on everyone, but she carried a heavy load. She ran, but that dark prince of hers ran after her. Not saying it was perfect after that, but Maddox didn't let her go, and they both healed a lot while they traveled their bumpy road. He didn't give up on her, not once, no matter how hard she made it."

"Where did she go?" I question further, not able to keep from prying even though I have a feeling that his answer will hurt.

"She went home."

I sit up straighter in my chair and turn around to look at him.

"You don't mean …"

The sad look in his eyes says it all.

"I do precisely mean that. Right to those horrible people genetics claim are her parents. Don't worry about anything except the knowledge that her man was the best kind of persistent."

"Something tells me it wasn't remotely as smooth as you're making it sound."

"Well, life rarely is. Wouldn't you say, Coopie?"

My eyes close, and I let that stupid fucking nickname wash over me.

"Point is, honey buns, when she left here, there was a void. We all felt it just as heavily as we felt when losing you. She just up and left without trusting her family. Some could say ... there's a few parallels there, hmm?"

"Can't change the past, Sway," I grumble a little harsher than I had intended. His words hit hard, his aim true—right to the gut, simmering and burning, just as they were intended to do.

"Not saying you should. What I was hoping you would see is that no matter what her reasons were then and how those of us she left behind felt about it—" He gives me a pointed stare before continuing. "What matters is that she eventually came home, and this family healed a little. We weren't as solid as we were, but we will be now. Marinate on that, stud. Sounds familiar, darlin', and I know you see that. There's a whole hell of a lot to say about getting the missing piece back and feeling that peace when it slides into its spot after being missing for so long. There's not a lot of room for anger when you're weeping for joy, falling on the grateful knees you've spent all that time praying for a miracle on."

His words slam into me.

Not softly, either.

He's wisdom and learning about Emmy eases some of the trepidation I had felt about what's to come. Solidifying what I thought to be true before leaving Boston—the one that drove me back to Hope Town—I'm not the only one who needs this. I've felt that missing piece that losing them left behind. The void and vastness of my family within that spot inside me has burned bright with pain since the day I left them.

I can only imagine what it feels like for them.

They just didn't know they weren't praying for something hopeless.

"Now I know you said that man you were was long gone," he continues. "Honey, I find it pertinent to inform you ... that man never left, and he's most certainly back in focus."

I shake my head but don't reply. There's no need. He isn't wrong. Each day since I found his note, I felt like I was coming back to the person I thought was gone forever. A person, if I'm honest with myself, I missed more than I ever thought possible.

"Tell me about the rest of them. I need to hear it before I go back to the person I was. I need to know that even though I left them, they eventually were okay."

He places his hair tools down on that cart and walks around the chair I'm in. When he stands in front of me, he bends his knees and crouches to look into my eyes. Both his hands reach out to take mine into his warm grip. I briefly wonder if it's comfortable to sit like that on heels that tall, but all other thoughts go out the window when he starts speaking.

"Are you sure you need that?"

"I need it as surely as I need air to breathe."

"Things weren't always as golden as they are now for everyone."

"What is it you just told me? That life rarely is?"

He makes a sound in his throat.

"Please, Sway," I ask softly.

"Let me keep doing your hair, darlin'. I'll talk while I cut."

He stands and grabs his comb and scissors, starting back at my hair before he speaks.

"Your brother struggled to find his footing, at least he did in the beginning. He was lost and he took your death real hard, sweetness. Those men around him didn't let him stumble, but it was his woman who didn't let him fall. The first time I saw him hold your son? I knew a big piece of his heart had been repaired. Zac, your boy, he's incredible. Next best thing to Zac and Chelcie that your brother could have is you … and you're about to make two Cooper men feel like they've been given the biggest gift someone could get in their whole lifetime."

I swallow thickly at the mention of Zac, choosing to change the subject instead of focusing on it. I betrayed my brother by leaving like I did. I'm not surprised that he stood up and raised him, but I didn't see him ending up with Zac's mom. I couldn't think of anyone else to raise the son I didn't know about. Hell, he probably did a better job than I could have at that time in my life. He was my hero growing up, and I would never have been able to raise a boy to be as good as I knew he did. "Chelcie is good?"

"She's absolutely wonderful. They had a second boy, Jaxon. The way

165

Asher tells it, those two are spitting images of both of y'all growing up. Almost the same age gap as you and your brother, too."

I picture Ash in my mind, and how we were growing up when times were good, they were some of the best moments of my life. Hell, even when they were bad, they weren't *as* bad with him there for me. I love that those boys have the bond we did without the harsh life. Those boys, well … men now, they have no idea how lucky they are that they have that gift of each other. I'm thankful as fuck that my brother loves my son as his own. I have no doubt they have a close relationship, and I need to tread carefully. He may be my biological son, but he's not *my* son. Something I hope Asher understands. I don't want to get ahead of myself when I think about Zac. He's not a child anymore. I missed him becoming the man he is. He doesn't need me to be his dad, but I hope he lets me in his life.

"Dee and Beck have a boy." Sway continues, pulling me back to the conversation. "Liam. Goes by Lee, and he's the spitting image of his father. Handsome as can be. He's a cop here in town, and his wife, Megan, she's a writer. They have two kids, girl and boy. Those two kids weren't the first to make one of those studs grandfathers, though," he adds, and I can't believe my ears.

Grandparents?

"Who was first?" I question, my voice thick with emotion at how much I've missed.

"Oh honey child, you're gonna love this."

I frown not understanding.

"Axel and Izzy were first."

"Nate?"

He nods. "And at the same time, Axel and Izzy were becoming grandparents, Greg and Melissa became grands, too." He snickers a little under his breath.

I frown, not following.

"Dani, short for Danielle, Axel's little princess and the one and only Cohen Cage. Those two were burning bright and denying it for a long time before they finally got together. I'm pretty certain those two will follow Cohen's parents lead and keep popping out kids until they can't anymore. They have three of them now."

"I bet Ax loved that." I feel a little more of the dread I felt when I sat down earlier lift away. Beyond happy for my friends and for the lives they're living.

"It was a sight to be seen, that's for sure. Though it was even better when Axel's baby boy fell in love with Maddox's baby girl. Those two might give Dani-Belle a run for her baby making money."

He goes on to tell me about Greg and Melissa's other children, Maddox and Emmy's daughters and his own daughter, Stella.

My mind whirls as I take it all in. They've created one hell of a life and while I'm sad that I wasn't a part of that journey with them, I know those lives they have may not have ever happened if the day I "died" went differently. I had been so lost in my thoughts, I didn't even realize he had finished my hair until I hear the buzz of his electric shaver. I don't look up, not sure I'm ready to look at myself yet. He moves in front of me, blocking my view anyway. Then he starts shaving off the last part of the man I had become so the ghost can come out of the shadows.

Ready or not, Zeke Cooper is back.

CHAPTER 22

Olivia

"GOLDEN HOUR" BY JVKE

I'm beyond exhausted.

I feel like I'm about to drop—both mentally and physically.

Davey, for a man, can shop. Shop until *I* drop, that is, because heaven knows he still had enough energy to keep going when I started waving the white flag. How that man can have as much vigor as he does, I don't think I'll ever understand. We didn't even stop to eat until well after dinnertime. Yet he was like the Energizer Bunny, not needing to power back up once.

My arms struggled to carry the bags from the trunk and on to the hotel's cart. We had picked up snacks, drinks, clothes, even a few new clothes for Zeke and me. Davey stating, at one point early in our shopping, that I should just trust him because he *knew* just what I needed. I didn't care. I was enjoying the distraction. Even with the heat my AmEx was letting off from being swiped so much today, it was just what I needed.

I'm pretty sure a big part of why I was so tired had to do with my concern for how Zeke was handling things. When I left earlier I could feel his nervous energy coming off him in waves. It was as if a beast had invaded and started filling up the space around us. Silent and steady in its stalking, but ready to jump at any given moment or sign of weakness.

He had assured me he was fine, but I knew he wasn't. As much as I wanted to rush back to his side, though, I knew my own worry and fretting wouldn't be what he needed at that moment.

So I shopped and channeled all my emotions into feeding the economy.

Davey stops me when we step off the elevator on our floor with a gentle hand on my arm. I keep pulling the cart, moving us out of the way of the elevator doors.

"You know what they've been doing in there, right?"

"I don't. I just could sense that it was something big and they needed this time together." The nervous energy I had beat back during the day starts to climb again.

"I don't know what he's been through since he left, and I don't need to know. I've been around these big strong men for a long time, but I still don't know what they're thinking most of the time. They've talked about him, you know. They've never let him die, sweet girl. I've seen pictures of him, yet even I struggled to recognize him as he is after all this time. He sure was something back then, and if my honey works his magic the way I know he will, I imagine you'll be looking at a different man when we open that door. He'll be stripped of a lot more than hairs. My honey has a way of cutting pain away as effortlessly as he does hair. I don't mean to pry, but are you sure you're ready for what's coming?"

Again, I nod silently, swallowing the thickness in my throat.

It isn't lost on me when we left and I saw Sway setting up a beauty station, that I was getting out of their for more than just a shopping trip. I wasn't lying when I told Davey I could sense something. I just knew as sure as the sun would rise in the morning and set in the evening, they needed to be alone. I'm sure I was driving him up the wall earlier, worrying about him, too. I'm not even a little upset that he thought this was something best to do without me.

"I'm ready, but even if I wasn't, I would stand tall and pretend for him. That said, I'm worried about how your friends will handle all of this. I think that pales in comparison, though, to my concern over how he's going to handle all of this."

His smile is small, but full of compassion, mixing with the understanding and caring light that he's had burning in his gaze all day.

"Oh honey, one thing about this family is they forgive just as fiercely as they love. There will be a lot of tears, that I'm sure of, but those tears will lead to something incredibly wonderful: their family will finally be complete with a piece they never thought they would fill again."

"You really think it's going to be that simple?"

He reaches out and takes my hand in his.

"There was a time that I would laugh and say nothing ever came simple for them, but now? They've all lived. They've *all* lost. Now, because of all that, each one of them knows how precious life is one way or the other. They might have stopped wishing for him to still be with them as often, but that isn't because they didn't wish that be the case with all they had. They had to stop bringing his ghost into their every day in order to move on. There's been a void as big as the Grand Canyon within them all since the day he left. I know you're worried and that you care deeply for him, but they aren't going to hurt him. Let me ask you, if you had this chance with someone you had lost, would you be angry or happy to have them back?"

His question slams into me. I hadn't let myself drift down this hole, but now that it's been asked, I can't help but imagine a life where my sister returned to us. Where Riley didn't have to know what it was like not to have her parents alive. Where my beautiful sister was smiling, happy, and breathing free? I know, hand to heart, I wouldn't even think twice about how I felt. I would live in that dream with so much happiness, all the pain from years before would be gone in an instant.

I jump when I feel him reach up and wipe away a tear I hadn't realized had started falling down my cheek.

"Yes, you get it, sweet girl."

He hugs me, and after a few deep breaths, we start pulling the cart down the hall.

"It would be the greatest gift," I tell him, finally answering his world-rocking question before I put the key in the door. "To have her back with me and Riley? It would be everything."

"People are given second chances for a reason. Life is meant to be lived and even through the hard times, there's always that question of what-if. We wouldn't be human without it. Sometimes it's hard, messy, or even beautiful. Sometimes it's all at once. Fear is a nasty companion

THE LONG WAY HOME

to ride you. Don't let it stifle your sunshine. You leave that in the past and you live your life big, bold and beautiful. Do it for you *and* do it for those people who you've lost who will not get the chance."

I hug him, his words wrapping around my heart.

"Thank you for that," I tell him honestly, taking his words and engraving them into my soul.

"Not necessary, sweet girl. What do you say we go in there and see what those two have been up to. I should warn you first, though … you should probably brace now."

"Brace?"

He nods, a secret smile curling his lips slightly.

"What does that even mean?"

He laughs but doesn't respond. Instead, he finishes unlocking the door for me and pulling the cart in behind him. I catch the door as it's starting to close behind him, right before it snicks closed, jarring me out of my confusion. I follow, still mulling over his strange warning.

Brace for what? Meeting the family that has thought Zeke was dead for so very long? I feel like I've been doing a dang good job of *bracing* if I don't say so myself. Running from this man isn't something I think I'm even capable of doing. Understanding came freely and easily. One would think, if I needed to brace, it would have been the day he told me he had been living with this secret identity. That, though, never once crossed my mind. Being mad at him? No way. Not when he was too busy hating himself for something he had no ability to control then. He's been a victim in this too. To keep his family safe, he had given that sacrifice. To live in pain. I wouldn't dream of adding to that. I know more than anyone how precious life is. Davey was right … in the same situation, I wouldn't be mad at my sister. I would cherish that gift with everything I had in me. I just pray that his family feels the same.

When we clear the threshold, I see Sway sitting on the couch in the hotel room's living area. He's got a big smile on his face, his eyes shining toward his husband. The room looks the same as when I left, so there clearly wasn't some big bad *thing* I should be bracing for when I walked in. I feel my brow furrow as I keep looking, searching, and coming up blank.

"He's in the shower, honey pie," Sway tells me, breaking into my scan of the room. "Now, normally Sway would leave you two lovebirds to the moment alone, but this is not to be missed! Never thought I would get my hands on that man, but whoa, nelly." He fans himself with his hand. "I would go as far to say it was worth the wait, too." He tosses his head back and laughs loudly.

"You seem way too happy about having your hands on another man," Davey jests.

Sway swats his hand in the air and bellows out another laugh. "As if he could handle me."

Davey walks over and sits down on the couch next to his husband. He gets a kiss the second his bottom lands, and I can't help but feel a little lightness as I watch them together. They're adorable and clearly still very much in love. They're touching, their sides meshed together even with space to allow another two people to sit. I understand their preference to be nearby. It's the same I feel toward Zeke.

"Ready?" Sway asks, gaining my attention.

"I'm always ready," I sass, the words out before I realized how they sounded.

"Noted." I hear spoken from behind me, the gruff voice of a man I find myself completely head over heels for gives me a thrill so violently strong, I feel my whole body react with a little shiver.

Sway's eyes twinkle, holding my gaze.

Davey looks on with a huge smile, eyes to the space behind me, and shock clear as day in his expression despite the happy smile is confusing. I don't have time to think about his weird reaction. Zeke speaks, and another shiver of awareness zaps through my body.

"Though, would prefer to be alone."

"Not missing this moment, Zachariah Cooper," Sway smarts back, eyes narrowing but still twinkling bright. "You made me wait for over two dagum decades for that. I'm going to enjoy watching her meet you again. Consider it payment for my services." He snickers.

"Pain in my ass," Zeke grumbles behind me. A beat of silence follows before I hear. "Turn around, Liv."

My heart pounds.

"Yes, Liv, turn around," Sway cooingly mocks.

I look at both the men on the couch, clearly loving this, and with a calming inhale, I turn around.

"Holy shit," I whisper the second I get my first glimpse.

He doesn't speak, giving me the time to study him. The new him. No, not the new him … the new old him. He's no longer Drew, not even is he my Zeke … in front of me might as well be a stranger—he looks *that* different. Had I not seen him without his contacts before now, I'm not sure that I would recognize him at first glance.

Those eyes though are all him.

"You're beautiful," I whisper, blushing instantly when I realize my thoughts had escaped my lips, my eyes still roaming over him, looking at the differences, but also seeing more parts of the man I knew him to be starting to stand out more in front of me.

He doesn't react outwardly, but I see his eyes catch fire as I continue my perusal. The blue as bright as the sky on a clear and sunny day. His eyes still crinkle in at the corners in the same way. His nostrils still give a little movement when he takes a deep breath in, almost like a fluttering beat. He still runs his tongue over his full bottom lip. His stance is still the same—shoulders strong, his fists slightly clenched, and his long legs planted wide on the ground beneath him.

I take a step toward him, watching his throat as he swallows thickly. Without his beard, the strong lines showcase the thick cords in his neck. His jaw ticks, those yummy flexes screaming look at me now that they aren't covered by hair. He looks so much younger. If I didn't know his age, I would put him in his early forties. Heck, maybe even his late thirties. His hair looks lighter now, too. The missing longer locks that had been more dirty than blond are a big reason he no longer looks like the same man. Blond and short, not dirty blond and long, trimmed at the sides with the length just long enough for me to run my fingers through it and make a mess on the top.

"You're staring pretty hard there." He breaks the silence with his low and steady words.

"You sound like you, but you don't look like you," I dumbly droll.

"Still the same me, Liv," he responds.

"No." I smile and take a step toward him. "You're Zeke."

"Like I said. Same thing."

My hands come up, and I frame his face, palms landing on the two dimples I had no idea the man I was seeing possessed. "Not even close. You're you, but you're also not." I rub my palms against his cheeks slightly, feeling the smooth skin that used to be covered up. His lips look fuller. His eyes brighter. "How do you feel?"

He swallows thickly again. His eyes dart a glance at the two men on the couch. It's only then that I realize he had been holding my hips because right before he opens his mouth, his fingers twitch and give me a squeeze.

"Like I might throw up."

"Let's not do that. You might mess your hair up." I wink, and his lips start to pull up into a small smile.

"Scared, Liv. I'm fuckin' scared."

I hear, Sway I think, make a small cry.

"Right here by your side, my handsome giant." I wink, taking a step closer and erasing the distance, no longer caring that we aren't alone. "I'm right by your side every step of the way."

"Not going to be easy."

"Nothing worth having ever is."

He grunts out a laugh, lacking all humor. Then he turns to look at Sway, without disconnecting from me.

"Make the call."

I hold his gaze, hoping he can see how much I love him. Gone is the tiredness I had felt before we entered the hotel room. In its place is steadfast determination to be this beautiful man's strength as he faces the family who thought he was dead.

Oh boy.

CHAPTER 23

Olivia

"STONE" BY WHISKEY MYERS

No one speaks.

We've been in the car for five minutes now, and the energy grows more and more electric as the time ticks along with the miles. You can taste it, it's that wild.

Zeke's been holding my hand so tightly, I lost feeling in my fingers a few miles back. I don't dare let go, though, or ask him to release the tightness some. I give him what he needs. I let him cling to me as if he's afraid he'll blow right out the window.

If I'm honest, I need it too. I need to feel like I was helping him somehow. Knowing how hard this was likely going to be for him. Who am I kidding, there's no way I could know what he's feeling. I'm just going to hold on as long as he needs me.

I can't imagine what's going through his mind right now. When he asked Sway to make the call, he tracked that man's every movement while Sway had paced the room, not looking away once. I couldn't hear whomever was on the other end of his call, but there was a small hum of their voice coming from the gap between his ear and the phone. That small space allowing the murmur of their voice into the room was all it took for me to feel the pain coming off him in waves. I don't know how

I knew for sure, but when his brother's voice was on the line, there was a small jolt that rocked his tall frame ever so slightly. My goodness, I pray with all that I have his brother doesn't make him fight for forgiveness.

When I glance over at him, I see the hard lines of his jaw as he clenches and unclenches. His dimple popping out with each flex he makes. I had no idea I had this big weakness for dimples before now. Maybe it's just because they're *his* dimples, but nevertheless … he's heart stopping with or without them. Even with so much trepidation radiating off him, he's breathtaking. I knew he was handsome, but I didn't know he was stop-your-heart-and-swoon kind of handsome.

I squeeze his hand and gain his eyes. "Are you okay?"

He glances down at our hands, lifting them up from where we had been resting them on the seat between us, turning them over with a flip before repeating the action a few times. His eyes study our connection silently. I wait, my heart picking up speed as the silence continues, but I give him what he needs and wait for him to answer me.

"I think …" He pauses and clears his throat. "I think I am," he responds a little lower the second time, for just me. "Thank you for being here."

"There's nowhere else I would rather be. It's going to be okay, honey. If you want to get out of there, just say the word and I'll make it happen."

"You gonna steal a car and take off with me?"

I hold his gaze for a beat. "If that's what you need? You bet your tail I will."

I get his smile. His real smile. Not the one full of worry and fear for what is about to come, faking it for me. I open my mouth, ready to say something to keep that smile on his face, but I don't get the chance before Sway clears his throat.

I had almost forgotten we weren't alone.

Almost.

"We're about to pull in, honey buns," Sway announces from the front.

When I glance out the window, I realize we're in a neighborhood. A big one, with tons of space between the homes. Houses that were meant to be the showcase of the land around them. As the car pulls us farther into the neighborhood, I realize that the space between each house gets larger and larger. Wouldn't it be something to have this much land? If I didn't love living in Boston so much, *this* is what I would want.

Sway pulls the car into a driveway, and I marvel at the beauty around us. Heck, no matter how much I love Boston, something as magnificent as this would be a huge temptation.

"They're likely out back at this time of the evening. When the sun starts going down and the grandbabies start getting tired, never fails to pull them around the backyard. We do monthly family dinners out here in their backyard. Older kids stay on the lake most of the time, but those grandbabies of theirs are passed around like hot potatoes for the adults that soak up the time with them."

"Been gone a long time," he murmurs, loud enough for Sway to hear him, pain thick in his words. "Somehow, it still looks the same."

"You're home now," he responds softly. "You've been gone, yes, but not sure it matters the why of it when you're back from the dead, honey child. Remember that."

"You've got nothing but faith this will work out, Sway."

Sway smiles at me before looking back at Zeke. "And you, my dear, apparently don't live only once. Why don't we squash that doubt now and yolt."

"What the hell is yolt?"

"You only live … twice." Sway laughs maniacally.

I watch some of the worry wash off Zeke. I have no idea what that meant, but it clearly means something to him. Enough to ease some of his worries and fears, at least.

"You've got all the time you need. Your brother is meeting me … well, us … in the home office Ax has. It's away from everyone. They're still out back. You and Asher talk first and then you decide what to do after. It will give you two the privacy you need. I should warn you, they know something big is happening, just unsure what."

"Cameras?"

"I texted Axel on the way," Davey starts. "He's reluctantly turned them off until you're inside, and I let him know it's clear to monitor the house again."

Zeke turns his gaze from the house, giving Sway a look of disbelief.

"He agreed to that?"

He holds his hands up with a small laugh.

"He's older now. His daughter, which I might add put every part of his overprotective nature in overdrive, is out of the house. Izzy is undoubtedly on his lap. He turned them off for me and not for long, but he did it because and only because he trusts me and everything he holds dear is already safe."

"I find it hard to believe that time could have cooled his protective nature."

Sway just laughs and shrugs. He and his husband step out of the car, shutting the door and leaving us in silence.

"Tell me what I can do?" I ask after a beat.

"Don't leave me," he answers with so much vulnerability in his tone.

"Never."

"No matter what happens, Livi. Don't leave me."

"Sweetheart, I'm not going to leave you. I'm right here, by your side."

His eyes, even in the dark, heat. He lets go of the hand he had been holding and frames my face with his large hands. His gaze holds mine, studying and searching. I take his handsome face in, the changes that just make him even more stunning, but those eyes are both the Drew I knew and the Zeke Cooper of his past.

"Wouldn't be here without you, Olivia. No matter what happens in there, you need to know that I'm thankful for you and that gift you've given me. Been dead a long time. Even without this"—he looks toward the house—"you have given me so much in the time we've been together that my life already was becoming beautiful. Can't imagine it can get much bigger than only everything in the world I every cared for in one place together. I know I wouldn't be here without what you and Riley have given me. I have no idea how this will go, but I know I can get through it with you."

He gives me a short but deep kiss, and when he pulls back, I can see the solid resolve and determination that's destroyed the fear in his stunning eyes. His whole body seemingly grows bigger and stronger in the darkness of Sway's car. I've seen so many sides to him over the years I've known him, but this is something to behold. I imagine, had I know him before the pain and years of being "Drew," I would see *this* man.

"Ready or not, darlin'," he says softly against my lips. "You only live twice, after all, so might as well make the second one count."

CHAPTER 24

Drew

"STARTING OVER" BY CHRIS STAPLETON

I'm going to be fucking sick.

Olivia's hand tightens in mine, and I release some of the tension I've been holding on to her with. I let my grip up some, but not much. I need her. I need that hold on her to make sure she's with me. That tether her hold gives me a feeling of safety that only she can provide.

It's not some grand big epiphany, this dependency that I have on her. Especially for this. If anything, it just drives home what I already knew about her and us together. I've been alone for so long, I had forgotten what it felt like to have someone who had your back out of love, not obligation. Even in the time "before," which I like to look at as the time I had with them in Hope Town before the shooting, I never had *this*. Sure, I had my brother by blood and the brothers I found in Axel, Greg, Beck, and Maddox. I knew, deep down, that the women in their lives had supported me out of love, not obligation, but that wasn't like the love that Olivia gives me. No, her love isn't the familial kind that the others gave me. It's the kind only found with your person.

Sway walks around me with Davey staying behind to take up the rear. He opens the door, the chimes making a little jingle that the alarm system does when the door opens. I follow as he enters, moving toward the home office that Ax has by memory more than because I'm following. My heart pounds with each step. I give Olivia's hand a little squeeze, relaxing slightly when she returns the gesture. We stop a little before the office door and let Sway go in first. I don't know what he says, but I hear my brother respond. First time I've heard him talk in so painfully long. I close my eyes and soak it in.

"Seems a little cloak and dagger type of mystery here, Sway. Isn't this a little different from your normal MO?"

"Oh hush, you. Not everything has to be done at a spectacular level."

Asher laughs. "Going to remember you said that."

Sway clears his throat, and I steady my breathing the best I can, bracing myself for what's about to happen. With a little flex of my fingers in warning to Olivia, I start walking and pull her behind me. She anchors me, holding me steady for the storm ahead.

My brother's back is to me, no doubt something Sway planned. His careful manipulations during the day to minimize the pain on everyone hasn't been lost on me.

I owe that man more than I'll ever be able to repay.

God, I take in my brother and feel that part inside me that has ached for him start weaving and mending. Each stitch making it feel that much closer to being healed. Full.

Even from behind, I would be able to pick him out of a lineup. We had a connection. Growing up with the evil mother we had, we struggled to find meals, and it makes you grow closer than most siblings.

Aside from his hair showing a lot more gray than blond, he looks the same even from behind. Same cocky stance. Same relaxed arms. That energy that tells people not to fuck with him.

Goddamn.

I've missed my big brother.

My heart picks up speed as I open and close my mouth a few times with no sound escaping. It feels too great, the emotions slamming into me so harshly, that if not for Liv, I would be on my ass. My words are stuck in my chest, too thick and clogged in the reaction to seeing and hearing my brother.

Olivia places her free hand on my forearm, and I look down at her.

Understanding, worry, and love in her eyes. Her touch calms my wrecked system enough for me to breathe. With a calming breath, I try to shake off a little more without success, and I clear my throat. My brother doesn't move much, but I see the slight tic that tells me Ash knows something big is happening. It's the same twitch he always had, ever so slight, and that left leg with the relaxed knee, clicks straight into place as he stands tall—no longer relaxed. He turns, slowly, and I see Sway in the corner of my gaze clasp his hands over his chest moments before my brother's eyes meet mine.

Fucking hell.

Emotions flash over his features.

So many of them, they blur into one of hopeful heartache deep within me.

I did that, caused that pain in his face.

Olivia hiccups.

Sway sniffles.

No one moves.

No one speaks.

My throat gets thicker when I see his eyes fill with unshed tears.

Still, no one moves.

Not one goddamn word is spoken.

Not for the longest fucking time.

In the next moment, before I even have a chance to react, I see him jerk forward. Though it wasn't the movement that shocked me the most … it was the anger that burned bright just before he did. It was enough to distract me, and I'll never for the rest of my life forget what happened next.

Sway screamed—later I'll look back on that shit and smile over how one grown-ass man could sound so high pitched and shriek-of-the-century loud.

Asher bellowed, warning me too late of the shitstorm coming.

It was Olivia who stopped my heart.

The sound she made when Asher's fist connected with her face mixed with the sound of shocked horror from my brother's, which only made Sway's screaming louder.

"What the fuck, Ash?"

"Me what the fuck? You what the fuck!"

"What the fuck!" I hear coming from the back of the house.

"Oh boy," Sway whispers, finally stopping that damn noise he was making.

"Come on, sweet girl." Davey steps into the crowd around where Olivia had stumbled after Asher's fist hit her. A fist meant for me that she stepped in front of. To protect me. My God, this woman. She knew exactly what he was about to do and put her own body in the way to protect me from hurting.

I don't deserve her.

I also know without a doubt that I won't ever let her go either.

"I'm okay," she whispers, her hand reaching out to rest her palm against my cheek. "Look at me, my giant," she says even softer. I look down and wince when I see the red mark already starting to bruise on her cheek. "You know that wasn't intentional, okay. You know that, honey. Do *not* let that moment affect this one, love. You've waited long enough for something you thought would never come—both of you have. Don't waste this moment by being angry."

"I can see his mark on your fucking face," I respond a lot calmer than I feel.

"Holy shit."

"Oh God."

I'm not sure who said it, but the various shocked proclamations come from behind us. I let Olivia's words settle and look up to meet my brother's gaze. The storm of emotions clear now, leaving only one thing behind.

Love.

"Hey, man," I rasp lamely.

He closes his eyes, dropping his chin down. His shoulders start to shake, and I feel my heart drop to my stomach. Then he looks up, and I realize he's laughing. Not even close to the reaction I thought he would have today.

"Over twenty damn years I think you're dead, and the first thing you say to me is 'Hey man' … Prayed for you every fucking day. For this very miracle. Not sure what I should address first, though—the fact that you think 'hey man' is a good lead or that my baby brother isn't fucking dead."

"Probably should start with apologizing to my woman."

He holds my eyes.

Dark blue against light blue.

Brother on brother.

And nods.

"I doubt I'll ever be able to express how sorry I am that happened. There's no excuse for my behavior or the pain that it caused you."

Olivia drops the bag of frozen veg from her face. When the hell did someone give her that?

Get your shit together, man. Stay alert, for fuck's sake.

"Please don't beat yourself up. That was unfortunate, but all things considered, I think you can give yourself a little slack. Let's forget this happened and focus on this beautiful miracle happening here."

"Not sure I can just forget that I punched a woman in the face away."

She lifts the bag back up to her face and shrugs her shoulders.

"Not sure I would call that a punch anyway." She smirks, placing the frozen veg back on her face.

My whole body relaxes with that little adorable twitch of her lips. God, I love this woman. She just took a fist to the face—for me—and instead of reacting how anyone would expect her to, she reacts with calm humor. No doubt minimizing her pain so that this night can be salvaged.

"Talk about an icebreaker, honey child ... next time, just use your shoe and whack one of the big guys. Closest one usually will do the trick."

"Hush, Sway," Davey scolds with a giggle.

"What? Am I wrong?"

"I've dreamed of this moment every goddamn day since I had to leave," I tell my brother.

I stand straight, my brother mirroring the movement, reluctantly letting Olivia's hand fall from my hold. I wouldn't have let go, but after that I need to know she's okay more than I need her as a safety blanket.

I see Olivia walk into Sway's awaiting embrace. She steps into his side, and his arm closes around her shoulder. I look from his hand to her face, meeting her uncovered eye and seeing only love reflecting toward me. I get that slight uptick of her lip that I fucking love and with a small nod to her, I return my attention to my brother. She's still feeding me strength, even from across the room.

"Never thought I would be here," I tell him honestly. "Didn't stop me from longing so deep in my gut for my big brother. Not once did I ever believe I would be in a position to have this moment. Spent fucking years with a hole inside me, Ash. One I know you felt so much bigger than I ever could because at least I knew you were alive."

Silence ticks on. The silence being what finally alerted me that, at some point while I was speaking, the room cleared, leaving just the two of us. My heart picks up before I remember that Liv is safe with Sway. Doesn't stop me from wanting her by my side regardless.

This moment, though, this is for the Cooper brothers.

"I'm so goddamn sorry, brother. So goddamn sorry for leaving you and the pain you felt believing I was dead. Never would have left you willingly, big bro."

A tear falls down his cheek at the same time one escapes to trail hotly down my own face.

He swallows, his throat working hard to keep himself from the same crack I feel ripping through the hold I have on my own emotions.

We both take the first step toward the other instantaneously, breaking the silent standoff. We wrap our arms around each other with a force that pulls a gruff grunt out of both of us. One arm around his back, and the other above his shoulders. His embrace mirrors mine. From the outside, we look like two dudes locked in a manly hug. However, inside our huddle, with his tears soaking my shoulder and mine doing the same to his—the Cooper men are healing.

We stand there, two brothers who lived through hell as kids together—surviving that hell … somehow and barely. We both wasted a lot of time holding on to that trauma and letting it shape our lives back then. In different ways, but still we never healed. We both experienced hell again when we were ripped apart. It didn't matter why I left. It didn't matter that I had to make the one person who always had my back the hardest—and everyone else for that matter—believe I was gone in a way I would never come back. None of the bullshit matters.

Nothing, that is, except for one thing; the two Cooper brothers back together and in each other's embrace finally start to feel that healing solidify.

CHAPTER 25

Olivia

"RUN" BY TAYLOR SWIFT FT ED SHEERAN

Holy crap, my face feels like it's going to explode, it hurts that much.

I'm not sure what I thought was going to happen when I jumped in front of Zeke. The only thing I could think of was keeping the man I love from feeling anymore pain today—especially the physical kind.

Was it smart?

No.

Would I do it again?

Absolutely.

If I have the power to keep him from feeling any more pain in his life, I'll do it again and again.

"Well, that was something." Sway sighs.

"You can say that again," Davey responds.

"Did a good job defusing the situation with your face, darlin', but let's maybe not to that again, hmm?"

"No promises," I whisper to the two of them, just beginning to notice the crowd in the room they lead me into when we left the brothers to have their moment together.

"Uh … hi?" I weakly wave. Then to my absolute embarrassment, my arm rises, and I point at my chest. "Olivia."

Nine sets of eyes look at me and the two men at my side from across the vast space of the most stunning kitchen. Based on what I know about these people, I have a pretty good idea who is who. I scan the faces of the people who loved my man years before. All of them look just as shocked as I'm sure they were when they realized who was in the office with Asher. It's one face specifically, though, the one woman standing without a man at her side, that I lock eyes with.

This must be Chelcie. The woman who had Zeke's child after they thought he was long gone. I can't even imagine what she's feeling right now.

I leave Sway's comforting hold and walk toward her. The room seemingly hangs on the edge of my movements. Energy electric coming off the big men in waves. I walk right up to her and wrap my arms around her, hugging her trembling body against mine. Her head drops, and she returns my embrace with a sob. Her whole body goes slack, and I hold her while she silently cries. My own tears stream down my face as she lets go and cries. I know from Zeke they didn't have the kind of relationship that would impact her life or marriage to his brother with his return. They weren't romantic. I can only guess that the enormity of her emotions have to do with not only worry for her husband but for her son as well.

"Thank you," I whisper in her ear, for her to hear only.

She leans back and studies me for a long moment. "For what?"

I smile sadly. "Raising a piece of the man I love."

Her lips tremble.

"It's easy to get wrapped up in sadness when life punches you in the gut. I don't even know you, but I'm sure you're one of the strongest women I'll ever meet. You all lost him, but you also had a greater stake in that loss. Could've not had the baby, but you did. So thank you."

"Hardly a baby anymore. More like a pain in my ass," someone grumbles.

I look from Chelcie to where I heard the voice come from.

Without the heaviness of the situation, I allow myself to look at the man who just entered the room.

Asher Cooper.

He looks so much like Zeke, but also so very different. Both extremely tall, both blond, both blue eyed … if I didn't know better, I would say they were twins. It's uncanny. They even seem to stand the same.

I look back at Chelcie, who is looking at her husband with so much concern. "Would you please introduce me to your husband?" I ask her, hoping that little request will urge her past the pain she was feeling moments before.

She nods, wipes her face, and we turn to walk over to the Cooper brothers. Zeke tags my hand the moment I'm within reach and tugs me to his side. His arm goes around my shoulders, and he pulls me into his side tightly. Chelcie walks straight into Asher's arms. I look away and up to Zeke once I see her relax into her husband's arms. I study his face, trying to read his emotions. He bends, placing his lips on my forehead, and leaves them there for a beat before pulling away.

"Asher." He clears his throat. "And Chelcie …" He pauses and dips his chin toward me. "Olivia."

I smile awkwardly.

"And this …" He trails off, and I feel him shifting us so that we're facing the rest of the people standing over to the side of us still. "This is my family."

His voice is so deep, gravelly, and full of oh-so-much emotion.

I wave, looking at each face.

He moves me to stand in front of him so he can look down into my eyes. "Give me just a second?"

"Of course."

He walks around me toward one of the couples—a tall, dark, and dangerous-looking man and the tiny blond woman at his side. She's adorable and looks like girl-next-door sweetness. The man, however, is the complete opposite. He looks like he could kill someone by just breathing.

Maddox and Emmy. It has to be them. Based on what I know about these people and the photos that I asked Sway to show me before we left the hotel room, I had a pretty good idea who was who.

Zeke stops in front of Emmy.

"Hey," he says low and thick with emotions. "Chin up, buttercup," he adds, lifting her downcast face with a finger to her chin to meet his eyes. "What do you say?"

"Oh Coop," she cries, wrapping her arms around him so tight he grunts. He returns her hug without hesitation, looking over her head to meet her husband's eyes … Maddox Locke.

Wow. This guy is really intimidating.

Emmy pulls herself back and looks up at him.

"You're really here?"

"I'm really here."

She lets out another sob, but this time moves into her husband's arms and continues to cry softly.

Maddox shuffles her with him when he reaches out, grabs Zeke by the arm, and pulls him close. He made it look effortless to pull a giant of a man around, too. I take it back, he's not just intimidating—he's intimidating *and* scary as all get-out when those almost black eyes look into your soul.

"I don't understand how, but my God is this one of the most magical moments of my life," someone says. Breaking my gaze from Locke, I look at the pretty redhead who spoke. Judging by the thickly tattooed mountain of a man holding her, I'm going to say that's Izzy and Axel.

"You can say that again, princess."

Zeke moves from the Lockes and walks toward the two. Izzy steps aside and the two men meet with another bear of a hug. They step back quicker than he did with Emmy, and both give each other a nod. Izzy gets the next hug, and she cries into his shoulder before her husband pulls—yes, pulls—her away. She drops her head into his neck and cries softly.

He moves to the two next to Izzy and Axel.

"Damn," he grunts before they hug. "Get in here, beauty," the man says, and the woman at his side wraps her arms around both men.

"That's Greg and his Melissa," Sway whispers in my ear.

Zeke steps away, taking a deep breath before moving to the last couple.

"That's Beck and Dee, sugar," Sway says, again low and just for me.

I knew from the little stories he has told me about his time with these people he considered his family that, next to his brother and

Emmy, he was closest to this man named Beck. This man who isn't even trying to hide the emotions written all over his face. Shock, pain, hopefulness, fear … hell, he might as well just be a giant mixing pot of every possible feeling one could experience. His tears, though, his tears show, which is winning—relief.

Dee gives him a hug first, looking up at him with a small smile and tears in her eyes. "It's really you," she whispers.

"It's really me."

She closes her eyes and smiles softly, then moves just to the side for her husband to take her place.

The two men give another one of those manly hugs.

The sound of each of them letting out a strangled sob in the quiet room seems to make every person jerk slightly. I don't need to look to confirm there isn't a dry eye in the whole room. There were three people who I knew would have the biggest impact on him today. His brother, for obvious reasons. Emmy, because of the friendship they had before moving to Georgia had kept them closer than the other females. And Beck, who I knew was the closest person he had aside from his brother.

These three were his rocks during a horrible time in his life. Each of them impacted him in distinctive ways to the other before and after he died. He missed all of these people, but he missed these three people just a little differently than the others.

I had just taken a tissue from Melissa's outstretched hand when Zeke was back at my side. I blew my nose quietly and dried my face before I looked up at him. He stood so close we were touching from shoulder to hip, his arm around my shoulder.

"This is my Livi. Olivia …" He pauses, and I feel the shuddered breath he pulls in. "Olivia, this is my family."

There are sniffles, someone sighs, and I hear someone else whisper, "Finally."

I'm not sure who it was, but they nailed it.

Finally.

His arm curls slightly, bringing me closer to his body. I inhale the delicious scent that is him. Smiling and meeting the eyes of the people in the room is a little intimidating when they're focusing right back on you this time. I give them a small wave and marvel in the enormity of this moment.

So this is what people mean when something means everything to them. It must be, because only "everything" could feel this monumental. Pure love, all of them, and a true family built on one heck of a solid foundation.

CHAPTER 26

Olivia

"WANDERING CHILD" BY WILD RIVERS

We stayed at the Reids' house for hours after the initial kitchen introductions.

At one point, I lost track of Zeke. Later, after we had gotten back to the hotel, he told me that he had stepped aside with Asher and Chelcie to talk about how they would tell Zac. Of course, Zac being an adult and all, he didn't have to get their advice or input on how to handle telling him, but I love that he did. It showed how much respect he had for both Chelcie and his brother as Zac's parents. I hope that it would help him understand that Zeke felt like he was Zac's true father and didn't want to take that role from him. He wanted his son to know that he was his, but also to know that his dad would always be Asher, and he wasn't going to threaten that relationship.

I love that he did that.

I love that he was asking for their guidance as well.

In the end, they decided that it was best for Asher and Chelcie to talk to Zac privately and then they would all go from there.

Personally, I had a feeling that Zac might be the luckiest man on earth to have both a dad and a father. Zeke might have just found out about him, but I don't for a second doubt that he would give his life for his son. He wanted to have a relationship with him, just not at the detriment to the one Zac shared with Asher.

That was two nights ago. Now, three days later, I was getting worried.

We've had a couple of great days here in Hope Town, but with no word on Zac, they came with a double edge to them. It was great getting to know these people, and watching Zeke heal a little more each day that he's with his family is a sight to be seen. However, knowing that with each great moment we had shared with everyone, there was a dark shadow that hung a little bigger each passing day that we heard nothing from Zac.

I walk into the backyard at the Reids', again marveling at the perfection that is their backyard. Talk about a secret garden.

One side is set up to be an outdoor kitchen with a grand seating area of a permanent solid wood table under a tall hut peaked roof. Instead of walls, thick white cotton drapes blew slightly in the breeze. They hung from rustic-looking hoops connected to metal beams that wrapped around each wall. There were so many chairs they could probably host a full football team to dinner. I was told earlier that was where they had their monthly mandatory family dinners. Over the years, they kept adding to it, improving and building it up, and just this year they had added the covered walkway to the outdoor kitchen—complete with a six burner stove, a flat top grill, and a pizza oven.

If that wasn't impressive enough, on the other side of the yard was a huge landscaped oasis that had me wishing I had my bathing suit every time I saw the Jacuzzi bubble or heard the crash of the waterfall (yes, the waterfall) over the chatter around me.

And finally, the icing on top of the backyard dreams are made of was what the pathway between the garden of flowers and colorful bushes. Once you cleared the canopy of low hanging trees, you were standing on the most stunning and peaceful lakes I had ever seen. It looked like heaven on earth, no exaggeration. The thick trees that hid the house from view while on the dock also gave it a barrier to the sounds beyond them. It's so still, calm, and quiet you would swear you were alone for miles and miles.

Now this kind of living might have a chance to sway me away from Boston. I can't imagine what it would be like to feel this every day. Could I have this kind of peace? In the city, impossible. But here? Oh, yes.

"Hey, girl!" I turn my head from looking at the beautiful lake footpath entrance and to see Emmy waving up at me from the porch. The other ladies sit around her by the firepit in cozy chairs. On our second night here, I discovered that Beck had built the chairs for Axel and Izzy's twenty-year wedding anniversary.

Could this family be any more perfect?

I wave down at her and had just dropped my hand when Izzy walks up behind me. I had walked ahead of her after she let me in, her waving me on to stop in the restroom.

"Incredible, isn't it?" she questions, looking around her backyard.

"I can see why you love it here."

"It's a lot of house without the kids home anymore, but I don't think I could ever leave here. Not just because of all this." She waves around her. "There have been so many moments lived within these walls and in this yard that I can still see them play through my mind as vividly as if I was watching them in person. These are the walls that watched me find my heart again, and again, and again. I thought they were done watching us experience miracles … until you walked in the door with our Coop, that is. Sway told me how important you were in him deciding to come home. I will never be able to thank you enough, Olivia. None of us will."

"You guys really aren't upset with him?"

She smiles softly, but with sadness pulling on her hard. "That day was one of the hardest moments in all of our lives, but it was also a defining moment that went well beyond our ability to understand at that time. So many moments in all of our lives were set into motion that day. I'm not sure some of them would have even happened had it not been for the way we dealt with the loss of Coop. Lives changed, all of ours and his. What good would it do any of us to be handed a literal God prayed for miracle and slap it in the face? Well … except Asher's hot head really makes me sound like a hypocrite, doesn't it?" She huffs a small laugh and frowns when her gaze moves to my bruise. "I still can't believe you stepped in front of Coop to take that hit. Talk about irony."

I frown. "What do you mean?"

She looks away from the yard and meets my gaze. Once again, I have to force myself not to think about how beautiful her pale-green eyes are.

"How much do you know about how he 'died'?" She brings up her hands to air quote the last word.

Thinking back on it, I don't know too many details, just that he had the opportunity and had to pull the trigger—literally. "I suppose just that he was shot in the belly the same day that he led you all to believe he had died."

She nods, the sunlight dancing off her silver and auburn strands of hair.

"What are you guys talking about?" someone yells from below.

Izzy holds up a finger asking for a second, looking torn, glancing between them and me.

"Maybe this is a conversation we should have with the rest of the ladies?" I hedge, guessing that's where she had been with her worry.

"Are you always this understanding?" she asks, smiling.

"Davey," I respond softly, as if that was answer enough. "I had a conversation not too unlike this one with him when I was worried that you all would be angry with Zeke."

"Zeke." She giggles. "Still throws me for a loop when I hear you call him that. I love it, it's just so … different. Anyway, I'm sorry for interrupting. Go on, please."

"Don't be." I clear my throat before continuing. "When I first met him, he was Drew. The day he told me about his past, I knew that he would forever be Zeke to me. I don't think he likes it from anyone else, though, which I don't understand but secretly love that it's just mine. He isn't my Drew anymore, but he also isn't Coop. Well, he isn't Coop to me, that is."

"What did Davey say?"

"To live life big, beautiful and do it right for those that don't get that chance. Well, to sum it up, at least that's the gist of it. I know what it's like to lose someone, too. He put it in perspective for me when I was worried how you guys would handle the shock of his return. If I had a chance to have my person back, it wouldn't matter to me how or why, just that I had them. There isn't room for anger to live for long when love burns so bright."

"You're a wise woman." She sniffles, wiping a tear from her porcelain cheek. "And so is Davey. I swear he is a healer for the soul."

We both laugh softly and I stop with a gesture to the stairs. "Let's finish our conversation with the others?"

I follow her, and we join the rest of the ladies. Everyone is here, except for Chelcie. Their daughters and daughters-in-law had joined us, and earlier, I met Dani, Lyn, Lila, Maddie, Ember, Stella, Nikki, and Megan. Sway had left earlier with Megan's daughter, Molly. Nikki's sister-in-law, Liberty, had joined us late. The various grandbabies running around the yard earlier had been music to my ears and made me long to have Riley here to meet them all. I had called earlier to check on her, and she sounded perfectly happy, making me miss her even more.

"So what was that all about?" Dee asks from her seat across from us, next to her daughter-in-law. Megan giggles at Dee's matter-of-fact tone.

"Well," Izzy starts. "I brought up her bruise and how I thought it was ironic how she got hurt protecting him. Standing in front of him to take the hit meant for him, to be exact."

A few ladies nod. Actually, looking around everyone seems to be nodding. Everyone but Liberty, that is. I look at her in question.

"Don't look at me. I'm new around here." She laughs, holding up her hands in mock surrender.

"Anyway," Dee continues, looking at Izzy like she's hanging on the edge of her seat. "Go on, please."

"Well, when she asked what I meant I asked her how much she knew about Coop's 'death,'" she says, again air quoting the last word.

"And she didn't?" Emmy says softly, guessing correctly.

"You're right. I don't know the details."

"Do you want to tell her?" Izzy asks Emmy.

I feel a shiver claw its way down my spine at the look that passes between the two women. I'm glad I had given myself a chance to sit down for this. When Emmy speaks, I can feel her pain.

"He took that bullet because he stepped in front of it … to save me," she tells me sadly, my mind flashing to the scar on his stomach. "I know because he had confided in me many years before, the only person who had ever put themselves in front of harm—for him—was his brother. Not a single other soul until you protected him like that, Olivia. It's ironic as hell that the woman he brings home with him for the first time was the second person ever in his life that took pain that another meant for him. And honey, I'd bet a lot of money that each time his brother stepped in front of something meant for him, they were absolutely life-changing moments in his life. I know that certainly was the case for me when he took that bullet that would have ended my life. All of that pales in comparison, though. You just proved to him what he already knew."

"Oh wow." I let the warmth of her words settle around me. I would take more punches if it kept them from him, in a heartbeat. "That's heartbreaking."

"It was … now, it's not so much." Emmy gives me a small soft smile, her beautiful face full of compassion. "It was a hard time in all of our lives, but we healed the best we could. And now, my goodness you have no idea what this miracle means to us. I understand he came home because of your encouragement, too."

I wave her off. "I didn't do anything. Sway did the hard work."

"You love him," Emmy says simply, her smile growing.

I nod. "Yes, very much."

"Then you did more than you realize."

"I still can't believe Asher punched you," Izzy adds, sniffling and wiping her eyes and –thankfully—breaking up the heaviness of the conversation's new path.

"He didn't mean to," I softly defend.

"He's still in the hotseat with me anyway. I can't believe he was going to punch Coop either."

"It's in the past. No sense in bringing it any attention." I shrug, hoping Izzy isn't too upset with Asher.

"Hard not to give it more attention with that shiner," Melissa jokes, pointing toward me, earning laughs from everyone, myself included.

I finally understand what it must have felt for him when I did that. He was upset with me, but more concerned with if I was okay. I kept insisting I was, but when the bruising started getting worse, it only made him more upset and wishing it had been him instead of me. When I asked him why he couldn't just drop it, he told me that he felt it eating his gut that I was hurt because of something meant for him. Using that logic for Emmy, I can't imagine what it was like for her when she thought he was dead because of a bullet meant for her.

Well, shit.

I don't regret it, but I hate that it caused him to fret.

"It was worth it," I tell Emmy.

She nods, one side of her lips curling slightly. "I see that now."

"We should make sure the two of them just stop stepping in front of harm," Maddie jests.

They all laugh weakly, that is until they start to trail off. Each of them glancing up to the porch area. A few soft gasps have me turning in my seat to see what's caught their attention.

Zeke stands there, phone in hand, and chest heaving like he just ran a mile. His eyes lock on mine, and he's completely disregarding the large mass of females around me. I'm on my feet, walking over to the stairs, not taking my eyes off him once. The air grows heavy around me as I look at his handsome ... but scared face.

"Honey?" I question, stepping into the space directly in front of him.

He reaches out and hands me his cell phone. With a slight shake to my hand, I reach out and take it. The text screen pulled up has a message from his brother.

Asher: Come over for dinner at 6. It's gonna be okay.

"You didn't answer him, honey?" I say softly, looking up at him from the phone. He looks worried right now. I hate that no one can do anything to change the way he feels. I get it, totally get it. He's about to meet his grown man son that he just found out about. That would be a lot for anyone. Then add in the rest of our reasons for being here? He's on emotional overload.

"I don't know what to say, baby," he responds so soft I have to strain to hear him.

"You tell him that you'll be there at six."

"We," he oddly responds.

"I'm sorry?"

"You type," he continues as if I hadn't spoken. "No matter what you say, though, make sure you say *we* will be there."

"Honey, maybe this should just be immediate family?"

He steps closer, crowding my space until the phone presses against my stomach and he's as close as he can get. I tip my head back and look up into his serious face.

"You want to stand here and tell me that doesn't include you? What do you think we're doing here?"

I blink.

"You *are* my family, Olivia."

Oh *my God*.

"Okay, honey," I dumbly say, my whole body coming alive. "Okay."

He bends down and nuzzles his nose along the side of my neck until his lips are at my ear.

"I can't do this without you," he whispers.

"You don't have to." My answer is immediate, and my resolve is solid. If this is something he needs, I'm going to make sure he has it.

"Not ever, Olivia."

His words slam into me, my eyes round, and I stare up at him.

"Not ever."

"Not ever," I echo.

Looking down, I wiggle my arms a little so I can bring the phone up between us. He gives me a little space, but not much, and I make quick work typing the response to his brother.

Zeke: We'll be there. Let me know if we need to bring anything.

The second I send the text, he shifts to wrap his arms around me, crushing me into his body again. He drops his head to kiss me softly on my forehead, dipping down to give me another across the bruise on my cheek, before I feel him let a long breath out. We stand there in each other's arms in this beautiful backyard haven, and I give him everything I can with this hug.

All my support, strength, and love.

CHAPTER 27

Drew

"IN MY VEINS" BY ANDREW BELLE FT ERIN MCCARLEY

Sway's borrowed car comes smoothly to a stop as we pull up to the curb at Asher and Chelcie's house. Cute older little ranch that you can clearly see has been well taken care of. The landscaping enhances the white brick house with a neat and well-manicured lawn. A few large trees grow out front, one with a tire swing that looks like it's had a lot of use over the years. If I didn't know better, I would assume a small child lived here.

Not a child anymore, though, is he?

My son, the boy who swung in that swing, has long since grown out of it.

And I missed every single day of his life.

Chelcie steps on to the porch with a small, too small, smile on her face. We haven't had much time to talk aside from basic pleasantries. Even though I had been giving them both some time to talk to Zac, Asher had still gone out of his way to spend as much time as he could with me.

"Hey," she greets us when we get closer.

"Hey," Liv responds, but I just nod, not trusting myself to speak yet.

"Can I talk to you?" she asks me, making it clear that she wants to speak to me alone when her eyes hit Liv before returning to mine.

"Don't want to sound like a dick, Chelcie, but that's what we're doing right now?"

She looks back at Olivia, then back to me. "I was hoping …"

"I know what you were hoping, and with all due respect, Olivia isn't going anywhere. I know this is hard—for all of us—but I'm not the man I used to be. The man I am now needs his woman at his side. Please understand, I'm not trying to be disrespectful."

She studies us for a beat before nodding.

"I … well …" She wrings her hands together, focusing on the movement before looking back up and meeting my eyes. Unshed tears fill hers. "I don't know how to say I'm sorry for not telling you about him. It … well, if I had known what would have happened … I would have told you the day I found out." She trails off and starts fidgeting again.

Doesn't feel right seeing her this worked up over something she never could have planned or seen coming. Just because I don't have romantic feelings for her doesn't mean I don't feel for her. She's my child's mother. My brother's wife. To the old me, she was just a body. We both knew what it was then, and it was fun, but if I was honest with myself now? I feel like an absolute ass for using her that way. It doesn't matter that she was using me just the same.

I hold up my hand to stop her. "No one could have predicted where our lives would have gone. You don't owe me an apology, Chelcie. It's me who owes that to all of you. Especially to you."

She shakes her head vehemently.

"Let's just agree to disagree then. The past can't be changed. Far as I can tell, I owe you a whole hell of a lot more than just an apology."

"You definitely do not," she answers.

"You had a baby when you didn't have to. Gave my brother a family when he didn't think he had one left. Loved them both, and I hear Zac's an incredible man, something else you're responsible for. All I did was one little part in those miracles, and we both know …" I hold her gaze. "We both know Asher is the dad I never could have been back then. It happened how it was meant to happen."

Olivia sniffles beside me at the same time Chelcie loses the fight with her tears, and they start to fall down her pale cheeks.

"I'm glad you're back," she finally says. "We all are."

I swallow thickly. Nodding, I don't trust my voice. "All of you?" Even to my own ears, my question sounds ripe with nervous fear.

"All of us. I mean it, Coop. Your brother, me, but most importantly —your son."

"I need to ask you something before we go in."

She wipes her wet cheeks and studies my face. After a moment, she nods and offers me a weak smile.

"Ash … he's his dad, Chelcie. I've been worried he's keeping his distance because he thinks I'll push him out of that spot. I need you to know I'm not. I might be the one who helped create him, but he's my brother's son in every way there is. He doesn't …" I let my words die, hoping she knows what I'm asking. It makes me sick just thinking that my brother could be avoiding me because he thinks I'm here to take that from him.

She looks back down for a beat before meeting my eyes again. "Please know that we didn't mean to take so many days to get to this point. Zac was working, but he also wanted to have a minute with us after we told him. He's not upset, not with you or anyone, just … well, our boy has a big heart, and he was worried about how we were handling things."

"Sounds like someone I know," I respond, that thickness getting a little harder to swallow through.

"He's a good person. Such a good man. He reminds us of you in so many ways, Coop. Ever since he was a little boy."

I nod again, mutely. I missed so fucking much. Then again, I wasn't lying when I told her that everything had happened the way it was meant to. Back then, I would have been horrible as a father. I glance at Olivia, not for the first time wondering if she's going to want kids of her own. I have to push that thought out quickly, liking way too much how that thought made me feel. Coop couldn't have been a good dad, but damn, I feel like Zeke could.

I glance back at Chelcie just when she looks at Olivia, thankfully stopping the onslaught of emotions being slung at me. Not sure if I can handle much more if I want to meet my man son without freaking him out.

"I'm sorry. I didn't mean to be rude just then. I understand why he needs you with him. His brother, well … let's just say those two might as well be two peas in the same pod."

Olivia giggles softly. "I don't think you were rude at all." She lets go of my hand and reaches out, pulling Chelcie forward with her hug. I want her back at my side the second she releases me. Chelcie holds my gaze over her shoulder, and her smile grows, and the sadness leaves her eyes. "I'm Olivia." She pulls back and keeps Chelcie at arm's length with her hands on her shoulders. "It's really great to meet you."

Chelcie nods slightly. "You, too."

Olivia lets go and steps back to my side. When her hand is back in mine, I feel my nerves settle a little more. I'm becoming addicted to her touch.

"Well, why don't we go inside? They're back in the game room. I figured that it would be good for you guys to be around manly things that can be good icebreakers and all. Would be better if we had the grill fired up already. I think men talk better around those, at least. Anyhow … it's this way."

I shake my head, a small smile forming. Same old Chelcie. We follow her. I keep my eyes forward, not wanting to look around just yet. My feet and my hold of Olivia's hand are the only things that I have some control over. My heart feels like it's going to pound out of my chest. Chills dance across my skin, and my stomach feels as if it rolled right down to my feet.

Fuck.

I should have asked for a picture. Hell, I should have asked anyone in the past few days what he would look like at the very least. I should have done something to prepare myself for what I saw when we turned the corner and entered the large room.

I vaguely see the impressive setup around me: pool table, arcade games, basketball toss, and a large bar in the corner—fully stocked if the amount of liquor is anything to go by. I can see a game on the large TV, but the only thing my eyes can focus on is the man in the room next to my brother.

The fully grown man.

Yeah. Should have asked for a picture.

205

Olivia gasps, softly. I relax the tightness of my grip on her hand. She tightens hers, and I'm pretty sure her shock is for the same reason as mine.

My boy looks just like me.

Tall, taller than my brother who's standing at his side. Blond hair, cut short and stylish, with a dusting of darker blond hair on his face that almost looks brown.

He shifts and takes a step forward.

When he swallows, I see his dimples.

He reaches one hand up and runs it through his hair and down to rest on his neck, looking down and flexing his hold on his neck, taking two more steps.

He's still looking down. When he looks back up and eyes identical to my own look into mine, I have to clear my throat.

Jesus.

I take a step forward at the same time he does. Olivia pulls her hand away with a gentle squeeze.

He reaches out.

I reach out.

I see my brother's approving nod and small smile moments before my son's body collides against my own. With a soft grunt from the impact, I hug him just as hard as he's hugging me.

I feel something settle deep in my soul. The warmth of it spreads out with the swiftness of a bullet, searing through all the tattered pieces of my heart and effortlessly repairing them. The few parts that hadn't been able to be healed by just Olivia's love. The ones that would have stayed broken without this reunion. Even with her light shining on them, there was only one way it could have been healed, and I've got him in my arms as the other looks at me from a few feet away with tears falling down her face without a single care.

I left this town a dead man, and right now, I feel fully alive for the first time in longer than I can remember.

I hug my son while he hugs me back, and thank God I'm alive. I realize I hadn't truly felt alive once in my entire life.

Not when I was growing up in the shitty house with an equally shitty mother.

Not when I had joined the Marines and found my real family.

Not even when I was screwing my way through life … searching for that feeling of being alive.

I was as close as I could get to it when Olivia gave me her light, but it was this piece that I never knew was missing that tipped over the scales.

We both pull back at the same time, and I look into eyes identical to my own as we both study the other silently. I was right. He's tall, maybe a hair taller than I am. I can tell he's got both my dimples, the nervous swallow giving them away. His hair, blond … no shock there. He kept it long on the top, styled in what I'm guessing is his fingers constantly pushing through the strands. The sides look light brown with the close cut he has.

He looks good. He looks healthy—if the muscles on him are any indication. He looks … hopeful.

"Not sure what to say when your dead dad comes back," he says with a huff of laughter at the end. He shakes his head, looks down at his feet, and rubs the back of his neck.

"Not sure what to say when I come back to life and meet my man son."

His lips twitch.

"You're happy?" I finally speak, my voice low with words meant for him only.

"Have been. But life got a whole lot sweeter today, though."

He reaches out and slaps my bicep.

"You only live once, old man," he gruffs out, that damn deep voice of my man boy. "Or so I've been told that is."

I clear my throat. "That's what I hear."

He grunts out a laugh and reaches out to give me another hug.

Yeah, he's taller than I thought he was.

"Wished for you every Christmas and birthday for as long as I can remember. There's no way I'm taking this gift for granted."

"I don't deserve that. Left all of you," I say, looking at my brother and Chelcie before focusing back on Zac. "I'm not sure I would have been the father you deserved, Zac. Looking at you, I hate that I missed your whole damn life, but I'm also thankful you were raised by two of the kindest people I know. Got their heart, I can already see that. Means the world that you want to know me. And … I can't wait to get to know you."

"You, too." He smiles, looking just like I did at his age.

"God, it's like looking in the mirror." I whisper the words low, just for him.

"Good to know I'll still look good when I'm an old man," he responds, a smile in his eyes. Those beautiful eyes of my boy.

"Sound just like I did at your age too."

"Not always a good thing." Chelcie giggles.

"He seems to attract just as many female *friends*, too." My brother laughs.

And Zac, the spitting image of me, does just what I would have done at his age. He winks at me, and with a shrug, he says all I need to know.

The apple really didn't fall far from the tree. My boy is good looking and sounds like he has no trouble finding a date. If I had known what kind of magic was waiting for me with the right girl—my Livi—I would have been more … selective back then. It's not my place to offer that fatherly advice, though. He either knows it or will figure out on his own.

"I'd like to get lunch, if it's good with you? Catch up on what I've missed?" I feel my awkward shrug like someone just put a spotlight on me. Why does this feel so damn scary?

He's quiet, looking behind him at my brother and his mom before turning around to face me again.

"I'd really like that."

It took me long enough, but fuck does it feel worth all that time it took to be right here, meeting my son.

My man son.

We exchange numbers and make plans to meet the next day for lunch. He steps away and sits in a chair next to the two couches, the rest of us scattered about with me and Olivia with a hyper Chelcie, fretting about making sure everyone is "refreshed and hydrated" before my brother forces her to sit and calm.

They look good together, Ash and Chelcie. He looks happy, and the way he has his wife pressed close to his side, he is also well loved. She's spent more time bouncing her worried eyes between both Asher and Zac since we arrived. It's good to see her relax when Zac sits down, relaxed and carefree.

I reach my free hand over and grab Olivia's hand that had been resting on my thigh, needing more contact. She's been curled into my side with my left arm swung over her shoulders—keeping her close. The conversation flows easily around me. I join in when necessary, but I spend more time marveling on how life-changing this moment is for everyone. I keep my hold on Olivia and let her tether me to the ground. The more I look around at my brother and son, the more I feel my heart beating faster, growing and filling wider than I've felt in a long damn time. I relax the hold I have on Liv, taking a deep breath to calm my thoughts. Using her to keep me grounded.

It's not just this night that has my heart racing and my nerves firing like madness. It's realizing just how much I owe the woman next to me for making this happen. For giving me back the life I had lost, the family I had left behind, and the son I have a chance to get to know now.

She has breathed life back into me, and what do I do to repay her love?

I keep a secret from her even larger than before. Hard to believe. I sit here with my family back, making promises together for our future now that we've reunited, and I'm keeping a monstrous secret from the woman who gave me the strength to take this chance I'm living right here in my brother's home. There's no way I could have done this without her, and for that, I owe her the truth. I can't let us continue to grow closer to that beautiful future without her knowing it all.

She's given me my life back.

I look around the room at the faces I never thought I would see again, the son I never imagined, and the woman who owns my heart.

This is what life is about.

Family.

Love.

What am I going to do if she can't forgive me?

I'm this fucking close to having a life I could never have dreamed of … and without her, I really would be a dead man, even with all of this.

My *son* laughs at something Olivia says. The rich sound fills the room.

I clear my throat and blink a few times. The emotions too damn thick as they war within me.

The pressure in my chest keeps growing as the night continues and conversations flow. The whole time, I'm too afraid to move far from her, my heart not able to calm without her touch.

Fuck me.

If she doesn't take what I have to tell her well and I lose her? I'm not sure my newly healed heart can handle that. It will break in a way I know not even this sweet life I've been given a second chance at will be able to mend it.

My son laughs again.

My mind goes to Riley, her sweet little giggle and crooked smile.

Zac was that little, and I missed it all.

Every damn step, word, and milestone.

His laughter booms around the room. In my mind, I hear Riley's echo in with the sound of his. I realize it was Olivia's sweet giggles when she moves against my side with each one. I have no idea what's so funny, having been lost in my damn thoughts for too long. It's hard to think of Zac, easily six and a half feet tall, being as little as Riley was. She's going to love him, too. Two giants for her to love. Thinking of Riley makes me miss her even more, which is saying a lot. In the months that I've been with her aunt, she's wedged herself a giant spot in my heart.

I look from Zac down to Olivia when her giggles become full belly laughs. I feel my lips tip as I watch her.

Yeah, I definitely want more kids to fill this life I'm going to build with her.

Marriage.

Kids.

I want to see her laugh like this with Zac. With Riley. And whoever we may add to our family there with us.

I want to live, dammit.

Maybe do that for the first time in my life, too.

God, please let her forgive me.

I look back at Zac, his eyes on me, and take a deep breath.

I can't have come this far to have true and honest happiness ripped from me the second I've found it.

Right?

CHAPTER 28

Olivia

"FARAWAY TREE" BY BOATKEEPER

He's been quiet.

The whole ride back to the hotel was filled with commentary from the sports station he has on the radio. I tried to get a conversation going, but he only muttered some grunts here and there, sticking to silence while he drives. I called Ella to check on Riley, but she had fallen asleep so it was a short call that didn't help fill the void. We had been having FaceTime calls every morning and night with our little bean, but still I missed her so much. I know Zeke does too. I saw how he was looking at all the kids that have been around our large group here in Georgia.

When we got back, I excused myself to use the bathroom, wanting to give him a moment alone after such a highly emotional day.

Before we left his brother's house, Zeke made plans to go to lunch with Zac tomorrow.

Zac.

He's such an incredible human. It's uncanny to look at him and see so much of Zeke in him. Chelcie and Asher brought some pictures out a few hours into our visit. We sat there, all of us, and looked through the albums. Zeke had been hyper focused on each photo and story. I could have kissed Chelcie and Asher for giving him that. Letting him watch his son grow through the years with each album we looked through.

After that, they pulled out the ones with a younger, wild-looking Zeke. Photo after photo of the man who I'm quickly finding has more layers than an onion.

The "old" him, the one that he was before I knew him ... aside from the initial shock of seeing the younger him and not seeing much of a difference in his son. They could have been twins. It's mind blowing. Not just because they look so similar, but because the Zeke I know now —the one who matches the man in those photos—looks so different from the Drew I knew. Three versions of the same man all so different from the other. Sounds just as confusing as it is to me. I go between sneaking little glimpses at him to full-blown staring.

One of these days, I might get used to how damn handsome he is, but that surely won't be today.

Secretly, I miss the beard. Though I will never admit that to him. Both shaved or not versions of him are simply perfection. However, I'm really going to miss that little burn I get when he kisses me deep and hard with that beard. Yeah, I'm surely going to miss that. His kisses are five star no matter what, though, so I'll live.

He clears his throat, and I come out of my lust-filled thoughts about him to give him my focus. I didn't realize I was just staring at him.

He settled in to the bed and put a basketball game on when we got back. Probably should just leave it and take the sign for what it was— that he wanted to be alone with his thoughts. Something not too easy to achieve when you're in a shared hotel room.

"I can go take a bath if you want some time alone to decompress, honey," I offer, standing on the threshold of the bedroom after finishing up using the restroom.

"I don't need to decompress, Liv." He doesn't look away from the TV.

"Maybe you don't think you do, but honey ... tonight was big for you. The adrenaline will crash soon."

He takes a deep breath and turns the TV off, turning his head to give me his attention. "Come here, Olivia."

"Maybe I'm good right here," I smart, leaning against the doorframe of the bathroom.

He cocks an eyebrow and gives me a playful smirk.

"I'm just worried about you," I tell him honestly. "Tonight was a lot. Hell, it's all a lot, honey. More than a lot of people can handle alone. More than the average person will ever experience. I don't know how to set aside that worry."

"Baby." He sighs, patting the empty side of the bed next to him.

"You have lunch tomorrow. You have lunch with your grown son, and you're watching a game like today was just a normal day. Honey, I don't know how to process the way *you're* processing all of this."

He lets a small laugh out.

"This isn't funny, Zeke."

His eyes flash.

His brow ticks up again.

"No way, mister. I know that look in your eyes."

"Then get over here."

I shake my head.

"Olivia," he says in a deep and dark tone.

I give a little huff that he only laughs a bit more at. My feet take me to the side of the bed regardless of the fact that he's now finding humor in my concern for him. I look down at the handsome man lying on the bed and marvel in just how beautiful he is. Something I've done quite a bit since his makeover by Sway. I can see a mix of the old him and the new him blended together, something I can say for sure after seeing so many photos of a young and carefree version of him.

"Come here."

"If I come over there, you'll just try distracting me by getting me naked."

He grunts out a laugh but just silently pats the side of the bed next to his hip. I sigh but sit. His hand takes mine, and those stunning bright-blue eyes of his look into mine. He looks down at our hands, his thumb caressing my skin slowly.

"I'm okay, Liv. Just taking the time to be thankful. Thanking God that he thought I deserved this second chance, and that he gave me you. No doubt, babe, I never would have gotten this gift had it not been for you."

I feel my brow furrow, watching his eyes when they go from mine up

214

to them. His free hand coming out to run one finger lightly down the bridge of my nose, soothing the spot between my brows first.

"Maybe tomorrow it will hit me. Maybe a month or year from now. That my boy is a man I didn't get to see grow, but today? Today, I'm going to keep riding this high you've given me. I might've missed his big milestones growing up, but now I get to get to know the man he's become and with any luck, he'll like the man I've become."

"He's going to love you, sweetheart," I tell him honestly.

"Maybe," he answers, small smile still on his full lips. Those dimples that have been causing havoc to my system pop out. Ever since the beard was shaved and they were uncovered I find myself rather obsessed with seeing them more and more. What I don't see are all the shadows that are usually riding him hard behind his gaze. There's something there I don't quite understand, but there definitely isn't sadness or pain.

"There's no maybe, Zeke."

"You may be right, Liv."

"I know I'm right," I smart.

His expression changes and the small smile he had on his face moments before turns into a predatory grin.

"You being smart with me?"

Placing my hand on his leg, I slowly start to move it up his muscular thigh. He cocks an eyebrow at me, but doesn't stop me.

"Who me?" I wink, my hand stopping at the thick bulge between his legs and he makes a primal sound deep in his throat.

That's all the warning I get.

His large frame lifts off the bedframe, and he pulls me over his legs. I let mine fall with his body between mine. The hardness of his erection presses against my heat, causing me to shiver. His mouth is on mine, kissing me deep, and I push my hands into his hair. The tickle of the shaved parts against my palm sends tingles of awareness up my arms. Our kiss is deep, slow and absolutely heavenly. His hands tighten on my hips, and he starts pushing up from the bed while his hold on my hips keeps me right where he wants me. I kiss him deeper when he rubs against my sensitive clit, pulling my head back and breaking our kiss with a gasp. His mouth goes to my neck, my hands to his shoulders, and he trails his hot kisses down the side of my neck and the exposed skin my shirt doesn't cover.

We're a tangled mess of limbs and fevered kisses as we try to get each other's clothes off. I lose his mouth when he pulls my shirt over my head. Sitting back on his thighs, I watch with complete transfixed lust as he pulls his own up and off—tossing it in the corner of the room with mine. His eyes are on my lace covered chest. The hunger in his expression as he looks at me only feeds my own.

"You're beautiful," I tell him.

"That's my line, babe."

I smile and lean into him, reaching out and framing his face. He watches me, hands rubbing my legs.

"You are, hands down, the most magnificent man I have ever known. I am so proud of you, Zeke, honey."

His hands still, and he tilts his head, studying me.

"You may never know how much, but I am. I know this hasn't been easy. I know you're hurting. I'm just worried about you."

His hold on my thighs tightens, drawling my attention. I had expected him to ignore what I was saying, especially given the heavy heat I saw in his eyes when he got my top off. When I look up and meet his eyes, I suck in a breath at what I see.

They're clear … almost completely so. Now that I get a good look this close, I can see a lot of the stress he had been carrying has melted away as well.

He looks lighter.

He looks happy.

He looks back at me like he's holding the whole world in his hand.

"I've been given a second chance, Liv. Something that *you* gave me the strength to reach out and take. I could look at the time I lost with Zac with regret, but that regret would root deep, and it's the kind of deep that leaks into any ounce of happy you could ever find. Too deep. Just can't do that, sweet Liv. I can't give life to those thoughts. If I do, everything I could gain from having my family back will be for nothing because the pain of that would be too much to bear. I know I did what I needed to do then and I'm more thankful that I can ever express that they're so forgiving of what I did. The rest, well … I have to let that go so we can heal."

I study him, trying to see the truth in his words.

When I open my mouth to say something, he lifts his hand and gentle places one finger over my lips.

"Trust me, Olivia. Right now, after the past few days we've had, I'm breathing easier than I have in decades. Only everything I have been missing with my family and the girl—no, both my girls—that made it all possible are all that matter to me right now. I could get lost in the past, it would be easy to, but instead I have one hell of a future opening up to me and *that* baby is what is important. I get to hold my girl in my arms and let me tell you, that right there would have been enough to ease my mind of any troubles. And baby, tomorrow I get to take my son to lunch. Nothing but up from here."

"I trust you. I do," I whisper, my eyes getting heavy with unshed tears. "It isn't that I don't believe what you're saying. I'm just worried, that's all."

"I love you. I'm okay, Liv. I really am."

"I love you, too."

He smiles, that heart stopping grin of his that never fails to melt my panties. Now that his cheeks aren't covered by facial hair, those dimples are able to shine bright. Once again I'm struck with just how perfect he is.

"I've got everything I need, baby. Riley, my family here, and you. Only everything I have given up ever believing I would have right here and mine for the taking. Far as I can tell, I just took the long way to get to where I was always meant to be. One day …" he trails off, his mouth coming to my collarbone where he trails kisses up my neck. His warm lips pressing against my sensitive skin before his tongue dips out to give my lobe a little lick. The cool air making me shiver. "One day, you'll take my name, my *real* name, and you'll bless our family with more babies like our Riley girl. One day, we'll bring Riley down here and she'll meet my family. She'll have all those kids to play with, all these adults to love her, and we'll take each day we've been given and treat it like the gift that it is."

"That's a lot." I smile at him. "I'm not sure that I can just turn off the concern I have when it comes to you, but thank you for giving me all of that." I look down, trailing my fingertips over his chest and down his torso. His stomach flexes as I move over his skin with the light dance of my fingers. The light dusting of hair on his chest making my mouth water. "You're going to marry me? How do you know I'll say yes?" I wink at him, and his smile grows.

"Way I see it, I wouldn't be given the gift of a second chance without you by my side. You gave me this, Olivia. You made all of this possible."

I shake my head. "I didn't do anything, honey."

"You did everything."

His mouth is on mine before he even finishes speaking. Our tongues dancing together as our hands move quickly to remove the remaining clothing from our bodies. All the while, our mouths stay connected. His hands, warm on my bottom, give a little flex and his fingers dig into my flesh. My core clenches in need for having his hands this close. One more flex of his hands and he shifts us so that I'm lying with his body between my legs. His hard cock settling against my wetness and he rocks his hips gently, the tip of him hitting my clit and making my body fire at a fever pitch. I feel him everywhere except where I want him the most.

We feed on each other's mouths, our kiss turning hungrier and hungrier. I roam my hands down his back and lift my legs to wrap them around his back. My hips coming off the bed, begging him without words to take me.

His mouth leaves a trail of fire as he moves down my chest.

"Oh my God," I gasp.

He curls his tongue around my nipple, his mouth open wide as he sucks as much as he can into it. He goes from licking to sucking, his mouth magic against my nipple. I could come from this alone, I just know it. He lifts back slightly, trailing kisses across the path to my other breast. The nipple he just released already begging for more. He rubs his face against my chest, breathing in deeply, before he starts feasting on the other.

"Baby," I whine. "You feel so good."

"Going to show you now," he states with a deep, lazy drawl.

"Show me what, baby?" I breathe, my eyes rolling closed when he takes my nipple in his mouth and pulls in deep. No one has ever made me feel like this from simply playing with my breasts.

"My love."

He tenderly takes my hips and runs his hands down my thighs to spread them even wider. Not looking away from my eyes, he lines himself up and slowly sinks inside me. The sound that comes out of my mouth only seems to fuel him because his eyes flash moments before he presses his hips against mine and pushes as deep as he can get inside me. His body blanketing mine, arms tucked under my body and his hands cradling my hands in his palms. I am wholly and completely his to take.

Boy, does he.

Zeke makes love to me slowly, tenderly and not once does he look away from my eyes. There's so much said between us without words at that moment. We move together in this dance as our bodies climb the fever pitch we're creating. He pulls all the way out and I almost don't recognize the sound that comes out of my mouth. It sounds wild and needy.

"Not going fast tonight, baby. Feel me. Feel it."

He continues to glide in and out. I can feel how wet I am when a little of my arousal trails a wet path down to my ass before falling on to the bed. The hairs on his chest tickling my sensitive nipples. Every single nerve ending firing at once. He bends, nose to mine—tip to tip—and pushes deep, causing me to scream out in pleasure. That seems to be the straw that breaks the camel's back, my scream. The vibrations of his approval coming from deep within his chest, causing ripples of goose bumps to dance across my skin. He keeps his pace a few more thrusts before he plants one hand in the bed and the other goes to my hip. He curls his fingers around and pulls my body up with each thrust he plants deep. The new position makes him hit deeper than he ever has.

I lose ability to do anything but *feel* as he takes me slow and deep. His gaze never leaving mine. Not even when he plants himself deep and his groans and mixing with my screams as we find our release at the same time. I gasp, my over sensitive body waring with the need to try to figure out what I just saw pass through his gaze. Gone so fast, I'm convinced I made it up.

Fear?

No, that can't be it.

I try to find it again, but all I see is overwhelming love in his sleepy observation. Not wanting to sour the moment, I shove it aside. Maybe I was seeing things.

"Thank you."

"Not sure what you're thanking me for, honey." I laugh a little, causing his thickness to slip free from my heat and my laugh turns into a breathy moan.

"My girl likes me inside her."

"You girl *loves* you inside her."

He smiles, shifting our bodies so his back is on the bed, and I curl into his side, resting my head against his chest.

"Thank you for bringing me back to life." He tightens his arms around me and kisses the top of my head. "I love you so fucking much," he whispers.

My eyes start to burn as the tears start to build.

"Honey," I gasp on a quiet sob.

"Yeah, you'll say yes."

My mind goes back to his declarations earlier. Yeah, he's not wrong. I know without a doubt in my mind that when he asks, the answer will now and forever be yes.

CHAPTER 29

Drew

"SALT AND THE SEA" BY THE LUMINEERS

I wasn't expecting the uniform.

I knew he worked, Chelcie and Ash had mentioned it a few times. I should have asked, but I didn't want to fuck up and ask the wrong question and lose how open he was being. I want to know everything, but I want him to *want* to give it to me when he's ready. I may genetically be his father, but I'm not his dad. That honor belongs to my brother. I want to be in his life, but not taking Asher's place. This is Zac's show, and I'm not going to rush him.

He moves through the restaurant with an easy gait, relaxed but still alert. He smiles at a few people as he passes and I feel my chest get tight.

I've missed so much of his life. Had it not been for Olivia, I would have missed it all. It's a miracle that I've been given this chance at all, no way will I take this for granted.

"Hey," he says to me as he bends to slide in to the booth across from me. "Sorry I'm late, I had to finish up a call before I was able to head over. I wasn't sure how much time you had, but went ahead and had someone cover the rest of my shift so I wouldn't be rushed to leave."

"How long have you been a cop?" I ask him, looking down at his uniform. The bold "COOPER" I see makes my throat feel thick.

My boy.

A cop.

I make a mental note to have the guys check into his unit. No such thing as being too careful. Most cops I know are damn good men, but there's a few that aren't. If my boy will be out there risking his life to protect Hope Town, I'll make sure he has a captain that would risk his life to protect his men.

"Couple of years. Went to school, but couldn't see myself stuck with a job that would have me glued to an office. Lee had been trying to get a few of us to join the force, but it was important to Mom and Dad that I finish school first."

His cheeks get a little color on them at the mention of Asher and Chelcie. I hate that he's feeling any bit of uncomfortableness over this.

"Hey, let's just get this part over with. Asher will always be your dad, Zac. I'm not trying to replace the role he's had in your life. If you want to think of me as a father, damn that would be fine with me, but Ash is your dad."

He studies me, stirring his spoon in his coffee while he does. "No one said I can't have two."

Well, fuck me.

"That what you want?"

He places his spoon on the napkin it had been resting on and holds my gaze, showing me just how much he wants that without words.

"I wasn't joking when I said I spent years wishing for you every chance I got. Dad and I talked about what happened and why you did what you did. I understand it, even if it sucks that it had to happen. I'm thankful …. *Now.* Now I have both of my dads. Just not sure what to call you, to be honest."

My body moves with silent laughter. "You can just call me Coop, bud. No need complicating things. Something else feels right, then go with that. There's not a single rule to this and, way I see, we can figure it out together."

"Sounds good."

"You always like this?"

"Like what?"

"Reasonable."

He laughs, the rich sound so much like my own. "I can be as

222

unreasonable as it comes, but I'm not stupid. You saved lives that day and sacrificed your own so that everyone that matters to both of us were safe. Mom told me you didn't know she was pregnant. Doesn't seem right to continue punishing a man who's doing a real bang up job of punishing himself. Don't you think?"

I nod, a small smile curling up one side of my lips.

A pretty young lady comes up to the table before either of us have a chance to speak again.

"Hey there." She smiles at me and looks over at Zac. Her smile falls off her face slowly. "Zac."

Looking over at him, I see some of the cocky confidence sparking fire as he looks up at the server with nothing short of a predatory grin.

"Bess. Looking nice today."

"I look nice every day and you damn well know it." She looks back to me and replaces the annoyed look she had given Zac with a friendly smile again. "Can I get you something to eat?"

"Not going to offer to take my order?" Zac continues.

I lean back and feel something shift in my chest. It's like looking back in time and seeing a younger version of myself. The only thing my mind ran on was pussy and food at that point. I ate both because I enjoyed the fuck out of it—searching for anything that would make me feel *full*. God, I had been such a fool. It's something he'll learn one day —judging by the scowl Bess keeps gracing him with, making his cocky grin so much like my own grow. Bess doesn't know it now, but if she's what he wants I have a feeling nothing will stand in his way.

"Surprise me," I tell her, bringing her attention back to me.

"Surprise you? Can't say I've gotten that before."

"Yeah, surprise me. Good with coffee, but bring me a water too please?"

"Do you eat meat?"

"Look at him, Bess. You think he doesn't?"

"You look just like him and I haven't had you order a thing with meat in it for two years."

Oh, my boy … you are in trouble.

"I eat meat. Nothing I can't have. Really anything is fine. I'm not picky and I like food."

223

"Okay, sounds good. What about you?" She frowns down at Zac.

"How about you get me a steak, Bess?"

"Smart-ass," she mumbles, scribbling on her notepad. When she finishes, she looks back up and focuses on me. "Anything else?"

"Yeah, actually. Can you put in a to go order when we're finishing up? Hamburger with onion, lettuce and tomato. Ketchup and mustard on the side, please. Fries and veg for the sides. To-go Coke as well. Oh, and some apple pie."

She finishes writing it all down and looks back at me with a twinkle in her blue eyes. "So you do care what you eat?"

I smile, big. "I care what my woman likes to eat."

Her own smile grows. She's pretty. Young and innocent-looking with something wild behind her eyes. The kind of woman I would have avoided when I was his age. She might as well have a billboard over her that announces she's the type you don't screw around on.

"Right on, mister. Lucky lady."

One more smile for me and a scowl for Zac, she walks back behind the counter.

"Wanna talk about that?"

"Nope."

I grunt out a laugh. "You change your mind, just let me know."

"Wanna talk about why you keep looking at your lady like she might disappear?"

My brow furrows, but I stay silent.

"It was quick, but I saw it."

I take a deep breath. "Heavy conversation for the first time I take my boy out to eat."

"Nothing about this whole situation isn't heavy."

Bess comes back, bringing my water. She places one on the table in front of Zac a little harder than she did mine, splashing water over the edge and down on to the table. Zac just smiles sweetly at her, grabbing a napkin to clean the spill. When she leaves, he looks back at me, and one dark-blond brow goes up silently, encouraging me to talk.

I don't know why, but I open my mouth and begin to talk. Telling him about Ray, Olivia, and Riley without reservation. He lets me speak, focused completely on me and what I have to say with rapt attention.

Bess comes back and places our food down, a big-ass steak and potatoes for both of us. And still, I talk. Seems like once the floodgates opened, there was no way I would be able to stop.

"When you go big, you really go all out, don't you?" He rumbles out a small laugh and takes a big bite of his food. "You need to tell her, you know that … so why haven't you?"

"Million-dollar question, isn't it?"

"Not really." He takes another bite and washes it down with a big pull of his water. "See how she looks at you and it's just how my mom looks at my dad. She'll be mad, maybe even big mad, but a woman doesn't look at you like that and not forgive you. Cheat on her, that's a different story—but they're born with forgiving hearts for the people they love. Keep the days ticking by without telling her and it'll only be harder."

His words, simple and no-nonsense, hit their mark.

"You're one hell of a man, my boy," I softly say, and I feel ten feet tall when I see my praise made him happy.

"Damn right I am."

We both get busy eating more of our food, swapping out simple conversation back and forth as we get to know each other. My mind continues to wander back to Liv. He's right, something I already knew and have known for some time now. The longer I let this go, the harder it'll hurt her, and I just can't have that.

Fuck me, she's going to be pissed.

225

CHAPTER 30

Olivia

"NOBODY" BY KEITH SWEAT FT ATHENA CAGE

I look terrible.

My eye, the whole left eye and the area around it down to my cheekbone are *colorful.*

The colors of my bruise have started to change into a deep black. It makes it look like I took all the blacks, blues, and purples of my eye makeup and went to town.

To be honest, I look like I ran smack dab into a wall going about sixty. That's putting it lightly.

With a sigh, I pick up my foundation and pray for a miracle. The way I see it, I might as well get to work on trying to camouflage this hot mess express the best I can. Not because it bothers me but because it bothers Zeke. I don't want him seeing it and thinking negatively about his brother. It wasn't intentional. He knows that, but that doesn't mean the alpha male in him is soothed by that knowledge.

It doesn't take me long to make some progress in hiding the bruise. Axel's wife, Izzy, had given me some tips on how to hide it. I didn't have the heart to ask, but something tells me she had way too much talent and a clear practiced hand at concealing. I also have a feeling that she learned it out of necessity.

I sit back in my chair at the vanity and look at my handiwork.

Well, not too bad.

It's clearly still there, given that my eye is swollen, but it doesn't look nearly as bad as it did.

It had been a long day, waiting for Zeke to come back to the hotel after his lunch with Zac. I had gone out with the ladies earlier, but now the only thing left was tidying the room up and packing. Tomorrow was our last day, and I didn't want to waste what time we had to spend with his family by having to pack.

My phone rings as I place my suitcase on the bed, and I can't help but smile huge when I see Ella's name come across the screen.

"Hey, gi—"

"Livi," Ella cries softly.

"What is it?" I ask, instantly alert at her tone.

"There's been an … accident." She pauses, and I swear my whole world falls at my feet while I wait for her to continue. "Riley is fine. We're at the hospital getting her checked out. Just a little bump on her head."

"What kind of accident?" I wheeze, eyes shooting up the hotel door when it bursts open and an out-of-breath Zeke comes rushing in. His wild eyes search until he sees me standing next to the bed. He rushes over. "What accident?" I ask again, my voice low and panicked.

"I don't even know what happened, Liv. We were standing outside of the shop one second, and the next, I had two big bodies on top of Riley and me." She takes a breath, and thank God, I braced. "Someone was shooting at us, Liv. God, I'm so sorry."

"You're okay?" I question, body numb.

"Just a little scratch. Riley hit her head when Hunt and Evan …" She trails off. "They saved us, Liv."

"Are they okay?"

Zeke nods, and for the first time, I notice the phone pressed against his too pale face.

"Yes. We're all okay."

"You promise she's okay?"

"God, Liv. She's so brave. She's fine, just the bump. She's more worried about her, and I quote, 'giant's friends.'"

I close my eyes and drop my head to rest against his strong chest. I can feel the wild beat of his heart.

"I'll call the airlines now and get the next flight out. You really are okay?"

I can hear it in her voice. She's not okay. Hell, I'm not okay.

"I will be, Liv. I will be."

I lift my head to wipe my eyes, seeing the makeup that was left behind on Zeke's black shirt. I just stare at it.

"Who did this, El?"

She's quiet, and I pull the phone away to see if we're still connected, only to have it pulled from my hand. I watch with my jaw slack at Zeke places the phone to his ear.

"I'll make sure she's on the next flight out. Just got a call from Saint. I'll fill her in."

He hangs up, then tosses my phone on the bed and reaches out.

I step back. I don't know why, but I need answers, and I feel like I'm about to come out of my skin. My girl is hurt, my friend is hurt, and I'm hundreds of miles away. The urge to run to her is so strong, I feel like I'm going to puke.

"Baby," Zeke softly says, reaching out again.

I hold up my hand.

"Tell me why you have that look on your face," I whisper. He looks worried, of course, but he also looks … terrified.

"Let me hold you," he responds.

"No. Tell me." I back up again and stop when I feel the bed at the back of my legs. "Tell me what has you looking scared."

"Liv," he utters with a hint of desperation to his voice.

"This is it, isn't it?"

He stops advancing, dropping his arms to his side and his gaze to the floor.

"This is the why to you sticking close to us, isn't it?"

"It's not the only why, baby, but yes … it's part of it."

Rage like I have never felt ignites, and the feel of it rushing through my veins steals my breath. I feel weak with it. I want to scream. I want to fling my arms around and hit anything in my way. I want to cry with the fear that wars with my rage, making me anxious with the need to rush back home and see for myself that Riley is okay.

"I'm going to call the airline and get the flight switched." His words do nothing to ease the way I'm feeling right now. If anything, I just want to lash out even more.

Don't let your anger lead without thought.

Words long since forgotten come rushing to the forefront of my mind. Words that I used to say to my sister when her temper would fire, and she'd be ready to fight a battle she had no chance at winning. It doesn't douse all the rage, but it makes it so I can take a little bit bigger of a breath.

"She could have died." The words are out of my mouth before I have a chance to stop them. Seeing them hit their mark only makes me feel worse. Regardless of the reasons, I *know* he wouldn't have done anything to intentionally hurt her. He cares about Riley just as much as I do. "I didn't say that to hurt you, Zeke. It's the truth. She could have died, and you were the only one who knew there was something—someone—out there who could hurt us. I asked you when we first started why you were there so many times, and not once did you tell me something was out there that could hurt her."

"I wasn't the only one," he whispers so softly I almost didn't hear him.

But I did.

"What do you mean, you weren't the only one?"

"That's why Evan and Hunt were there."

"What does *that* mean?"

"I'll tell you everything, baby. Let me call the airlines and get this sorted first so we can get back to our girl."

Our girl.

My God. Like a cold shower, his words slam into me and shock the anger right out of my body. I can see it clear as day in his beautiful blue eyes that he's just as upset as I am. Because he loves her like I do. Like she is his own.

I just don't know if I can trust him anymore.

The thought alone is like ripping out my own heart.

My fight with him can wait. My girl needs me.

No, I think … my girl needs us both.

After one last look toward Zeke, I see his pained eyes on me and nod. With one last wipe to the tears streaming down my face, I turn to pack.

CHAPTER 31

Olivia

"HERE, RIGHT NOW" BY JOSHUA RADIN

I shift in my seat, trying to find some space where there is none to be found.

Everywhere I try to shift, a large body blocks my movements.

"Sorry," the large, unfamiliar body to my left grumbles.

I shift to my right as the arm around my shoulders flexes and pulls me even closer.

Zeke.

He knows I'm upset with him. Hell, I haven't so much as spoken one word to him since he informed me we were leaving in an hour and, I quote, "would have company." Had I been in the right frame of mind, I would have questioned how he had sorted everything so quickly *and* had us leaving in an hour. Having flown into the airport only once was all I needed to know that Hartsfield-Jackson Airport is a hot damn mess, and no one gets anywhere in just an hour.

Imagine my shock when we were picked up by Asher, Beck, and Maddox. All of them coming to our hotel door with silent and stoic expressions. They pulled Zeke aside, talked to him in hushed words, and then announced it was time to go.

I didn't ask any questions.

If it gets me to my girl, I would do anything.

When we get down to the lobby, the three men move to surround me. One Cooper brother on each side, with Beck trailing us. It's been bothering me since, seeing them move into a protective stance the moment we were in public. I didn't ask. I kept my silence and prayed that Ella wasn't underselling how Riley was.

"We're here," Asher says from the front. I look up and catch his gaze in the rearview mirror. Eyes so similar to his brother's.

The doors start opening, and the men start filing out. Zeke grabs my hand, and I let him help me climb down from the SUV.

"Where are we?"

"Private airport. Seems a few talents were picked up over the years. Maddox is flying us up."

I glance over at the dark eyes of the large silent man. Man, he's intimidating. How sweet little Emmy can handle all that silent brooding, I don't understand. In the limited interactions I've had with him, he's hardly spoken.

"Just leave your bags there, sir. I'll get it all loaded up for you, and you guys can head up into the cabin."

Zeke and the guys place our luggage on the cart the man indicated and walk up the plane's stairs. Without a choice, I follow their lead. I don't pay much attention to the very opulent surroundings. Instead, I take the first seat I pass and settle in to look out the window. My thoughts are too turbulent for me to do much more. Beck and Asher pass by me, taking seats farther back in the cabin but close enough that I can hear their low conversation about football. Maddox goes to the front, and I see him take the pilot seat. A man I don't know next to him.

Zeke sits down next to me. "It's not a long flight, but the car ride was long enough for the silence, Liv. Please talk to me."

"Who is up there with Maddox?"

I see him turn his head from the corner of my eye. "Helps out on long flights. Maddox brought him in case we need any help while in Boston."

"What kind of help, Zeke?" I turn, looking him in those beautiful eyes, and feel my heart speed up. "Are we in danger?"

For a man who was so good at hiding what he was thinking for so long, he's doing a crap job of it now. The expression on his face is nothing short of wrecked, and I hate seeing it there. No matter what I'm feeling now, I love this man. I know deep in the pit of my heart that he would never do anything to intentionally hurt us. It's just taking me for one hell of a ride that he felt he had to hide something from me. Regardless of the reason, I wish he would have trusted me enough to give it to me.

"I'll never let anything happen to you or Riley."

"But something *did* happen, Zeke. Something did."

He closes his eyes and leans his head back against the seat. His chest moves rapidly, jaw clenching and those dimples popping. As upset as I am with him, he still steals my breath away. I don't understand why he couldn't talk to me and tell me what was going on instead of building something with me on a foundation of omissions.

He's beating himself up harder than I am. My thoughts give me pause when I was about to speak.

I look at him.

Really look at him.

He looks terrible. Handsome as always but terrible. His eyes have been dull all day. The brightness in his clear-blue eyes, the brilliance that had stolen my breath the first time I saw him without his green contacts, hasn't come out from beneath the clouds once. He's holding himself so tense I'm not sure how he's able to keep from crushing the bones in the hand he's holding. Not once since we got news on Riley and I found out he had been keeping something from me has he looked like himself.

He looks ... scared. And dammit, if that doesn't just break my heart.

"Looks like we have a straggler," Beck says from a few seats back.

I look out the window, and my eyes widen when I see the black Jeep speeding at an alarming rate toward the plane. I can't tell who it is, the windows are too dark, but whoever it is seems to be trying to get our attention if the horn, arm out the window, and flashing lights are anything to go by.

"Time to take off," Maddox calls from the cockpit. "Get his ass in here quickly." I see his arm reach out, and the door shuts a moment later. I guess that's all the warnings we get. No need to come over the speaker for someone as commanding as him.

Chatter continues, and Asher, having just walked past us from the bar area with water bottles, turns back and heads to the door. He tosses two water bottles in his arms over to his brother and lets out a little laugh when it lands in his lap. The other two—assuming for him and Beck—go to the small counter next to the door before he opens the hatch.

I had been so focused on what Asher was doing, I missed the airport employee moving the stairs back to the side of the plane.

"Party is here," the youthful Cooper voice of Zac announces. He dips his head and enters the cabin. He winks at me, giving me a smile almost as heart-stopping as Zeke's. Almost. "Couldn't let all the old men out of the state without a babysitter. Shiner's looking good."

"Sit down, boy," Asher groans, shaking his head with a smile. When he passes his brother, he leans down and looks him in the eye. "All you, baby brother. Same tact that you have in serious situations, too." A small laugh vibrates his chest. Asher looks over at me and gives me a small smile. Thankfully, he doesn't apologize again for the shiner Zac just mentioned. I know he feels bad enough.

"Jesus," Zeke breathes, reaching out to give his son a manly handshake.

"I can't wait to meet your girl," Zac tells me, honesty dripping from his words. "Pops says she's incredible."

Pops?

Oh … my God. He's talking about Zeke. I sneak a glance at him and see him staring at his son with shocked wonderment.

"She…" I clear my throat. "She is."

"Well, what do you say we get going so I can meet my soon-to-be little sister."

Eyes round, this time I don't sneak a glance, I gawk with my mouth wide open.

Zac, ever his *pop's* son, reaches out, and with one finger under my jaw, he closes my mouth. "Don't look so shocked." He leans in, over Zeke, and whispers in my ear, "Bet he's already got the ring, too." He grunts out the last word and stands while rubbing his stomach and smiling down at Zeke. He looks at me one more time with a wink before moving to sit behind us.

"Shit," Zeke breathes.

———

We'd been in the air for about an hour into our three-hour flight when I couldn't take it any longer. The turbulent thoughts pinging around in my head were violent enough to make me sick to my stomach. Maddox was flying this plane so smoothly, I couldn't even blame the sea of turmoil in my gut on the flight. Even the air around me seemed to be humming with an undercurrent of troubled energy. The men, for their credit, didn't outwardly show that anything was amiss. They kept their conversations light: sports, meat, and who was paying next time they go play golf.

Zeke hadn't left my side.

Nor has he spoken once.

Not to the men.

Not to his son.

And not to me.

He had rested his head back about a half hour ago. Something, I should note, I watched from the curtain of my hair.

So I had hit my last nerve.

The proverbial straw snapping the camel's back in half.

I clear my throat, turn my body, and slide my hand from his. His eyes snap open instantly. I reach out, placing my hand on his cheek, and gently turn his head toward me. He hasn't shaved, and the stubbly hair on his cheek tickles my hand, sending shivers up my spine. My thumb moves without thought, soothing the skin beneath it. When he closes his eyes and his chest shutters, I almost cry. How can I stay angry with him when my strong man is starting to split apart by his own beating?

Leaning over while gently pulling him toward me, I place my mouth close to his ear. "Is there somewhere other than a bathroom back there where we could go talk?"

His heavy pull of air as he inhales slowly sounds like a bullet going off as it breathes the silence from him. His head moves, nodding and gliding against where our faces are touching. He reaches out, unsnapping my belt before repeating the gesture on his own. He stands. Bless the men around us, they don't pause in their conversation once. Zeke takes my hand and helps me stand. We walk past the few

235

rows of opulent leather seats, and he leads me toward the back of the plane.

I hadn't allowed myself to look around earlier, so the second door in the back takes me by surprise when he reaches out to take the handle. When it opens, it looks like a mini hotel in the sky.

There's a bed in the back of the space, something I avoid looking at too long. I might be mad at him, but I'm not immune to his …. Well, everything. There's a loveseat and recliner right inside the room, placed in front of a large TV. Mini fridge and a small table with two chairs connected to it by some windows.

It's intimate.

Private.

In any other scenario, I would have gone right to that cozy-looking bed … instead, I lead us over to the table. The loveseat would mean we would be right on top of each other, and … I needed the space to get this all out.

He folds his huge frame into the small chair and waits for me to speak. Letting me lead. I appreciate that more than he will ever know. I know it's not easy for a man like him to drop the lead in any situation.

"Why?" I ask, breaking the silence with one word that might as well have been a gunshot. His reaction, a flinch so strong his bulky frame jolted. "Why was our girl hurt, Zeke?"

"Ours," he whispers, word so heartbreakingly sad it's me that reacts with a jolt this time.

"Of course, she's yours too, Zeke. What on earth did you think we were doing here?" I ask, pointing at each other.

I see his throat work when he swallows thickly. He holds his finger up gesturing for me to give him a second while he leans forward, elbows to the table, and drops his head into his hands. My mouth opens slightly and I know I'm seconds away from crying when I see his shoulders shake slightly.

If I live to be a hundred, I never want to see him look like this again.

Not ever again.

"Zeke," I whisper, reaching out and placing my hand on his shoulder.

"Done a lot in my life but seeing your face when you got that call about Riley will forever be at the top of my scariest moments. I'll never forget seeing that fear and pain on your face. I put that there."

What?

He really believes that.

"Did you hurt her?"

He looks up, fat tears ready to fall from his eyes.

"Would you have left with me had you known there was a threat out there?"

I shake my head, confirming.

"You would have been there. Riley would have been with you and wouldn't have been at the shop that long."

"Do you think just by me being there it would have been different? She wasn't there much longer than she would have been if I was home to be at the shop."

"She wouldn't have been there that late and you know it."

"We could argue over this all night, Zeke. Me being here with you was a choice I do not regret. It's also not the reason something happened to her. Something you need to explain to me."

"Goddammit," he hisses. He leans back and runs his hand through his short hair. "I never wanted you to find out, Liv. I don't know that I would have ever told you either. He might have been the reason I started walking with you two, but he has nothing to do with me falling in love with y'all. Not one thing."

I open my mouth to ask who *he* is, but shut it when he holds his hand up.

"Please, just let me get this out. Knowing I hurt you is something I'm struggling with, Liv. The fact this will hurt you too is like someone has a gun to my head asking me to physically harm you. Don't like hurting you, baby."

He clears his throat, eyes holding my worried gaze. "My last job with this great country of ours was to kill Riley's father."

He could have punched me, but it wouldn't have rocked me as violently as what he just said.

"I'm sorry, what did you say?" I utter through the shock and terror.

"Ray's alive, and I've been hunting him."

"You know," I start. "There's really only so much that one person can take before her brain explodes. There's no way. They said he died, Zeke." Fear rushes back through my body, replacing any anger I had left and blanketing everything else in its sticky grasp.

"Best guess is these days he's a few teeth shy of a full set."

Leaning back, I let the enormity of his words settle. If this is correct, I've been in danger since the day my sweet sister left this earth. Riley hasn't been safe one single day.

It would have happened even if you hadn't fallen in love with the hunter.

Like a cold shower, the thought envelops me tightly, and I gasp. Zeke looks up, worried gaze on me.

"Have we ever been safe?"

He looks away, inhales deeply, and holds it before slowly releasing the air. When he looks back at me, I see a little of *my* Zeke coming back. His eyes getting brighter and brighter as something I have never seen rushes to the surface. Gone is the shell of my man and in its place is … well, a warrior. He looks bloodthirsty and ready to kill.

"I will never let anything happen to either of you, again."

"That isn't what I asked you."

"You've been safe."

"If he's been alive this whole time, I haven't ever been safe."

"You've never been alone, Olivia."

I frown, not understanding.

"How long have I been coming into your shop?"

"Since right after we opened."

"Every day between that one and the first day I walked you home were torture for me guarding the woman who called to every part of the man I was then and now. I never believed it was possible to have the kind of life a woman like you would give me. Not after I had been living like a dead man for so long. You woke up a dead man the day you first greeted me in your shop. The only part of why I had even been blessed to cross your path is because I had been given the job of securing Ray. Maybe I would have found you another way, but I did because I needed to hunt that piece of shit out. I didn't know you aside from a folder of words explaining who you were. Then I walked into the shop, and you stopped being a file and started being personal. You were mine that day.

Took a while for a dead man to thaw back to life, Liv. You did that. Every day until I couldn't stay away."

He holds my gaze, strong and sure. Then blows me away. "I didn't tell you because I thought I could control the narrative. I was selfish and thought I could spare you the pain of ever knowing he was alive. I didn't see a point at first, and then I couldn't handle the thought of giving that kind of pain to you. Hurt you double because of it."

He leans in and takes my hands. "You've been safe because the day Ray died he was on our radar. The team was in charge of watching you in shifts then. I didn't meet you until the shop opened. That day it was me and only me that guarded you from the shadows. The team monitored Ray's movements and waited until he died on his own accord or ran out of money and came back to America. We knew where he was every step of the way. It wasn't until he started moving back to the US that we lost him. The timing couldn't have been worse, and I was distracted."

"Zeke ..." I exhale, and my words trail off. This is so much to process. Too much, really. The rational part of me can see and hear the truth in his words, but he hurt me, and that isn't something I can just brush off that easily.

He's been through so much in his life. More than any person could even fathom. Who am I to punish him when he's done that enough for way too long.

My thoughts once again beat their way to the front of my mind.

"Why didn't you tell me after we became us? After you became my Zeke, why not then? Surely you had to trust me when you told me who you truly are? Even then you didn't trust in me ... or maybe us ... enough to tell me why you had started coming around."

"It wasn't that I didn't trust you," he answers immediately.

"Then why? Help me understand it."

"The thought of hurting you is worse than anything I have ever felt in all fifty-two years, Olivia. I knew telling you about Ray would hurt you, but I also knew telling you and telling you I kept that from you would hurt you. It was an impossible situation that I had no chance of controlling. I really believed that I could handle it, and you wouldn't have to feel any of that hurt."

"Life isn't much of a life without the hurt that makes you grow, Zeke. You should have told me. You should have told me and then you could have helped me through it."

"Know that now, baby. I know that now, and I'll never be able to say I'm sorry enough."

"I don't need you to, Zeke. I need to know that you'll not keep things from me again. I know you're sorry, so no more of that. Tell me now, will we be safe now? Is he gone?"

"He will be."

I take a deep breath. "What does that mean?"

"That there's a reason this plane is full of the men who had my back every day until they couldn't. My team now is good, but these men are better. You'll be safe because we're going hunting."

"Hunting doesn't mean Bambi, does it?"

"Hunting means you and our girl will breathe easy for the rest of all of our lives."

I don't ask. Not because I don't want to know, but because I don't need to. What I needed to know he just laid at my feet. He didn't hurt me intentionally. He's done nothing but give me as much of him as he was able. He's lived half a life dead to protect those he loves. It's all he's lived for the other part of his life. If it wasn't for Riley, I would have lost my reason to live when I lost Emma. Even with her light, those days where the hardest I have ever lived through. This big strong man had to do that with no one.

"I can see how much this is hurting you. We have to find a way for you to forgive yourself. You didn't hurt Riley, honey. And you'll make sure that man never does either, aren't you?" He nods his head once. "I love you, Zeke Cooper, but don't you dare lie or keep things from me again."

His whole body deflates when he lets out the tension he had been strung tight with.

"My God, I love you too, Liv." He reaches out and pulls me into his lap, taking my face in his warm hands and presses our foreheads together to look into my eyes. "I'll spend the rest of my life making sure I never am the reason for your pain."

"Rest of my life, hmm?"

Despite the heaviness of moments before, I watch in fascination as his whole face changes. The stress falling off him as an expression I haven't seen yet takes its place. He looks cocky in a way that is so attractive. He looks like the younger him I've seen in photos during our time in Georgia.

"My boy wasn't wrong," he oddly adds, giving me a wink before pulling me in for a deep kiss, then pulling back to speak again. "Had it for a while now."

"Had what?" I rasp, lips tingling from our kiss.

He pulls back and looks down at my hands clenching his shirt. He takes my left one in his and just smiles. "Your ring."

I wheeze and choke on the air.

Oh. My. God.

CHAPTER 32

Drew

"YOU WERE MEANT FOR ME" BY JEWEL

"What's the plan?" Beck asks, the first to speak after Olivia and I return from the back. If they noticed us looking disheveled, they didn't let on. I got on this plane thinking I had lost my reason for living, only to be gifted with her forgiveness and her body before we had even landed.

"When we get back, Zac will take Olivia home and stay with her and Riley."

"Okay ... and the rest of us?"

"We're meeting my team at my place. Evan is on his way with Ella—the friend—and Riley. They've laid the base of our work out for us. We've got a lock on his location. Hasn't moved since last night. Saint got off one shot, and there's no way he's going to a hospital. Best case, he's already dead. Second best, he will be soon."

Olivia's hand flexes in mine, and I look down at her. She swallows and gives me a small nod to continue. I would love nothing more than to spare her from this part, but after thinking I had lost her, I need her by my side until we get back, and I leave her in my home with my son to watch over her and Riley. It's going to be hard as fuck to leave the two of them.

"Who is this guy?" Asher asks.

"Ray Graves. Piece of shit that makes deals with the devil for firearms. He's had a few years running flesh, some running drugs, but he was real good at running his guns. That is until he got on the wrong side of some powerful men with the Italian mob. He already had the Mexican drug cartel after him for screwing them out of a lot of product. After he faked his death, he took all his money and ran to Europe. Been bouncing around there going through money and whores like they're water."

"Actually, it was all my sister's money." Olivia's voice cuts through the silence, drawing the attention of all four men. "He killed her before draining her bank accounts."

I take a moment to really look at her. There's a hint of sadness, but with color high on her cheeks, I have a feeling she's feeling the need to avenge her sister right this moment.

"Baby," I softly say to her. "Next is gonna suck to hear, and I wish I could shield this from you, but no secrets, right?"

"Just say it. I'll be okay." She takes a few deep breaths.

"You will be," Maddox speaks, getting all of our attention. "Won't feel like it immediately, but you will be. Strong women don't fall easily."

"This woman doesn't fall at all," she tells him.

"Don't imagine you will." He looks at me briefly before back to her. "I see why my wife likes you."

"Feeling is mutual."

"So what's the plan after we get the girls settled with Zac?"

"We're going to head toward his location and make sure he doesn't ever touch my girls again."

"Whatever means necessary?" Beck asks.

"No civilian crossfire. Isolated hit, and then we call in the cleanup team. You don't have to do more than watch my back. In and out."

"Better shut your mouth with that in-and-out shit before you jinx us," my brother grunts.

I lean forward and hold his gaze. "This piece of shit ambushed her friend and our girl at their place of business. You don't have to do more than watch my back because no one else gets near him but me. Your hands are clean, and you're in and out. I'll take care of the rest."

"Yeah, not going to work like that," his brother responds. Maddox and Beck nod in agreement. "We didn't get you back to lose you again."

"He's mine," I tell them.

"No doubt, but we won't just be watching your back. If he poses a threat, whoever gets the shot takes it."

I want to argue. I want to demand that I get justice for him hurting Riley and scaring Olivia. I want to say fuck it all and run off half-cocked, ready to bash that fuck's head in. However, when I look down at Olivia and see her worried expression, I know they're right.

"I'm done after this," I tell them. "He's my last job and … my most important. The only one who gets the shot is me."

Silence follows, each of them looking at me with understanding.

Each of these men, well maybe not my son, knows what I'm feeling right now. All aside from Zac. I pray my boy doesn't know what we do—what it's like to avenge the women we love. If he does, I'm thankful he'll have the same army at his side that I have.

My worlds collide, giving me everything I had never dreamed possible. It's up to me now to protect them for good.

CHAPTER 33

Olivia

"ONLY EVERYTHING" BY QUINN LEWIS

The ride from the private landing strip to Zeke's place felt like it took an eternity rather than the half an hour it did. Being this close to Riley but not seeing her yet makes me beyond anxious. I need to see with my own eyes that she's okay.

By the time we pulled into the parking area for Zeke's place, I had my hand on the door and was ready to bolt.

"Easy," Zeke whispers in my ear. "Let them get out first and make sure everything is clear."

How easy it was to forget, even for a moment, that a threat was out there. I nod, and it takes a lot of effort to sit back in the seat and let all the men climb out.

"I'm excited to meet Riley." The voice comes from behind me, and I jump, forgetting that Zac had climbed into the back of the large SUV. His head pops between Zeke and me. So close I lean back to put some space between us and smile at him. He looks ridiculous, having climbed his big bulk into the trunk area of the SUV when we realized we didn't have a big enough vehicle waiting for all of us.

"She's going to love you," I tell him.

"How do you know?"

I look around him and meet Zeke's eyes. Seeing them next to each other this close steals my breath. It's wild how much they favor each other.

I clear my throat, blushing when Zeke smirks at me knowingly.

"Let's just say she's got a thing for tall men."

Zeke starts chuckling, and Zac's smile grows.

"That sounds interesting."

"Just watch your junk if you plan on having any babies. Her little feet know no limits when it comes to climbing."

"Climbing?"

This time, I laugh with Zeke.

"You'll see," he adds.

The door next to Zeke opens, and Asher pokes his head in. "All clear."

We climb out, and someone pops the back hatch to let Zac out. We all move toward the elevator as a unit with me in the middle. It's unnerving. However, it's probably one of the safest places I've ever been. I know Zeke would protect me with his life, and he wouldn't have these men at his side if they wouldn't do the same. I pray it doesn't come to that.

I don't take a full solid breath until we're in the back elevator that will bring us directly to his door.

To my Riley girl.

The ping of the elevator reaching his floor makes my heart speed up. I move, pushing to the front with Zeke at my back, and wait for the door to open.

"Auntie!"

I lean back into Zeke when I hear her sweet voice, but only for a moment do I allow myself that relief to show. I push forward and drop to my knees in front of her. My eyes roam all over her tiny body, from the top of her head to the bottom of her feet.

"You got a boo-boo, too, Auntie?" She reaches out and pokes my cheekbone. "How'd you do that?"

"Walked into a wall, if you'd believe it," I tell her, figuring this is one of those times when it's best to omit the truth.

"Me, too!"

I frown, looking at her and waiting for her to finish. I know very little about how she got the nasty scrape and bump on her head.

"You walked into a wall?"

"No," she sings. She was about to say something else when the rest of the group with me must have been noticed. "Wow."

I feel Zeke move to my side before he bends down. Riley moves to stand in front of him, her little arms coming up and her hands going to his hair. She gives his short locks a little ruffle before she frames his face with her tiny hands.

"You look different."

"I do."

"You sound the same."

"I do."

"Okay."

And to Riley, that was that. She gives him a big hug. I'm guessing that's when she gets a really good look at the rest of the men in the room. Her little eyes go huge, and she looks at me with a twinkle in her eye.

"You brought me more giants," she whispers, looking over my head. Her little face lit up. "Who are you?"

I turn to see who she is looking at, not even a little surprised that it's Zac.

"Whoa," she exhales. "You look like my giant."

"I do?"

She nods and looks at Zeke. "He looks like you."

He bends down, and Riley follows his movement. "That's because he's my boy."

She looks back at the boy in question, little brow furrowing. "He isn't a boy. He's big like you."

"Get over here and give me a hug, kid," he grunts a laugh out, clearly not going to entertain that conversation. She wraps her arms around him, and he moves to stand with her in his arms. She gives a squeal of happiness when he stands to his full height with her arms around his shoulder and bottom supported by his forearm.

"Well, you sure did bring home some extra baggage than what you left with." I turn to see Ella standing with Evan's arm around her shoulders. It looks more to help hold her up than anything else.

"Oh, El," I cry, moving from our little huddle to my friend. When Evan doesn't let go, I know he is without a doubt holding her up. "Are you okay?" I ask when I step in front of her, not sure if I should hug her or not.

"I'll be fine. Just a little sore, that's all."

Evan snorts and rolls his eyes. "Understatement."

She narrows her eyes at him. "When we don't have little ears. We've been over this."

I laugh lightly.

"Livi, I'm going to show my new giant where the toys are!" She rushes past me a second later with Zac's hand in hers and his big frame walking behind her. He looks over his shoulder and gives me a wink, lifting his arm to give me a thumbs-up before they vanish around the corner, and I hear them move farther into the apartment.

"Now that the little ears are gone," Ella starts, her body leaning heavier into Evan. "I'm so sorry, Liv."

"Don't," Zeke says. "You have nothing to be sorry for."

"It isn't your fault. I swear, Ella. You saved her life. Don't you apologize for someone else attacking y'all."

"He almost had her. I had my hands full and turned to lock up. It happened so fast. You'll see the bruise later, but all five of his asshole fingers were so tight on her little arm, it left the perfect impression of his hand. That's how close he was. I thought Evan had forgotten about us, and I was too busy stewing in my snit. I wasn't paying attention."

"This is NOT your fault," I reiterate. Wishing my friend wasn't hurting.

"We're going to have to agree to disagree, babe."

"Thank you," Zeke interrupts, moving slightly so I have to step over a little. "Thank you for protecting our girl."

Her eyes come to mine and I can see all the comments she's not verbalizing. I also can see happiness, for me and for Riley.

"Seems like we have a lot to catch up on," she says low toward me. She glances back at Zeke and gives him a weak smile. "I'd do it again and again if it meant she's safe." She opens her mouth, but closes it before speaking. I wait, knowing she isn't done by the expression on her face. "Kill that son of a bitch." The anger and vitriol in her tone are a stark comparison to the one only moments before.

Zeke nods and Ella looks relieved. I have a feeling she knows more about what these men do than I did before the past few days. She wasn't saying that to be flip, she truly meant it. Evan's arm moves and he guides her back tightly to his side. She leans in and settles.

Isn't today full of surprises.

CHAPTER 34

Drew

"SHOW ME WHAT I'M LOOKING FOR" BY CAROLINA LIAR

"This is the place," Saint speaks ahead of me, holding his phone up and checking the screen again. "Yeah, on the left." He points at a building that looks like it saw its best days about a century ago. Abandoned and standing by the grace of God only.

"How the hell do you know this is the place? All these shit buildings look the same," Beck questions.

"See this." He turns his phone toward our small huddle and shows them his screen. "When Evan got close he planted a tracker on Ray. He'd never find it. Micro as hell and undetectable. All he had to do was get close enough to tag a part of his skin and boom—he's ours until I stop transmitting."

"Impressive tech," Maddox grunts, leaning in to tap the screen.

"You'd be surprised what the government's got hiding for our use these days," Hunt says.

"What's the plan?" Asher asks, standing by my side. I glance at his vest and almost smile, remembering how he threw a tantrum when he demanded we all wear them. I gave in the second he looked at me and said he wouldn't lose his brother again. I took it from him in the next breath and said nothing else.

No one was dying today except Ray Graves.

250

"Two on each side of the perimeter. Beck and Evan, you're on the left quadrant—two windows and no exit door. Saint and Hunt, you two take the right—same as the other, one window instead of two. One of you needs to stay near the back and monitor the windows there as well. The fire escape from the second floor is rusted and broken. It won't be a problem, but it still needs to have eyes on it. Maddox will enter the back and start to clear the rooms. Asher and I will take the front and do the same, meeting at the staircase in the middle. Best guess is he's gone high and burrowed deep. He won't see us coming until we're on him if that's where he went. Saint ran thermal earlier, and unless he's moved, that's where he is. Only way out is to jump, so keep eyes on the windows. We'll try to get another thermal read if there's an opportunity before we breach the stairs."

"And if we find him?"

"Then you fucking wait and call for me."

All six men nod, understanding what I'm asking of them. The vengeance for not only harming what's mine but also for taking Olivia's sister and Riley's mom from them. Ray won't be breathing after we finish, and it will be the most rewarding kill in my career. I'll get back home, and my reward for the life I lived, lost, and lived again will be waiting for me.

"Comms check," Saint says.

We each make sure our mic and earpiece work.

"Let's get to work, boys."

Those are the last words I speak before we go silent and not even our steps can be heard. We move like a team that has always worked together instead of two units that just met. There's a reason I trust Saint, Evan, and Hunt as much as I do. A reason that the two units are working so flawlessly together. They're the only men I've ever met who reminded me of the ones I've lost—the bravest, strongest, and most skilled.

I see Beck and Evan split from our huddle, still moving in sync with our steps but taking them to their post. Saint and Hunt break off next, getting a little closer to the house before they move. I look around, not the least bit surprised that Maddox is nowhere to be seen. The man's always moved like a damn ghost.

I glance at Asher, his face cast in shadows and only his eyes showing through his gear—black cap pulled low and black cloth covering him from his nose down, same as the rest of us. We're moving with the wind and in the shadows. I wait for him to nod before we sidle our backs to the front door.

"Everyone in position?" I speak softly into my comms. I wait for each man to confirm, then nod to Asher. "It's party time, boys."

We move.

Silently.

Dancing with the shadows.

I have no doubt the rest of the men are following their orders to a T. Asher and I move with an ease that returned instantly, like we haven't been without each other for two damn decades. The only sound coming from the shell of a building are from the outside. Not so much as a breath is heard.

It's too quiet down here. If Ray's hurt, which I know he is, he wouldn't be able to keep this still unless he was dead. I pray that isn't the case and I get to watch him take his last breath.

We clear the rest of the lower level and meet Maddox at the base of the single staircase. It's your typical shit hole with one way up and down, no windows and vast blackness.

Shadows.

My old friends.

I know how to live in these. Hunting won't be a problem.

I look down when I feel something tap my arm. Maddox has his arm stretched out. Hanging from the tip of his fingers are two night vision goggles. I should have known he'd have them ready to go. We all pull them over our heads, waiting to snap the glasses in place. I wait for Maddox to finish, seeing him put up the thermal he had been running while clearing the floor.

He points up and moves his hands in a way that tells me exactly where I'll find Ray. Each deliberate movement of his fingers conveys a specific communication, something we learned over our years working together in situations much like this one. There's a reason these men came into this building with me. This being one of them. I glance at Asher and see his nod; knowing he understood as well is a relief. He wasn't in our unit, but we did enough jobs together. This was one of the first things I taught him.

I give them one finger, then another, then point up. Each of us pulls the glasses down, and the room around me fades to a green haze clear enough to move freely in the darkness. Man, whoever invented this was a damn genius.

Thirteen steps.

We move soundlessly down the long hall. Asher slides into the first door we come to, Maddox in the next. I keep moving, my heart steady and calm.

Each breath slow and measured.

Calm.

The hunter in his element.

Three more doors.

I glance in the first, seeing a small and very empty bathroom. Asher comes back to my side when I get to the next.

It's not that one. I can feel it. I give him a nod, and he enters slowly. I keep walking, not worrying about anything other than my mission.

I hear it before I get to the next door. The labored breathing and hiss of pain. That fuck has no clue he's being pursued. No damn clue he's about to see the last person he ever will on this earth. He thought he was running from some bad people, but he has no fucking clue.

He's about to meet his worst nightmare.

And for touching my girl, I'll make sure it's slow.

Starting with his hands.

We enter the room, the door silent despite the fact it looks like it's about to rot off the hinges. Thanks to the glasses, I can see him in the corner before I even take two steps.

Back to the door.

Fucking moron.

Asher and I move our guns up and train them on him in perfectly synced movements. It would be so easy to just take out the trash like this. Something he won't get the satisfaction of being blessed with.

"Ray."

He jerks when I call his name.

"Who's there? How do you know my name?"

I turn my flashlight on, already trained on him, and feel my lips curl. Well … I'll have to remember to pull those out of his cheek when I'm done here. If the purple puff ball is anything to go by, I'm pretty sure those are Ella's keys.

"Seen better days, hmm?"

"Who are you?" he slurs. I imagine it's difficult to speak with the new accessory.

"You made a mistake, bud. You should have just stayed dead." His eyes widen at my words. The irony in them not lost on me.

"What? Look, if this is about the guns, I can tell you where they are."

"Do I look like I want your guns?"

"I can't really see you, with the light and all." He follows that bullshit up with some weird giggle.

This motherfucker. I move my aim and let one silent bullet fly. It hits him in the thigh, and his scream gives me a little satisfaction. I crack my neck and breathe in deep, feeling the odd gratification of knowing my last hit will close the door of one life while knocking all the walls down that separated the two. I get to be both men and step out of the fucking shadows.

"The fuck was that for?"

"Only one person will ever be allowed to be a smart-ass with me. On her, it's cute. One, you don't have her laugh. Two, you damn sure don't have her sweetness. And lastly, you don't have the ability to make me forget who the fuck I am."

"Who … Who are you?"

I step forward, Asher's light shining behind me while I keep mine trained on Ray. It looks like he's huddled in my shadow now.

"You tried to take something from me today, Ray. Something I care a whole lot about. Care to tell me what that was?"

"Look, man, I don't want any trouble." He holds his hands up, Ella's keys jerking and jingling against his cheek.

I'm going to make sure that girl gets whatever the hell she's ever dreamed of for this. I knew she fought since she damn well broke two of her ribs. However, it seems that Evan left out that she stabbed Ray in the face when he told me what went down earlier.

When I'm right in front of him, he seems to realize just how fucked he is. My smile grows as he weakly tries to grasp his gun. His arm reaches out and falls a few times.

Dislocated.

Goddamn Ella, the fucking magnificent.

Going to buy her a car for that one.

I bend, picking up his handgun. "Is this what you want, bud?"

He whimpers but doesn't speak.

"You know, this would have ended much differently for you, Ray. You just had to put your hands on my girl."

"Look, man, I didn't know she was yours. I was just getting the kid."

"The kid?" I whisper, deadly and low. It sounds evil even to my ears.

"THE KID IS MY GIRL!" I roar, grabbing him by his shirt and pulling him to his feet. Well, his feet dangle somewhere above the floor, the short fuck.

"Wh-What? That's my daughter," he gasps, hands trying to pull at mine to release him. His feet knock my shins while he struggles. "What the fuck, man? Let me go."

"Not your daughter. You lost that right when you killed her mother, you piece of shit. That beautiful little ball of happiness doesn't have a single ounce of you in her. She's my girl. You're one lucky bastard that her aunt cared more about her innocence than she hated you. There will be no more stories about how her daddy died some good man, either. From this day forward, you will never be spoken of. There will come a day when she'll come to me, the man who raised her like she was his daughter, and she'll say…" I tighten my grip and bring him closer. "She'll walk up to me, smile on her beautiful face that looks like her mama's side, and say, 'Daddy, tell me about my birth father,' and I'm going to sit her down and tell her *just* what kind of man you were. She'll take it hard because she's got her aunt's heart. But she'll be just fine because that girl will be so loved that anywhere she lands will be soft."

"The fuck you will," he spits, waking up to the fact he's not getting out of here alive.

"Oh, I will. I earned this shot. You earned one, too, buddy … just not the kind of shot you'll like."

His eyes widen.

I take a deep breath, and I get to work ridding the world of the trash

255

that wishes to pollute it. I feel each layer of pain I had carried over the years fall off my shoulders. The incredible freeing feeling that I never thought I would feel again slams into me when I step back from Ray's prone form.

I've killed my last name.

And with his last breath … I took the first full one I've had in two long as fuck decades.

———

I enter my apartment and nod at Zac, sitting in the kitchen facing the door. Waiting. The place is dark, and I can tell Riley is sleeping by the lack of noise. The only time the apartment is this still is when she isn't here … or sleeping.

I drop my keys on the table just inside the room and toe off my tennis shoes. We had all brought our change of clothing, burning everything we had worn before we left the run-down area we found Ray in.

"Is it done?" Zac asks, his deep voice rumbling through the vast room like thunder.

"It's done."

I walk toward him, taking a beer from the fridge on the way. "You want one?"

"Yeah. Now that you're back, I'll have one."

"Good boy," I mutter.

"Nice keys," he says, pointing at the table I had dropped them on earlier.

"Not mine."

"I'm guessing there's a story there?"

"Oh, there's a story there. Story for another day, my boy. I need—" He holds his hands up with a wide smile, stopping my words.

"Say no more, Pops. You've got one hell of a good-looking family waiting for you in there. I'm glad to be part of that and so fucking happy you're alive."

"Fuck," I whisper, his words slamming home and mending the last piece of my heart I didn't know was still broken. "Me too, Zac. Me too."

He nods, smile still bright and eyes full of pure joy. "Try to get down to visit before I end up with another sibling. Would like to get to know the one who comes with your Olivia for a little first."

"No promises."

"I imagine so," he agrees on a laugh.

"Thank you for protecting them tonight. Hard to believe my new baby boy is big enough for me to say that to."

"I'll be back in the morning before we head home. I promised the little princess I would take her on a date to lunch tomorrow. Give you and Olivia some time alone without you three being apart for too long. I ran it by Olivia, but understand if you aren't there yet."

"Hey." I smile, walking up to him from where I stood just a few feet away. "If it's okay with Olivia, it's okay with me. She's a great kid, but I'm real happy she's getting you out of this to be her role model."

"See you tomorrow around noon, then."

"Your dad's downstairs," I call out, remembering Asher's request earlier to take all the time I needed, and he would be waiting for Zac to go to the hotel.

"You know, people will think my two dads are gay," he tosses over his shoulder, stepping into the elevator.

His toothy smile, so much like the one that used to frequent my own face, is the last thing I see before the doors slide shut.

Damn, that kid is incredible.

"He's pretty awesome." Olivia stands just outside of the threshold to my bedroom.

"I was just thinking the same thing."

We both start walking at the same time, her meeting me with a soft collision. She runs her hands down my arms and looks over my body while following her hands' path. It wasn't until she moved to drag them down my chest that I realized what she was looking for.

"Hey, I'm okay."

She looks back up with tears in her eyes. "Is …?" She trails off, one tear falling.

"It's over, baby."

She closes her eyes, and the tears start flowing freely.

I pull her close and hold her to my body. She continues to cry softly. I rest my head on hers and pull her as close as she can get comfortably. Her hands fist the shirt at my back. My eyes zero in on my bookshelf and that gold glitter. I stand in the same spot I had months ago thinking there would never be anything worth shining in my life. Now, now I hold my whole world in my arms. The rapid beat of her heart slamming against my body, mine answering the call with its own hurried beats.

"You have my word that I will never lie to you, omitting or otherwise, Olivia. I don't ever want to see you hurt, baby, and I'm so sorry I contributed to that feeling."

"Stop," she cries softly. "Right this moment, it's you, me, and Riley, Zeke. We aren't going to let this sour us. We will not let the gift you just left in Georgia be shadowed by this. We move forward, and we do that together."

"Just like that?"

She arches a brow. "Nothing in how we got to be standing right here was 'just like that.' I know I love you. I know that the thought of you hurting physically sickens me. When you look at Riley, I know you feel the same way I do. And I know when you hold me, I'm the safest woman in the world. What we have is something some people never find. I'm no fool, Zeke Cooper. I will not look this gift in the eye and spite it."

"Do you want that ring now?"

She looks adorable when she's confused. It takes her a second, but when she realizes what I'm talking about, the sassy woman I love comes rushing forward.

"When you ask me properly, which will not be standing in my underwear in your living room, mister."

"Noted."

"Take me to bed, Zeke Cooper. Take me to bed and let me show you how much I love you."

She takes my hand and turns.

And what do I do?

I follow, feeling better than I have in two damn lifetimes.

EPILOGUE

Olivia

"MAKE YOU FEEL MY LOVE" BY ADELE

"Are you sure you've got everything?" I ask Riley, again.

"Yes, Auntie," she coos smartly, rolling her eyes at me and giggling. "Why do you keep asking me that?"

"Well, my little bean … I just can't believe you're going to be gone for two whole weeks. Are you sure you don't want me to come?" I joke, knowing she will think it's funny since I've been asking her for the past two months that we've been planning her trip to Hope Town.

"You're silly," she hoots. Her tiny belly laugh making me start to laugh with her.

I reach out and wrap my arms around her, pulling her into my body and hugging her close. "I'm just going to miss you, sweetheart. You're going to have so much fun with your brother."

She makes a squeal of joy, just as she does every time I mention Zac. She started calling him her brother about six months after we had returned from our Georgia trip. It was a toss-up on who loved it more. Me, Zac or … Zeke.

"He said I get to meet more family, too. Kids just like me!"

"I know, baby. Zac even said he gets to take you in his police car for a ride!"

"Woohoo!" She jumps, almost knocking me in my chin.

259

"Knock, knock," comes from the hallway that feeds the elevator. "Zacky!"

And just like that, I'm forgotten. I love every second of it too. Seeing her this happy is worth everything I could ever give.

I smile and stand to my full height.

"Hey, Pops. How's it going, Mama Liv?"

"It's so weird when you say that, Zac." I laugh, shaking my head. My smile grows when I see Riley riding on his shoulders. He ducks so she doesn't knock her head on the door's arch, coming deeper into the kitchen.

"Where are your parents?" Zeke questions.

"Looking at an apartment. They're looking at getting a place that everyone can share. How do you not know this?"

"Why would I?"

"Well, I don't know … because?"

"Pretty good one there." Zeke laughs, reaching out to hug Zac. Riley giggles when they come together, and she has two giants' heads to softly pop.

"Is she all packed? I'm double parked, so I need to run."

Oh wow. I thought I would have a little time before I sent my girl off with new people and on a jet, no less. My stomach erupts in even more butterflies now that I'm closer to something else I'd been anticipating all day. I shake off the anxiousness and focus on Riley.

"Bye, Auntie! I'll see you in two whole weeks!"

"Little girl, you better get down from there and give us both hugs and kisses!"

She laughs even harder when Zac reaches up and zooms her to her feet. She has a little wobble before she rights herself and rushes over. Her little body collides with Zeke's legs.

"I love you, Pops!"

Oh my God.

My eyes find Zac's and see the same awe-dumbstruck shock I feel mirrored on his face. It's no secret that Zeke loves Riley as if she is his own. Their bond has done nothing but grow in the past year. I know he's even expressed to his son that he wished he could adopt her, having heard that from Chelcie after his last visit here. Zac's been waiting just as long as I have for this moment. I'm so thankful it happened at this exact moment, and he was here to see it happen. That man loves his pops, and he just got to watch him get the greatest gift ever.

Riley claiming him as hers.

I glance down directly at where she slammed into the man standing beside me. His large arms wrap around her tiny body, holding her close. His eyes on me, tears falling freely.

"I love you too, little girl."

She giggles.

He closes his eyes.

I turn away and look at Zac to see him wipe his own eyes, giving Zeke this moment to himself. I love that he isn't shy about showing or saying how he feels.

Riley gives me a hug next, and we all walk toward the elevator. We had stacked up her two suitcases and travel bag by the entryway seating area, so it didn't take long before I was waving at my little bean as the doors closed.

Zeke's arms wrap around me, and I take the comfort he's giving.

"Two weeks will be up before you know it, baby," he soothes.

"I know," I whisper.

"Then what's with all the tears?"

"She called you Pops, honey."

He leans back and smiles down at me. "Never heard anything sweeter. I love her, Liv. She's easy to love, but it's more than that. I'm so damn proud to be hers and that I get that honor from her. Never thought I would get this, raising a life. It's one beautiful life I never thought I would be living. Damn sure took the long way to find my home, and it's even sweeter than I ever dreamed, baby."

"It's going to get a lot sweeter, honey."

He frowns at me, not following. I step back and take his hands, smiling as the tears return.

"I'm pregnant, Zeke."

His hands jerk, squeezing me before relaxing. His mouth slack and eyes wide. I'm not even sure he's breathing. I'm just about to ask him if he's okay as worry starts to creep in, but with a jump, he turns and stalks toward our bedroom.

"Zeke?" I call after him.

He just lifts one finger in the air and keeps stomping toward our room.

What in the heck?

I start to follow, only to jump when he comes right back out the way he came. He holds my eyes, something I can't quite read in his. That is, until he gets closer. There's so much emotion behind those blue beauties. I've never in my days with him seen him look more like the younger version of him than right now. He looks downright drunk with happiness.

He drops down when he reaches me, landing on one knee before me.

I gasp when he takes my hand.

My knees get weak when he brings a stunning diamond ring forward and slides it down my ring finger.

Tears fall down my eyes faster than ever.

"You only had to wait another two weeks, baby. Had a big thing planned. It's been hard enough, waiting this long to get my ring on your finger where it belongs. You got my baby in your belly, you're not going to wait a second longer. Olivia Elizabeth Kelley, loving you has given me a reason to live again. You've given me beauty, love, and a home. All things I thought I had lost forever. I'll spend the rest of my life making sure I show you how thankful I am to be the lucky man to love you and be loved by you. Will you do me the honor of becoming my wife?"

I started nodding before he was halfway through.

"Yes! A million times over, yes!"

He stands, pulling me into his arms, and kisses me deep.

"What do you say we get packed and get our ass to the airport? I don't want to be away from our girl anymore."

Just like that, this man shows me that beautiful heart of his once again. Everything I never thought I would find. The man worth a million fairy tales. And he's all mine.

ZEKE

Now this is what living feels like.

I hold my woman in my arms while she has my ring on her finger and our baby in her belly.

Before the day is over, I'll have our girl with us, too.

Our family.

Family.

I've craved having this my whole life since I never had the traditional family growing up. I lost a huge chunk with my brother and my son. And now, after feeling as dead as I have been living, I get to soak up my rewards.

Only everything I'll ever need right here.

Man, this damn sure must be what living feels like.

"Maybe we can call them and ask them to wait for us. You know, give us a little more time to … pack," she says softly, voice thick with arousal.

Make no mistake, my girl has no intention of spending much time packing. I'm willing to bet she just tosses a bunch of anything into a bag and calls it done.

No, my girl is thirsty.

"Tell me what you really want, Olivia."

"You. Always you."

"You got it, baby."

I close the distance, and my lips land on hers. She jumps, wrapping her arms and legs around me. Our kiss is deep and wet. I move with purpose, taking us through the apartment and into our bedroom. I help her to her feet and start to peel off her clothing, slowly. She has other ideas because she's frantic in her quest to get me naked.

"Slow down, baby."

"I can't. I need you."

"You're going to let me take my time enjoying your sweetness, Olivia. Stop trying to keep my sweetness from me."

"I'm not …"

"Are you not rushing me?" I ask, pulling her bra off and bending down to pull her nipple deep in my mouth, rolling the tight bud with my tongue. She pushes her hands in my hair and pulls me closer to her tit.

I pull my mouth away, the loud pop echoing in the room and tangling with her gasp of pleasure.

"You feel how much I love your sweetness?" I ask, grinding my cock into her belly.

"Yes, baby," she whines.

"Get naked," I demand, hooking my thumbs in my waistband and pulling my pants down. My cock springs free, and her tongue comes out to lick her lips. "Now, Olivia. I'm hanging on by a thread here."

She rushes, almost falling over, and kicks her panties and pants off in a huff. Her hair falls into her face when she reaches to unhook her bra. My eyes go to the smooth skin of her belly.

My baby is in there.

A life that we created together.

One that will know nothing but love and I will spend the rest of my life protecting.

Just like I will Olivia, Riley, Zac and everyone else that I hold dear.

"Lay down, baby," I tell her, not trusting myself to touch her yet.

This woman, she has no idea. Not one clue how much she means to me.

I climb over her body, her legs going around mine right away, and I settle my hips against her core. She lets out a mewl, pulling me closer. Her tits press against my chest. I look into her eyes and pray she can see what I wish I had the words to express.

I lift my hips, and I feel my cock glide toward her opening. Reaching between us, I guide myself into her body … slowly. Her eyes never looking away from mine. Tears filling her lips. Smile blinding.

I start moving, reaching out I take the hand that now has my diamond on it and place it against my chest. With each thrust of my hips, another tear falls.

"You brought me back, baby," I murmur. "You healed me. You continue to heal me."

"Oh baby," she cries out, her body clenching around mine.

"There will never be a day that I don't make sure you know how loved you are. Thank you for giving me a family, Olivia." I push myself in as deeply as I can go. "I love you so much."

"I love you too, baby."

We don't say anything else. I take her slow and don't lift my lips from hers until we're both swallowing each other's cries.

It turns out, my family didn't mind waiting for us. Not one complaint for the two hours that they sat there. When I locked eyes with my brother and saw the knowing smirk on his face, I didn't even feel bad about making them wait. My future wife by my side, our girl sitting next to my grown son and my brother and sister-in-law all here.

Together.

Damn does it feel good to be alive.

THE END

For real this time.

MESSAGE TO THE READERS:

Where do I start?

How do I even begin to thank you all for the love and unwavering support?

How do I express just how much you all have helped carry me over the past few years.

I can't.

There will never be enough words *in any language* to thank you all for being the incredible humans you are. There were times that I doubted I would ever be able to see this book to completion. There were times that I almost just gave up.

Then … there you all were. It never failed, if there was a day that doubt was winning, I would see someone mention these amazing characters and it was as if I had been zapped with magic fueled by you all.

Every single word you just read was is for you all.

This book is *you*.

It's for every single one of you.

Every person I said would never see this book—I'm sorry for going so many years making you think this would never come.

269

Thank you for welcoming me home. Even though I took the long way back.

I've missed you all.

You only live once … right ;)

To my daughters: McKenzie, Taylor and Audrey … You three are the strongest ladies I know. You've been through more in your little lives than a lot will ever face. I'm so proud of your strength and resilience. I'm blessed beyond measure because I get to be your mom.

To my parents: thank you … *for everything*. For never letting me fall and loving the girls and I as fiercely as you do.

A special thank you to Kat, Georgette, Michelle, Stacey, Heather, Tracey, Jo-Anna and Jenny. <3

My Babes—my tribe—you all are EVERYTHING. Simply everything.

Made in the USA
Las Vegas, NV
02 May 2024

89405611R00157